Mackenzie Bell

A forgotten Genius Charles Whitehead

A Critical Monograph

Mackenzie Bell

A forgotten Genius Charles Whitehead
A Critical Monograph

ISBN/EAN: 9783337337322

Printed in Europe, USA, Canada, Australia, Japan

Cover: Foto ©Raphael Reischuk / pixelio.de

More available books at **www.hansebooks.com**

A FORGOTTEN GENIUS:

CHARLES WHITEHEAD.

A Critical Monograph.

BY

H. T. MACKENZIE BELL.

' Alas ! for all the miseries that strew
  The common path our trackless footsteps make,
As we creep on this maze of darkness through :
  The hearts that break, the hearts that cannot break,
  The hearts that bury their last hopes and take
E'en comfort from the grave and struggle still,
  And lingering on for very misery's sake
Live—not because they would but that they will ;
And die when baffled Death is left no power to kill.'
CHARLES WHITEHEAD.

LONDON :
ELLIOT STOCK, 62, PATERNOSTER ROW, E.C.
1884.

PREFACE.

Vicissitudes of fortune are as frequent in literature as in other departments of intellectual activity. The rank held by an author is constantly liable to change. Literary reputation is frequently a thing of chance, and is due almost as much to a favourable concatenation of circumstances as to intrinsic excellence. Perhaps it is an error to conclude that merit is the final test to which fame is brought, that the guerdon of praise is the ultimate and certain recompense of genius. We know that it has sometimes happened that men whose work has eventually proved to be good and even great, have been for years, perhaps for generations, unrecognised. The inference is a reasonable one, that,

but for some accidental circumstance, they might have
escaped observation altogether. It certainly does not
often happen that a man of unmistakable genius, after
he has once attained to recognition, falls entirely out
of sight. Charles Wells and Ebenezer Jones—not to
speak of William Blake—are, however, examples of men
who have suffered such freaks of fortune. I believe
Charles Whitehead to be a further example, and I
have undertaken this work in the hope of doing justice,
however tardy and inadequate, to one whom I regard
as a neglected genius. My attention was first drawn
to Whitehead and his works by observing the high
estimation in which the late Dante Gabriel Rossetti
held the latter, both in verse and prose. Since then,
I have discovered that Christopher North admired
Whitehead's early poetry, and that at least one of
Whitehead's novels inspired Dickens with warm admiration. Some of Whitehead's surviving friends consider that in natural powers he was hardly less gifted
than Dickens himself, and that, had it not been for

a single infirmity of temperament, he would have achieved the highest distinction in one or both of his walks in literature. Unhappily, he was beset by a great weakness: his life was overshadowed by the same serious failing that lends so sad an interest to the life and genius of Poe—an author to whom White-head, on one side, and one side only, bears a curious affinity. It will be agreed that a writer who has called forth so many and such warm eulogiums from competent critics as it will be my pleasure to quote is at least deserving of consideration; and it is in the hope that, thus late, the public will give him a fair and sympathetic trial, that I now present this monograph.

My best thanks are due to Mr. George Bentley, Mr. E. L. Blanchard, Mr. Cornelius Pearson, Mr. A. Schulze, and to Mr. F. Blackburn, for valuable information most kindly given respecting Whitehead's private and public life.

I have to acknowledge my obligations to the

publishers, who have generously permitted me to quote from copyright works. Wherever I have been cognisant of copyright claims I have been careful to recognise them. Any omission in this respect will, I trust, be regarded as an inadvertence.

H. T. MACKENZIE BELL.

LONDON : *May,* 1884.

CONTENTS.

PREFACE.

PAGE

Literary Vicissitudes—Neglected Genius . . . v

CHAPTER I.

BIOGRAPHICAL AND BIBLIOGRAPHICAL.

Birth—Parentage—Early Efforts—Successes—Christopher North and Charles Dickens—Critical Verdicts—Writing for a Living—The Mulberry Club—Personal Excesses—Failure in Life—Emigration to Australia—Still Lower Depths—Death from Destitution . . . 1

CHAPTER II.

WHITEHEAD AS A POET.

The Solitary—Jasper Brooke—Ippolito, The Cavalier, etc. —Of the School of Shelley—Forecastings of the School of Rossetti 36

CHAPTER III.

WHITEHEAD AS A HUMOURIST.

Jack Ketch—English Highwaymen—Grimaldi Memoirs, etc. —The Forerunner of Dickens—The Manner of Victor Hugo 95

CHAPTER IV.

WHITEHEAD AS WRITER OF SKETCHES.

Smiles and Tears—Francis Loosefish—Edward Saville— Confessions of a Lazy Man, etc.—Later Contributions to Periodical Literature—*The Wife's Tragedy—The Spanish Marriage* 126

CHAPTER V.

WHITEHEAD AS A ROMANCIST AND HISTORIAN.

Earl of Essex—His Relation to Queen Elizabeth—To Bacon—To Ralegh—*Sir Walter Ralegh*—Spelling of the Name—As Poet and Man of Letters—As Statesman —His Conduct in Ireland—Summary of his Character . 162

CHAPTER VI.

WHITEHEAD AS A NOVELIST.

Richard Savage—The Eighteenth Century Novelists— Whitehead's Methods—The Richard Savage of History —Johnson, Boswell, etc. 206

CHAPTER VII.

CRITICAL SURVEY.

Whitehead's Place as a Poet—As a Novelist—His Ultimate Rank 291

Chronological and Bibliographical Table . . 295

A FORGOTTEN GENIUS.

CHAPTER I.

BIOGRAPHICAL AND BIBLIOGRAPHICAL.

IT is a melancholy reflection that as fast as a man of letters rises into repute he may sink into obscurity. Between popularity and fame there is, of course, a wide difference ; fame is that higher kind of distinction which, as Falstaff says of honour, cannot usually live with the living, because detraction will not suffer it. "It keeps company with the man who died o' Wednesday." Fame is essentially a dead man's possession, and of him who has ever possessed it, it were not rash to say that, whatever the nature or quality of his doings, he is never wholly forgotten. That lower kind of reputation called popularity has usually another fate. It is almost entirely a living man's possession. It never kept company with " the man who died o' Wednesday." At whatever part of a man's career it begins, it perforce ceases at his tomb. It is' the inheritance of every ephemeral demagogue, who no sooner makes his exit from his little stage of life than popularity deserts him, and he remains only open to the test of how far he is or is not an inheritor of fame. And as popularity is necessarily the commoner, and fame the rarer possession, what a mighty sweeping-down of the world's little deities every succeeding age must of necessity have witnessed! It is well that it should be so: well that the great army of momentary heroes should give place to the much smaller company of Time's true great ones. But, in the general deluge, it sometimes happens that great men with little ones are submerged: often disappearing entirely and for ever out of the world's cognisance: occasionally rescued from the densest obscurity by the labours of the student who rummages in forgotten corners.

Marlowe is not, strictly speaking, a forgotten contemporary of Shakespeare; but there is a sense in which he could almost be said to be so. We do not read his plays as we read Shakespeare's: we *never* act them. He is in the hands of the specialists, not the people; and who shall say how far the championship of such men as Mr. Swinburne contributes to keep him in memory? Yet Marlowe was the master of Shakespeare, and was doubtless at one time the more popular of the two. Beaumont and Fletcher are of course remembered, and so are Webster and Ford; but there may well be a difference of opinion as to the value of the reputation that is limited in its operation to a comparatively small circle of enthusiastic readers. But, outside these greater names, who shall say how long is the list of the contemporaries of Shakespeare who are entirely unknown to the general reader, and therefore practically forgotten ?

How many, too, of the contemporaries of Pope are in a like position ! Not to speak of the large corps of criticasters headed by Dennis, or the small corps of poetasters of whom Tickell was the tail, there were not a few men of rare and high genius, like Christopher Smart, the author of *The Song to David*, who are now no longer remembered.

To come to later times, we find that Keats's gifted friend, the author of the Scriptural drama of *Joseph and his Brethren*, has only within recent years been revived. Within our own time, also, Thomas Lovell Beddoes, the Elizabethan poet of the Victorian era, Alexander Smith and Sidney Dobell, the leaders of what was called the Spasmodic School—high as their several ranks were in their day—have for all practical purposes, so far as vital poetic existence is concerned, been permitted to fall largely out of sight.

And now I take upon myself, with all modesty of personal motive, but with all possible admiration and enthusiasm for my subject, to endeavour to show that the world has permitted itself entirely to forget a man whose genius is exceptional in several walks of litera-ture, and in one of those walks falls short only of absolute greatness. Charles Whitehead is a name so largely forgotten, though the owner thereof is little more than twenty years dead, that I can readily amuse myself by fancying I overhear the remarks which the title-page to my volume will call forth :

" Charles Whitehead, does he say ? Oh yes, I know. But does he not mean *William* Whitehead, the contemporary of Colley Cibber, and his successor in the laureateship ?"

There is one fact of Whitehead's life which makes the obscurity of his name a thing of the most melancholy interest. That fact may be stated at once without further reserve. Whitehead died from the effects of want in a hospital at Melbourne, Australia, after living for some years in that colony, without relatives, entirely friendless, and alone. The pathos, the abjectness, the squalor of poor Whitehead's end, make up as sad a record as can be conceived. It is no less than the truth that this man had written one of the most remarkable novels produced in his time ; he had written a volume of verse that had enjoyed the recognition of one of·the most powerful critics of his age ; he had written a play which, whatever its success as an acted drama, had been compared with Massinger as a literary product. For thirty years he was actively engaged on the best periodical press in London : his name was widely known there ; he was at one time the friend and colleague of Charles Dickens, the club associate of Douglas Jerrold, and the acquaintance of Thackeray and Lord Lytton. From one sad infirmity of character, this man was driven from the only city in the world that was fit for him, to a country opposed to all his instincts, his habits, and his weaknesses, and he died there in obscurity and of destitution—unknown and almost unnamed, probably without a line in the local newspaper of the city of his adoption, certainly without fitting record in the proper places at home.

When we think of men of letters who have been cruelly neglected by the world, the mind turns first to Otway, dying of the results of a fit of gourmandizing after a period of destitution; to Chatterton in his garret in Brooke Street, Holborn; to Schiller, huddled at last into a deal coffin, for which his family were scarcely able to pay ten poor shillings, and all but borne to the grave by hirelings, and buried at midnight and as if by stealth; and among the poets of our own time, the mind turns to poor James Thomson, composing his weird poem, *The City of Dreadful Night*, in the weary vigils he kept, night after night, in the streets of London, walking there from sunset to dawn, knowing not whither or wherefore, only that by so doing he seemed to chase away the poverty and misery that hung about him as a load that was pulling him down to the grave. But none of these sad examples of men of letters on whom the world turned its back—not Otway's case, nor Chatterton's, nor Schiller's, nor Thomson's, nor yet Savage's case, though he died in a debtors' prison in Bristol; nor Steele's case, though he was banished from London at the end; nor Sheridan's case, though his creditors tried to arrest him even while he lay dead; nor Burns's case, though on his deathbed he was tormented with anxiety as to how to save himself from arrest at the hands of the hosier to whom he owed £10—not any of these seems to me a case of neglect of high genius more complete than that of Whitehead, more cruel, more tragic.

The materials for a biography of Whitehead are so scanty, that it is doubtful whether any such phenomenon of inadequate personal data exists in the case of any other man of letters of modern days. It would appear that his near relatives are all dead, and of his intimate friends there survive only one or two. Any more perplexing problem, therefore, than that of writing a biographical sketch under these conditions can hardly be conceived. Nevertheless, I have, after much effort, brought together a number of facts, which, meagre though they are, yet afford a realizable idea of the man, and a sufficiently connected account of his career.

He was born in London, in 1804, and was an eldest son. His father was a wine-merchant in the City. He was a genial old man, and on the day he attained his seventy-fifth year, he slapped his son Charles on the back, saying, " Well, my boy, when I have lived twenty-five years longer, I shall be a hundred." He died the next year by an accident. One of Charles Whitehead's brothers was dearly loved by him, and it would appear from a note appended to the first edition of *The Solitary* that this brother was drowned. His early and untimely death is the origin of some of the most beautiful and pathetic stanzas in that poem. Charles had two other brothers, Alfred and Frank, and one of them, probably Alfred, assisted Charles in writing one of his earlier romances

—*Jack Ketch.* He had three sisters, Clara, Esther, and another of name unknown. Esther had literary ability, and she appears to have possessed practical qualities, which the subject of this volume lacked.

Both Alfred and Frank wrote for the magazines. Alfred died early, and long before Frank. Brothers and sisters are all now dead, and probably Charles was the last to survive. Charles had not a University career, but otherwise his education was carefully attended to. There is an impression that he was a Christ's Hospital School man, but this seems improbable, for the head-master, who has kindly searched the registers, tells me that Whitehead's name does not appear there.

Whitehead began life as a clerk in a commercial house in London. He first appeared as an author in 1831. *The Solitary* was his earliest work, its publisher being Effingham Wilson, who about the same date produced Tennyson's first volume of poems—that is, the first volume written solely by himself.

The Solitary appeared in a thin octavo, and was prefaced by an introductory poem in which the author spoke touchingly of his personal isolation—an isolation for which there seems to have been scarcely so much foundation in fact as might be expected from a sincere writer, for there is little reason to doubt that at the time in question Whitehead was living in complete harmony with his family, as yet undisturbed by death. To deny to a young writer, however, a certain

Byronic license to suck the eggs of a sweet melancholy
would be to deprive him of a dainty, if not a very
substantial dish.   Whitehead's melancholy has at
least the merit of being poetical.

> " Of joy, or pious sorrow, to rehearse;
>   Or sweet affections, often told in verse;
>   Or all the blessings of a sylvan state;
>   Or all the wretched splendour of the great;
>   Or all the comforts that, unbidden, come
>   Like pilgrims, to the simple latch of home;
>   The father's tender smile—the mother's kiss—
>   And all the dear security of bliss;
>   These are not mine : expect no gentle theme,
>   No graceful woes that lovers best beseem,
>   No soft Italian tale, or Oriental dream.

> " My Muse vouchsafes me but a little space,
>   And leaves to swifter feet the longer race;
>   Th' o'erburden'd heart of sorrow, ere it break,
>   Trembling with jarring harmony, to wake;
>   To fling a reckless hand along the chords,
>   And dash the unform'd breathings into words;
>   To wrest one satisfaction from the tomb,
>   And, if I can, anticipate my doom;
>   This, Fate permits me ; should we meet again,
>   Why, then I have not struck the lyre in vain;
>   If not, I do not owe the less to thee
>   Who would be blind, tho' all the world could see:
>   Meanwhile—nor hope, nor fear—I am content,
>   If, when this sickly dream of life is spent,
>   When Hate has done his worst, and Fate is past,
>   I anchor in the bay of Truth at last."

The reception of the book seems on the whole to
have been favourable.   The *Athenæum* accepted it as

a protest against those old poetic heresies which required that poetry should be stripped of all its mystery, at the same time that it recognised in the author one of those followers of Shelley who were said to measure their depth by their darkness, and to fancy themselves profound when they were merely perplexed. Speaking of the moral habit of mind whence *The Solitary* had emanated, the critic protested against the disposition to be moody, melancholy, and full of complaint against Life, Hope, Time, Pity, Youth, Manhood, Old Age—everything, in short, that exists, has existed, or will exist in this world, where there are six days of labour for one of rest.

"A little super-transcendentalism," says the *Athenæum*, "we have no objection to, upon occasion, nor, upon occasion, to a good, and if melodious, hearty fit of passion with the world and its inhabitants ; but when we get nothing but sighs, and tears, and groans, witherings of spirit, blastings of memory, scarings of brain, and drying up of heart—when poetry is turned into Niobe,—and without having lost nine children,—it is hard, first, to help laughing, and, next, to avoid feeling a stern regret at such gross misapplication of mind and sensibility. Melancholy and levity are in their extremes alike irrational. We now bid ' The Solitary ' farewell, hoping to see him again, purified from what looks like affectation, and writing as good verses as we think he has power to write."

The *Literary Gazette* a year later, takes shame to itself that *The Solitary* should furnish matter for review in 1832, and asks the author's indulgence when it makes the acknowledgment that the poem, in which power and beauty are so unmistakably evident, should have been reviewed months before. But perhaps the warmest tribute of praise came three years after the publication of the poem, when Professor Wilson wrote as follows in the *Noctes Ambrosianæ*:

" NORTH. No politics, Sam.   Pray, did either of you ever read 'The Solitary,' a poem in three parts, by Charles White-head ?

" BOTH. No.

" NORTH. It is full of fine thoughts and feelings, and contains some noble descriptions.   Some of the stanzas committed themselves to my memory, and I think I can recite three, suggested by the quiet of this scene, for they are pregnant with tempest :

" ' As when, of amorous night uncertain birth,
        The giant of still noontide, weary grown,
    Crawls sultrily along the steaming earth,
        And basks him in the meadows sunbeam-strown,
        Anon, his brow collapses to a frown,
    Unto his feet he springs, and bellows loud,
        With uncouth rage pulls the rude tempest down,
    Shatters the woods, beneath his fury bow'd,
And hunts the frighted winds, and huddles cloud on cloud.

" ' Nor rests, but by the heat to madness stung,
        With headlong speed tramples the golden grain,
    And, at a bound, over the mountains flung,
        Grasps the reluctant thunder by the mane,
        And drags it back, girt with a sudden chain
    Of thrice-braced lightning ; now, more fiercely dire,
        Slipt from its holds, flies down the hissing rain ;
    The labouring welkin teems with leaping fire,
That strikes the straining oak, and smites the glimmering
        spire.

" ' And yet at length appeas'd he sinks, and spent,
  Gibbers far off over the misty hills,
And the stain'd sun, through a cloud's jagged rent,
  Goes down, and all the west with glory fills;
  A fresher bloom the odorous earth distils;
A richer green reviving Nature spreads;
  The water-braided rainbow, melting, spills
Her liquid light into the air, and sheds
Her lovely hues upon the flowers' dejected heads.' "

Such an allusion to this poem seems all the more valuable when we remember how severe a critic Christopher North usually was. He found practically nothing to admire in Keats, but little in Shelley, nothing in Leigh Hunt, and a good deal to reprehend in Byron, his admiration going out mostly to the Lake School.

It would certainly appear that for some years later *The Solitary* had its special circle of admirers, probably among the young poets of the school of Shelley; and, due no doubt to this encouraging reception, Mr. Bentley re-issued the poem in 1849, together with a drama, some narrative poems (*Jasper Brooke, Ippolito*, etc.), lyrics and sonnets composed in the intervening eighteen years. The late Dante Gabriel Rossetti, who among his other distinctions enjoyed the rare and enviable one of having an eye constantly open for merit in obscure places, and who was the chief agent in the revival of Charles Wells and Ebenezer Jones, was an ardent upholder of Whitehead. In his posthumous letters* he writes:

* *Recollections of Rossetti*, p. 252.

"I'll copy you over page a sonnet, which I consider a very fine one, but which may be said to be quite unknown. It is by Charles Whitehead, who wrote the very admirable and exceptional novel of 'Richard Savage,' published somewhere about 1840.

"'Even as yon lamp within my vacant room
    With arduous flame disputes the doubtful night,
    And can with its involuntary light
But lifeless things that near it stand illume ;
Yet all the while it doth consume,
    And ere the sun hath reached his morning height
    With courier beams that greet the shepherd's sight,
Then where its life arose must be its tomb :—

"'So wastes my life away, perforce confined
    To common things, a limit to its sphere,
It gleams on worthless trifles undesign'd,
    With fainter ray each hour imprison'd here.
Alas, to know that the consuming mind
    Must leave its lamp cold ere the sun appear !'

I am sure you will agree with me in admiring *that*. I quote from memory, and am not sure that I have given line 6 quite correctly. . . ."

And again, (p. 195) :

"Charles Whitehead's principal poem is 'The Solitary,' which in its day had admirers. It perhaps most recalls Goldsmith. He also wrote a supernatural poem called 'Ippolito.' There was a volume of his poems published about 1848, or perhaps a little later, by Bentley. It is disappointing, on the whole, from the decided superiority of its best points to the rest. . . . But the novel of 'Richard Savage' is very remarkable—a real character really worked out."

Though not limiting his claim to that of a poet, Whitehead appears to have exercised his poetic function down to the last years of his life. It is doubtful, however, whether any subsequent poetic production enhanced the reputation secured by his first effort. What further triumphs he had to win were to be achieved in another department of literary activity, that, namely, of the poetic romance, and his first essay was certainly not of an ambitious character. It was entitled *Lives and Exploits of English Highwaymen, Pirates, and Robbers*, and was probably produced merely for what it would fetch as literary task-work, the conditions of which it must surely have satisfied, for the book passed through many editions. The *Athenæum* gave a lengthy review of the book, censuring the author for trusting to unreliable authorities for his materials. It animadverted on a rather foolish paragraph in the preface, in which the author speaks of his work as a "collection of biographies of two distinct classes of persons, interesting in themselves, and displaying actions and adventures which are never likely to be performed in this country, or by the natives of these islands, again :" after which it referred in detail to some of the contents of the book, and wound up by drawing a fanciful and amusing picture of the education and training of the man who should be fit to undertake worthily this task, in which Whitehead, according to the critical journal, had egregiously failed.

In the same year Whitehead published anonymously the romance of *Jack Ketch*, with fourteen illustrations by Kenny Meadows. The book was for the

most part a farcical travesty on the broadly grotesque
and semi-gruesome idea of the inner life of the public
hangman.   Nevertheless, it contained passages of the
utmost seriousness, and of almost pathetic gravity,
evincing throughout the dexterous hand of a skilful
literary workman, and in its more notable passages
the powerful grasp of a master of tragic art.   The
book was received with a good deal of favour, which
was, naturally enough, not unintermingled with some
good-natured banter and some censure on the choice
of a ghastly theme.   The *Examiner* said:

" Well hath he performed the interesting and subtle task.
We have little doubt that his book will prove as tempting a
piece of literature as the admirers of ' Moll Flanders ' have
for a long period encountered.   We wish it may force its
way into a few of her more immediately devoted subjects :
it inculcates a capital lesson, and might serve to give a
genteel young hero pause on the path of glory leading to
the felon's grave.   Much of the same sort of power, indeed,
that belongs to Hogarth's graphic biography of the ' Idle
Apprentice ' distinguishes the production ; and we may, in
conclusion, remark that the woodcuts with which it is illustrated would scarcely, some of them, have been unworthy of
Hogarth.   They present admirably characteristic likenesses
of the hero of the tale under various circumstances—displaying, in all that villainous compound of vulgarity, the
accomplished depravity which belongs to inveterate scoun-
drelism."

The *Athenæum* was more severe in its strictures.
After admitting that nothing tends more to harden
the heart than that pampered sickliness of feeling
which refuses to contemplate the dark consequences

of crime or error, the journal says that while it may be well occasionally to look into the unblessed haunts of the profligate, and to hear the clank of the prisoner's chain, the impression which such scenes leave on the healthy mind is rather one of humiliation than of gratified curiosity. There can hardly be a doubt that there is justice in this view, but it opens up a much larger question as to the use of the horrible in art than can properly be discussed in this place.

"Thus it is," continues the *Athenæum*, "with the book before us; and while we acknowledge the coarse power with which it is written, we cannot say that its perusal has given us pleasure; the history begins in low crime, proceeds through scenes of profligacy and murder, and ends with the appointment of its hero, Jack Ketch, to his odious office. We feel that he is well worthy to be so promoted; the progress of his villainy has been sufficiently laid before us, and were it only for the brutal indifference with which he could regard the breaking heart of his innocent and gentle wife, who may be likened to the flower trampled on and crushed by the criminal on his way to the scaffold, we are sure that he has nerve and cruelty enough to discharge the duties of his calling, and are content to leave the rope in his hands and to see its fatal coil twined round his picture. The characters throughout are well sustained. Misty, the poor patient schoolmaster, with his nose pink with dram-drinking—Wisp Haynes, the conscience-stricken rogue—Snavel, the dishonest attorney, and Mr. Wilmot, who avenged his knavery, have all individuality and distinctness. The *Confession of James Wilson*, too, is a fearful story. Still, we shall make no extract from the book, and while we leave it, expressing our conviction of the power its author has put forth in its pages, we must also express a hope that when we next meet him it will be under a pleasanter guise than the executioner's mask, and in a less dismal place than on the drop."

It will be seen that this notice, whilst fully admitting the power of the book, takes exception to its occasional ghastliness, and it cannot be doubted that there is propriety in this view. Were it not for this defect, the book could not fail to take a high place, for there are passages in it which are descriptive and analytical of emotion of the highest order. It has passed through numerous editions.

I have little doubt that the success of this book gave rise to one of the most interesting incidents in Whitehead's career. Whitehead was now about thirty years of age; he had probably relinquished commercial pursuits, and was devoting his talents and energies to literature. He must have been reasonably prosperous in the profession he had adopted. He was a fecund and facile writer, whose books found acceptance. Moreover, he must have contracted an intimate alliance with more than one publishing-house putting forth periodical literature, and it would appear, from an allusion in Forster's *Life of Dickens*, that in 1836 Whitehead was acting as the editor of a library of fiction. In this connection arose his intimacy with Dickens, then a young writer producing his earliest sketches. Mr. George Hodder, in his *Memories of my Time*, says that at this period Whitehead was asked to associate himself with Seymour in the production of the book which afterwards became famous as the *Pickwick Papers*.

I have sifted this statement and find it to be correct. When the publishers, Messrs. Chapman and Hall, offered Whitehead the commission to write to Seymour's sketches, he declined it on the ground that he was not equal to the task of producing the copy with sufficient regularity. He then recommended to the publishers the young author of the *Sketches by Boz*. As a result of this piece of good fellowship on Whitehead's part (which was doubtless warmly appreciated by Dickens), the two writers continued good friends for some time. It is even possible that the title *Pickwick Papers* may have been suggested to Dickens by a passage in the preface to *Jack Ketch*, where a humorous allusion is made to the possibility of the author producing " his more mature experience under the unambitious title of *The Ketch Papers*."

Charles Whitehead soon afterwards became a dramatic author. On the 15th of September, 1836, a play by him entitled *The Cavalier* was produced at the Haymarket Theatre, with Vandenhoff and Miss Ellen Tree in the principal parts. I shall elsewhere detail in full the plot; it is sufficient here to say that the scene is laid in the years immediately succeeding the Restoration, and that the play deals with somewhat delicate questions. It was performed occasionally in the provinces, and in 1850 it was revived with great success at Sadler's Wells.

The issue of the *Examiner* succeeding the first production of the play contains a long and very severe critique on it, probably written by Leigh Hunt. One of the chief allegations against the play is its want of originality of theme, and this much may to some extent be conceded, but the admitted excellence of the dialogue ought surely to have redeemed it in the eyes of the severest censor. The *Times*, after detailing the plot, proceeds to censure the piece for its supposed improbability. But it admits that the first two acts are written " with considerable talent," and that " the language is highly dramatic without bombast." It condemns severely the last scene, and says that the curtain fell amid " a conflict of hisses and clapping of hands," and that when Mr. Haines (I presume the manager) came forward to announce the repetition of the piece, " the same struggle of ' Ayes ' and ' Noes ' took place." Having given a word of praise to the " excellent acting," the *Times* concludes its remarks by saying :

"Since these observations were written, we have received the following announcement : ' The catastrophe of the new piece will be altered.' "

The play appears to have found more favourable critics elsewhere, for after the first night's performance it was said that the plot was ably carried out to a touching and effective conclusion, and that the dialogue was written with so much passion and vigour as to be worthy of Massinger in its best passages. Mr. Hodder tells us that on the night of the production it was listened to with the profoundest attention, and was vehemently applauded throughout, until the final scene; but this being of too painful a character, the audience gave signs of dissatisfaction, and when the piece was announced for repetition there was a general cry of " With alterations." The alterations were made, and *The Cavalier* had a prosperous career.

The happier climax, however, certainly involved an artistic loss. *The Cavalier* was revived at the Lyceum Theatre in 1856, but soon gave place to *The Lady of Lyons.*

Whitehead is described as being at this period (1840-50) a man of singularly nervous temperament. Indications are not wanting that he was already becoming a victim to the infirmity which overshadowed his later years. That infirmity was, it is to be feared, the result of a passion for a certain type of social intercourse acting on a man of his years and temperament. There existed a tavern which has since been pulled down, called the Grotto, in Southampton Buildings, Holborn, and it was at this resort, which was much frequented by young literary men, artists, and some few actors, that a friend of Whitehead's, who has been good enough to give me many interesting particulars respecting him, first met the author of *The Cavalier.* This gentleman was attracted to Whitehead by his great geniality of manner and remarkable brilliance of conversational wit and humour. He, however, only went occasionally to the Grotto for the sake of the company, which was of the usual Bohemian order. Charles Whitehead was the leading spirit of the place, being there every night. Shortly afterwards Whitehead and his friend, my informant, were together elected members of the famous Mulberry Club, so called in honour of Shakespeare's mulberry-tree at Stratford-on-Avon. In this club were many persons connected with literature and the stage, and it was there that Douglas Jerrold gave forth many of the sparkling witticisms which made his name so celebrated. One can readily imagine what pleasurable gatherings must oftentimes have taken place: one can fancy the withering sarcasm and the sparkling repartee. The club first held its meetings at a tavern in Cockspur Street, but subsequently removed to a tavern which then stood opposite Covent Garden Theatre, in Bow Street, and on that tavern being demolished in order that Bow Street Police Court might be erected, they adjourned to the Wrekin Tavern in Broad Court, Bow Street. This last resort, however, has long ere this shared the usual fate of such places, and is now no more.

But few appear to have entered on life with fairer prospects than Whitehead. His family were in easy circumstances, and he himself was much beloved by them. He had been well educated, and had great and acknowledged talents, and, what is almost equal in value for aiding a man striving after fame, an excellent constitution and vigorous health. Moreover, I am told that on his father's death he received in all probability a considerable sum of money. He was acquainted with the most distinguished men of letters of his day, who all regarded him as a man possessing the highest gifts, and able, if he so willed, to achieve almost any position in literature. But all these advantages were rendered of little avail, and his career irreparably marred by one fatal propensity—a propensity which he acquired early in life, perchance at the Grotto tavern. He seems never to have conquered this baneful habit, and in time it led to his being often in most straitened circumstances, the force of which made him guilty of many little indiscretions otherwise foreign to his nature, and by-and-by the very friends who admired his genius most were compelled to shun him. Dickens, for instance, began to observe his weakness after a time, and was from this cause alone gradually compelled to cease to hold intercourse with him.

I must now speak of what is unquestionably White-head's greatest work. *Richard Savage, a Romance,* appeared in *Bentley's Miscellany* for 1841-2, and before the close of the year 1842, was published separately in three volumes illustrated by Leech, who had also illustrated it in its serial form. The *Literary Gazette* thus speaks concerning the book:

"This romance has been running for a good many months in 'Bentley's Miscellany,' and is unquestionably one of the most interesting productions of its class which has appeared in that way. The actual record of Savage, as left us by Johnson and other biographers, is one of such deep diversity and incident, and appeals so forcibly to the mind, that it needed only an author of such talents as Mr. Whitehead possesses to make the foundation and staple of a narrative which should throughout possess very strong attractions. And such is the work before us, elaborated with much skill and power, never flagging, and cleverly embellished with characteristic scenes by John Leech. So generally read as the portion has been which has appeared in Bentley's popular periodical, we may well dispense with the custom of quotation, and leave 'Richard Savage' to the public favour he so truly deserves."

The *Athenæum*, however, is more severe :

"Unpleasing subjects are not less destructive of a writer's chances of popularity than that mode of treatment which concerns itself only with the mean or repulsive objects of humanity. The clever author of 'Richard Savage' would do well to lay our remark to heart. There was force and talent enough in his 'Jack Ketch' to set up half a dozen novelists. But the story was one of naked want, crime, and cheatery ; and where is it now ? Thus, again, 'Richard Savage' contains conceptions of character and pages of dialogue beyond the reach of the common-place observer of human nature, or the common-place reporter of conversation ; and yet the work is so disagreeable, that few will have patience enough to read it, still fewer to give it credit for the talent which it contains, rather than exhibits."

It must be acknowledged that there is considerable force in the objections urged against the book in the earlier part of the latter notice. It may fairly be maintained against Whitehead that he is too fond of depicting the mean aspects of humanity, and that, in all probability, his stories would have been much more popular had he dealt with brighter themes. We must, however, remember that the tendency to depict the sad and terrible in life was his natural idiosyncrasy, and having chosen a character such as Richard Savage, with a substratum of historical fact pertaining to it, it was impossible to delineate his hero in any other manner than that which he has adopted. In any case the *Athenæum's* remark "that few will have patience to read it," is an instance of misjudged opinion. The book passed through at least three editions, and was included in Mr. Bentley's "Standard Novels" at a popular price. The *Examiner* contained a long review of *Richard Savage,* and it is worthy of note that the review preceded one of Dickens's *American Notes.* Severe censure is passed on Whitehead because in the scenes of strong emotion the style is said to be jerky. Doubtless it is so; but when did anyone make an oration while strongly agitated? A well-known modern writer makes a most pertinent remark concerning such a point. She says that every true critic can readily distinguish between the roughness imparted to style by the literary artist for the purpose of effect and the angularity arising from crudity and inexperience. Undoubtedly in this instance the reviewer in the *Examiner* was deficient in critical insight. His lack of perception is further shown by quoting with warm praise the long and somewhat tedious account given in the book of Savage's treatment and conduct when apprenticed to a cobbler. His remark concerning Ludlow—an altogether fictitious character, and in most respects Whitehead's greatest creation—"that he is no less intelligible when mad than when supposed to be sane," verges on the ludicrous. Altogether, however, it is quite evident that, despite these faults which the critic finds with his work, the *Examiner* places a very high value on Whitehead's powers. *Richard Savage* is dedicated to a Mr. Elton, probably the same to whose family Dickens was so kind after Elton's unfortunate death by drowning.

One of the most important pieces of intelligence that I have received is from Miss Hogarth, who tells me that she had often heard Dickens speak with "great admiration" of the novel *Richard Savage*.

Charles Whitehead's next work was *The Earl of Essex*, an historical romance in three volumes, published by Mr. Bentley in 1843. It is in some respects the most popular and interesting of his works, using the words in their colloquial sense, and contains passages full of vivid writing. It deals with that portion of Essex's career subsequent to the rebellion of Tyrone. The *Literary Gazette* has a favourable account of the book; but as I have already given such frequent extracts from contemporaneous criticism, I must refrain in this instance from making an excerpt.

In 1847 appeared *Smiles and Tears, or the Romance of Life*, in three volumes, the publisher being again Mr. Bentley. This work consists mainly of a reproduction of numerous tales and sketches originally contributed to periodical literature. There is much in the book which is humorous in the highest degree; there are also tones of deepest pathos, and here and there there are passages rising to the dignity of real tragedy. The volumes are, therefore, fitly named. It is worthy of note, however, that long before this work appeared, there came into existence a volume called *Smiles and Tears*, consisting of collected essays by various writers. But in all probability Whitehead never heard of this book, and he certainly borrowed none of its contents. Respecting the later *Smiles and Tears* the *Athenæum* says:

'Those, like ourselves, whom Mr. Whitehead's former imaginary productions have prepared to expect clever and vigorous writing from his hand, will not be disappointed in his 'Smiles and Tears.' His touch, however—to borrow a painter's word—is hard rather than sweet. He seems to catch hold, by instinct and predilection, of the sharp corners and blemishes of life—to know all its wants, without comforting himself sometimes with thoughts of its riches. Such a tendency is a serious drawback on the success of a humourist. The reader becomes tired of meanness and folly and distress; and though the sort of optimism and false pathos in which too many comic writers find relief and refuge is, to ourselves, little more moving and genuine than the maudlin benevolence of a gentleman 'in his cups'—the very recourse to the expedient clearly shows the nature of the contrast required. The public is not so nice as the professional critic in discriminating the paste from the real diamond—the rant of the stage from the utterance of real passion. Thus much to account for the comparatively limited success of Mr. Whitehead, as compared with that of others to whom he is superior. For the rest, we need but say that we apprehend these 'Smiles and Tears' to be a republication of papers which have already appeared in the periodicals, and that they make up a good parlour-window book after its kind."

Whitehead's last book was *The Life of Sir Walter Ralegh* in the Illustrated Library, published by N. Cooke. This volume was issued in 1854. The work is an excellent one of its kind, showing the author in the capacity of a competent and conscientious book-maker, and not destitute in occasional paragraphs of valuable historical criticism. Naturally, however, it would not be right to judge of the book by the high standard which we can apply to some of his other efforts.

In addition to the more important works, which I have here enumerated at some length, Charles Whitehead revised the *Memoirs of Grimaldi*, edited by Dickens under his pseudonym of " Boz," and this was published by Mr. Bentley in 1846. The book has run through many editions, and in a recent one issued by Messrs. Routledge, undated, but probably published between 1876 and 1880, Charles Whitehead's name is not given on the title-page, though his notes are used. I only mention this as a most striking instance of how utterly a man of rare and conspicuous genius may be forgotten. It was not thought worth while to mention that the work of Dickens's juvenile pen had passed through the hands of a novelist of whose genius that great author had a very high opinion. Whitehead wrote much for periodical literature, largely, but by no means exclusively, for *Bentley's Miscellany* and it is probable that he at one time edited the *New Monthly Magazine*. He also did a good deal of journalism, though for what journals he wrote I have been unable to ascertain.

It is always a tempting study to seek to discover in an author's writing hints of his own personality, but in this case the task is not an easy one, for Whitehead's prose is of so objective a character, that it is difficult to trace the individuality of the writer in it. It might be said that *Richard Savage* had some angles of resemblance, and this no doubt is to some extent true. A man does not go out of his way to depict with every show of sympathy a singular character, without having some subjective impulse; and that Whitehead was in some sense a Richard Savage in his pride, in his suspicion of those who did him favours, and in his irresolute moral character, must be sufficiently obvious. But that Whitehead should himself desire to repudiate the allegation that he had drawn from himself in the person of Savage is not to be wondered at, especially when we remember that the book was written before its author had fallen into the lowest depths of that abject condition of which it is my melancholy task to speak. In the preface to an early edition of *Richard Savage* the author says :

"I have drawn his character to the best of my ability, and as I believe he himself would have portrayed it, for Savage was never careful to conceal his faults. To those who have hinted I drew from myself, I have nothing to say. Words are wasted upon men who from malice will not, or from ignorance cannot, dissociate the author from his subject. The calumny or dulness, as the case may be, is old, applied to those who write fiction in the first person.'

However this may be, I am myself fully persuaded that into the person of Misty, the poor outcast schoolmaster in *Jack Ketch*, Whitehead put a great deal of his own personality. Misty is described as a man of highly strung poetic nature, entirely destitute of practical genius, being buffeted about by a cruel world until he falls into habits of intemperance as a relief from the pressure of untoward circumstances, and all the best aspirations of a lofty soul are bartered and sold for a dram. Nothing can exceed the picturesqueness or the pathos of the conception or the rendering of this character, which in its vivid humanity leaves little doubt that the author was drawing from his own character for the backbone of sentiment to a story in which the individual incidents are of course wholly fictitious. Readers will be glad to have the following masterly passages reproduced :

"It was very early in my youth that I discovered that I was not constituted as other natures are. A mellow evening, a tone of voice that struck upon the chord of memory —the tone, I say, and not the thing spoken, whatever it might be—a trait of generosity in others, a word of praise spoken to myself—all these would bring tears into my eyes, and sometimes induce a melancholy that preyed upon me for hours. I had been taught to look up to my father as to a superior being ; and his invariable harshness and cruelty to me helped, perhaps, to break my spirit, and to poison my nature. Do not mistake me ; my nature was gentle, but it was not healthy ; it was inoffensive because it was weak. I

became distrustful of everything—of everybody—of myself.
I dare not appear to feel, when not to feel were to be a
brute; I was afraid lest I should be made a mockery—lest
I should be held up to the world as one upon whom it might
exercise its scorn and ridicule with success and impunity.

*   *   *   *   *   *

"'Depend upon it, my good friend,' resumed Misty,
' that a wounded spirit must be assuaged, or healed, or got
rid of, by some means or the other. Hence drunkenness,
desperation, suicide. The first frequently precedes the other
two, and sometimes causes a recourse to them; but drinking
will suffice to keep out the foul fiend Despair for many
years. I invoked the aid of the benignant spirit Drunkenness.

*   *   *   *   *   *

"'Oh, Mr. Ketch, how dreadful a thing it is to be proud
and poor! I felt it—it was hell to me : not the physical
want—not starvation—not tramping the streets all night
without a shelter for the head, or a resting-place for the sole
of the foot—but the insult—the contumely—the scorn : I
felt it until my nature was changed—until my feelings turned
into gall, and burst forth into bitterness. The proudest man
must condescend to live; and to do so without means, what
must he do? Beg. I could not do that. You may naturally inquire how a man of my education and acquirements
could possibly be suffered to linger in penury, if I made
known my capabilities to the world. Alas! I was not the
man to blazon my own merits, such as they were; besides,
I would rather have broken stones on the road than be at
the mercy of men who, aware of the superiority of another
in mental endowments, vindicate their actual superiority in
secular advantages by compelling him to feel how dependent
he is upon their bounty. For these men do not feel, or will
not acknowledge, that the services you render are the labour
for which you ought to be paid, but pocket the advantage,

and lay claim to the merit of benevolence. Better for a proud man, Mr. Ketch, to be far below his real station than just under it; it is easier to bear extreme poverty—nay, want—-than to endure the unworthy insolence of a patron, a friend so called. To friends, therefore, I applied but seldom, and never with much advantage to myself.

*   *   *   *   *   *

" ' You have never, perhaps, seen your face in a particular looking-glass after an interval of some years; if you had done so, you would have detected the changes that time had worked upon you in a moment—a change which your daily looking-glass had failed to discover to you. This is association. In like manner a scene—a place—the home of your youth, familiar to the past, brought before you once more, discloses the altered aspect of the mind within.' "

Whitehead was very dilatory in his habits of work, owing doubtless in a great measure to the sad failing I have named, and after receiving a sum of money from his publishers in advance, he was too ready to neglect the punctual performance of his task, until importuned by them to do so. He had also family troubles. There was the hereditary taint of insanity in his race, and his brother Alfred, as well as one of his sisters, became mentally afflicted.

He resided in various places, but remained for a long while in "very mediocre apartments" on the first floor of a house in Great Ormond Street (probably the third on the right, entering from Southampton Row), and he was living here when *Richard Savage* was passing through the press. Mr. Hodder tells us that when he knew Whitehead (about 1852), the novelist lived in a little back street off Red Lion

Square. A striking picture is given of the poverty of his surroundings. His study was a little parlour on the ground floor, with no better prospect than the gutter below. As a literary craftsman it may be said of him that he made but few alterations in his proofs, and rarely an erasure in his MS., unless he took the trouble to re-copy the whole passage. His reading of the period of Queen Anne to George III. was extensive, and Mr. George Bentley, who knew him well and loved him, and retains an affectionate respect for his memory and a high opinion of his gifts, says that he spoke of Steele as if he had known him and spent some time with him. Nothing that could be said in description or criticism could bring us closer to the man Whitehead than this happy and penetrating observation. Whitehead possessed an extraordinary fund of humour, and in his early years was well-fitted to be the life of any company into which he was thrown. One of his early friends tells me that, were he now able to recall a number of Whitehead's puns, they would give him distinction in that lower department of humour; he remembers Whitehead telling him that he hoped *Jack Ketch* would not be considered " a Ketch-penny publication "! As a young man, one of Whitehead's whims was to project ridiculous works with impossible titles. He once informed the friend to whom I refer that he intended to write a book to be entitled *The Flash Cove's Vade Mecum: or Every Man His own Vagabond,* the volume to consist of short whimsical rules for the performance

of various peccadilloes. As might be expected of a
man of his temperament, he had a keen apprecia-
tion of the ludicrous, and could- amuse his friends
with felicitous sallies of wit, and could recount his
own experiences with great point and comicality. I
have been favoured by several friends with a minute
description of his appearance in later life, and although
it will perhaps be thought that some of my previous
remarks are inconsistent with a man so described,
it must be remembered how time changes even the
least mutable of us, and most of all a man who,
like Whitehead, had been long buffeted by a relentless
fate. He was tall, and of a dark complexion, with
a hollow chest and stooping gait, giving the appearance
of great fragility. He had a long, careworn face.
His voice was pleasant, but very low-pitched, and
sometimes in conversation he spoke so low as to
be scarcely audible. His manner was modest and
diffident; so diffident indeed, that except to his
intimate friends he appeared almost too shy and
sensitive. One of his favourite attitudes when talking
was to stand with arms folded across his chest, and
he sometimes seemed awakened by a remark, as if
his thoughts had previously been far away. One
who knew him slightly tells me that Whitehead looked
to him " the personification of one of the authors
of Grub Street." The handwriting in which he wrote
reports on books for one or two of the publishing
houses was peculiarly small, but very precise. Owing
doubtless in a great measure to the one pernicious

habit, the influence of which he could never throw off, his natural vivacity deserted him as years went on, and he became often moody and morose, and sometimes, when not sober, even quarrelsome. His wife is described by an acquaintance, as a very retiring lady; a friend, however, who knew both husband and wife for years, says that she was not without a temper of her own, and was a little inclined to shrewishness. Though not what may be described as an amiable woman, and not by any means one of education, she seems to have been a woman of some force of character, and, as such, a very suitable wife for a man so deficient in practical resolution. There is evidence that she exercised a salutary control over her husband. It would appear, also, that in his better moments his conduct towards her was exemplary. At other times he doubtless gave way to the irritation peculiar to men of his habits, but on the whole it may be said that his domestic relations were all that could be desired. Unfortunately for Whitehead, his wife died before him. They had no children. As years went on he began to experience a certain want of success, and this feeling probably became gradually intensified rather than diminished, primarily, no doubt, from the mental and physical effects upon him of his deplorable habits. He was now in his fifty-third year—an age long before which a man's ways and modes of thought have been moulded into their life-long shape. A man can rarely emigrate with success after middle life. The emigrant should always be young; for if not, however friendly the people with whom he casts in his lot, there still remains the inevitable change of scene, and altered conditions of existence and modes of thought, which make travelling to the young so delightful, and to the agèd so irksome. It was therefore unwise of Whitehead to change his sphere, notwithstanding the known hospitality of the people and the delightful climate of Australia. It was, as Mr. George Bentley fitly remarks, "carrying an eighteenth-century mind into a twentieth-century country, with certain collapse." Perhaps Whitehead thought that the voyage would improve his health, and possibly even permanently renovate his already shattered constitution. He left London, accompanied by his wife, in 1857, having accepted a literary engagement on a Melbourne newspaper, probably the *Melbourne Argus;* but I am told that at the time of his death, which occurred at Melbourne on the 5th July, 1862, he was a "Free Lance," writing for any journal which would take his copy; and this statement is confirmed by an entry in the books of the Registrar-General's Office for Victoria. He is therein described as being "engaged on newspapers," fifty-eight years of age, and having died in the Melbourne Hospital. It is also certified that he had been five years in Victoria. The pathetic and the commonplace are oftentimes one, and surely never more so than in these few prosaic words narrating Whitehead's end. How low had sunk the author of *Richard*

Savage, The Solitary, and *Jasper Brooke,* when the only epithet suitable for him which occurred to the clerk who made the entry was that of "engaged on newspapers"! The last and saddest fact made known to me concerning Whitehead comes from the secretary of the Melbourne Hospital, who furnishes me with an entry from the books stating that Whitehead died from the effects of destitution.

Whitehead has been compared to Thomas Lovell Beddoes. They were certainly alike in some respects. Both were wanderers from their earliest and probably best friends, and from the land of their nativity; both died in hospital, and both were, in all probability, interred in that peculiarly mournful plot of ground wherein rest the remains of those whose last days were frequently days of more than ordinary suffering and sorrow, and who died, knowing that the last sad offices would be done to them by strangers, and that their burial would be unhallowed by the tears of their kindred. Viewed as a whole, Whitehead's was a strange life, a sad life, but by no means a life without a moral.

CHAPTER II.

WHITEHEAD AS A POET.

As a poet Charles Whitehead clearly belongs to the school of Shelley, with a certain affinity to that of Keats. *The Solitary*, the first in order of his collected poetical works, is a poem in the Spenserian stanza. It is a poem of reflection rather than incident, with here and there a few lines of description, but mainly depending for its interest on the originality and force of its abstract reflections.

It is here, on the very threshold of his book, that we first perceive unequivocal signs that Charles Whitehead was no mere writer of verse. Had he been so, he would most probably have conceived it impossible to write anything which the world would care to read, on subjects which have been the staple theme of poets for the last thousand years. *The Solitary* is a noble poem, full of thought, and dealing with many of the constantly absorbing themes of life about which, from a true poet, we are never tired of listening, and which, according to Mr. Matthew

Arnold's theory, it is the highest function of poetry to discuss.

In some important particulars Charles Whitehead seems to have been the forerunner of the modern School of Poetry, known by the slang title of " Æsthetic." This he was in a similar sense to that in which Cowper was the harbinger of the romantic movement at the beginning of this century, though Whitehead was obviously a lesser agent. He is master of much of the technical perfection which has become indissolubly associated with the names of Mr. Swinburne, and Dante Gabriel Rossetti ; he has also a great deal of the weird supernatural quality so prominent in the latter poet. His life was sad, and his poetry reflects without affectation the mournful side of his career. Charles Whitehead may thus be said to have stood between Coleridge and Rossetti, and though most painfully unequal, he is, in my judgment, in his very best moods not far below the average level of either, and assuredly much above the lowest level of both.

In the poem of *The Solitary* we see with quite remarkable clearness some incidents of the poet's inner life. It would appear from the scattered and somewhat mystical allusions which float into a poem like this, that Whitehead had a brother who was accomplished and highly gifted, but that he died before he " spoke to fame." Whitehead tells us in a powerful and touching passage how at the grave of this brother he resolved to consecrate his life to noble purposes ;

but how, at first insensibly, and for a long time so
gradually that he scarce perceived it, he drifted from
this secure anchorage into a stream of evil tendency,
which, broadening and increasing in strength, carried
the hapless barque on its bosom into a maelstrom
of utter ruin—in other words, he fell away into a
species of deep social degradation, from which, as
we know, he never wholly extricated himself. The
poem is full of reflections on life and its varied
emotions, on sin and sorrow, from the standpoint of
one who, in the circumstances I have sketched, suffers
from the world-weariness that springs partly from
remorse. A few examples of these reflections will
perhaps be welcome.

Whitehead is notably a phrase-maker—one who
loved nicely to balance his words until he obtained
the exact shade of meaning he required. Many of
his phrases are so felicitous that they can hardly
fail to live in the memory. To this quality of his
writing the following extracts will bear abundant testimony. The first extract is a passage of personal
recollection respecting the brother* to whom reference
has been made.

> " A sweet and lovely evening :—Heaven and earth
>   Do lend each other beauty, and the cloud
>   Blushes auspicious of to-morrow's birth.

---

* The following note appears in the 1831 edition of
The Solitary : "The author's brother was drowned some
years ago at the age of seventeen."

Let not thy spirit be too rudely bow'd
By the tumultuous throng and busy crowd,
That memory doth ev'n by this scene restore ;
    And bid my throbbing heart speak not so loud ;
For oh ! my brother, crush'd and stricken sore,
Unto thy silent grave I bend my steps once more.

" And many a Spring hath died above thy head,
    And many a Summer flower that blooms to fade ;
And Autumn many a leafy offering shed,
    Whereof the Winter his cold couch hath made :
    The young green tree affords an ampler shade ;
And many a musing stranger, wandering by,
    Hath pass'd the lowly turf where thou art laid,
And heav'd perchance the involuntary sigh,
Since thy neglected grave thy brother hath been nigh.

" And now he comes—ah ! can he be the same
    That with religious step, in early youth,
Awe-struck and trembling to thy chamber came
    And kiss'd thy forehead pale—in earnest sooth
    Vowing to dedicate his soul to truth,
For ever, for thy sake ?   Ah ! bootless vow !
    But pity, fare thee well, and thankless ruth—
For they must reap who sow, who sow must plough,
And as thine ashes then, cold is his bosom now."

The closing lines are inexpressibly sad. It is in
truth the cry of a weary soul, who has the unutter-
able wretchedness of feeling that most of his sorrow is
self-inflicted ; the cry of one who bitterly bemoans his
pitiable state, and would willingly escape from it ; of
one, the fortress of whose moral courage has been so
sapped by the enervating influence of excess, that he

is no longer able to break through the barriers which environ him.   All this may have been autobiographical, or it may have been merely an idea dramatically projected into art; in any case, it remains what I have described.

The next passage I would quote is striking, coming from such a man.   It is a subjective word-picture in verse of such an one as Richard Savage, whom Charles Whitehead has elsewhere so vigorously delineated in prose.

'Judge him not harshly ; he is sunk too low
   For thee to exalt thy worthier self upon ;
The happiness he sought thou canst not know,
   The misery he found thou hast not known :
   The meed of glory was not his alone :
Bare is the summit of Parnassus' station,
   And cold the fountain pure of Helicon,
Thou hast not felt the great, the mad temptation,
The hell—the heaven—the paradise—the deep damnation !'

This is what Charles Whitehead has to say about unrest — the longing and vague disappointed hope which men such as he so often feel :

"Why not content ?   The hour runs to its close ;
   The day, the month, and the unfruitful year ;
The jet of life more free and wider flows,
   As Youth's contracted channels disappear :
   O Youth ! false treacherous stream, for ever dear,
We turn—the better prospect dim is seen
   Before us, and we wipe the bitter tear ;
The shallop in the haven rides serene ;—
Oh for eternal shores, and fields for ever green !"

These lines strike a higher note in the gamut of
Truth :

> " Oh ! better not to live than live the death
>   Of being without impulse, and supply
> A daily portion of superfluous breath
>   To animate a pulse that scarce can die :
>   The strength to soar, without the will to fly ;
> The soul still brooding on its own estate
>   Like desolation aping destiny ;
> The heart that will not love, and cannot hate,
> For which Heaven hath no joy, and Hell can find no bait."

In this stanza we see a notable example of Whitehead's phrase-making.   It would not be easy to find a
more succinct phrase to denote the existence of those
who, with food and raiment and with a sufficiency of
worldly goods, abandon themselves to a life of virtuous
sloth, than in the line—

> "A daily portion of superfluous breath "—

and, which is more, not only do we find this phrase to
be succinct, but we feel it, notwithstanding its withering sarcasm, to be true.

In the following lines we perceive that Whitehead,
with the instinct and some of the egotism of the
true poet, discerns at once one of the real rewards
of the muse to be the sweet conviction which she
imparts to her true disciples, that they alone can
analyze and exhibit to the world the mysteries of
our sorrows and the beautiful phantasies of our
dreams.

> " Nor for herself, nor for the wealth she brings,
>   Is the Muse woo'd and won ; but for the deep,
>   Occult, profound, unfathomable things,
>   The engines of our tears whene'er we weep,
>   The impulse of our dreams whene'er we sleep,
>   The mysteries that our sad hearts possess,
>   Which, and the keys of which, the Muse doth keep.
>   Oh ! may the trust her young disciple bless,
>   Whene'er she yields her gifts in faith and gentleness !"

In the following stanzas Whitehead deals with the
interesting subject of the isolation of great natures.
Such lines remind us by inverse association of what
Byron says in the third canto of *Childe Harold* on
the loneliness of greatness—that worst form of loneliness which is most frequently felt amid crowds—
even when these are crowds of admirers. The
concluding lines of this passage are truly magnificent.

> " Meanwhile, these Alpine natures, plac'd alone,
>   Wrapt in the clouds, a frozen harvest reap
>   Of an unkindly seed too early sown ;
>   Nor can they the precarious summit keep,
>   But rush untimely to the gloomy deep :
>   As though an avalanche, hurtless before,
>   The sunbeam's nearest favourite, should leap
>   From the high cliff which its vast pressure bore,
>   Never to threaten fate or tempt the thunder more.

> " Alas ! for all the miseries that strew
>   The common path our trackless footsteps make,
>   As we creep on this maze of darkness through :
>   The hearts that break, the hearts that cannot break,

The hearts that bury their last hopes, and take
E'en comfort from the grave, and struggle still,
And lingering on for very misery's sake
Live—not because they would, but that they will;
And die when baffled Death is left no power to kill."

Whitehead had a great admiration of Shelley; witness the following passage:

"Ah ! would I could recall him from the past,
Untimely, sudden, and for ever gone ;
That gentle spirit to the waters cast,
Whose restless planet, edg'd with darkness, shone
With mournful light and yet of Heaven alone ;
Who with intrenchant shield and temper'd sword,
Plume-crested, like a new Bellerophon,
Had with fresh strength a nobler verse restor'd,
And left a name for raseless marble to record.

"But he was sunk in the devouring wave,
Wak'd into rage by Ocean's tyrannous nod.
Masterless Ocean, ne'er but once a slave,
Then only to the only Son of God,
Who, on his neck proud-lifted, meekly trod
And smil'd him into peace—shall he withhold
His vengeance, lightning-wing'd and thunder-shod,
When the frail bark rips up his bosom cold ?
No—o'er that laurell'd head the atheist billows roll'd.

"Yet, lest Apollo, for the outrage done,
In mockery of his power, and in despite,
To his disciple and the Muses' son,
Should henceforth, in his all-resistless might,
Remit his beams, nor crown the deep with light,
The hoary monarch bade, with timely heed,
The auxiliar tempest to reluctant flight,
And summon'd all his billows in his need,
Bidding his daughter haste with more than utmost speed.

" And Arethusa came, and with dear care
     Rais'd the sunk form that ne'er should suffer more,
And strain'd the salt ooze from his clotted hair,
     And, laid in her cerulean bosom, bore
     The hapless bard to the Italian shore ;
And there he lay whom pity ne'er forgave,
     Whom life might ne'er recall, nor love restore,
A sight all powerful and strong to save
The souls of those who deem no life beyond the grave.

" Yet to his urn there came a motley crew,
     More base, more blind—and earthlier than the worm ;
Much marvell'd they, and sage conclusions drew,
     Much did their solemn minds rebuke the storm ;
     One beat his breast to keep his bosom warm :
The moralist pursued his saw, ' to die ;'
     The nice-brain'd sophist, full of phrase and form,
Affirm'd the wherefore, and assum'd the why ;
While ever and anon they shouted ' Charity !'

" Such charity as leaves all hate behind
     . In bitter earnestness of wrath—such speed
As oversteps the fleet feet of the wind,
     Bearing the sponge, the hyssop, and the reed,
     When Truth cries out in her extremest need.
Was theirs ;—such subtle praise as fain would be
     Reputed back as their own honour's meed ;
Such censure as the smirking Pharisee,
When he hath thank'd his God, was theirs, and their decree.

" Oh, Shelley ! not a word—no, not one word,
     The voice of censure or of pity's breath.
Take all that my unskilful hands afford,
     This bunch of cypress, this unfashioned wreath
     Hung at the postern of remorseless Death.

> Meanwhile, let be, if aught these words avail,
>   The sword of Justice laid in Mercy's sheath;
> Sure we are fallen enough, and false, and frail,
>   And have scarce space to pray—then wherefore should we
>   rail?"

Where could we find a finer poetical description of Shelley's death than occurs in these lines?—and how true it was that Shelley's

> "Restless planet, edg'd with darkness, shone
>   With mournful light and yet of Heaven alone."

The mythological conceit of Apollo sending Arethusa to succour his hapless disciple is at least pretty, and is artistically woven into the weft of the verse. Such classical allusions require the most skilful care and adroit handling; otherwise, especially in modern verse, they show a tendency to become insipid and inane. The foregoing classical parable, however, beautifies the passage, and in the concluding lines there is much forcible reflection.

In the following lines Whitehead beautifully states one of his conceptions of the true poet's mission:

> "To kindle soft humanity; to raise,
>   With gentle strength infus'd, the spirit bow'd;
> To pour a second sunlight on our days,
>   And draw the restless lightning from our cloud;
>   To cheer the humble, and to dash the proud;
> What heaven withholds more largely to supply,
>   And fringe with joy our ever-weaving shroud;
> Besought in peace to live, and taught to die;
> The poet's task is done—Oh Immortality!"

In these almost prayerful lines he touchingly asks
for the greatest of all gifts—the gift of Charity:

> "Oh ! grant us yet, nor be this prayer unheard,
>   Whatever else at our request denied,
>   Meek Charity in thought, in deed, in word ;
>   Humility that walks by the wayside,
>   And with the pilgrim Patience doth abide,
>   In such low state as the worn peasant knows ;
>   Content at least, whatever fate betide,
>   How few our joys, how multiplied our woes,
> To bear our life to its probationary close !"

Here are some powerful, though painful, lines on
baffled hopes, strikingly showing the bitter blight that
was even then—so early in his life—preventing the
fruition of his powers.   Such phrases as the following
live in the memory:

> "Time's December comes before our May,
>   Yesterday's to-morrow is to-day;"

and a line in a subsequent passage, too long for
complete quotation,

> "The present is the future of the past."

This is the passage referred to above:

> "And thus, and to this consummation wrought,
>   The Spring we yet were hoping fades away,
>   Even in the very ecstasy of thought,
>   And Time's December comes before our May.
>   The wintry sun looks down with slanting ray,
>   And something must be finish'd or begun,
>   And yesterday's to-morrow is to-day,
>   Commence the promis'd race you vow'd to run—
> Ah ! past-redemption wretch, thou art indeed undone !"

On one of Hamlet's pregnant themes Whitehead speaks thus:

"Strange paradox!   Eternal contradiction!
   Man!   Who shall know thee, who shall seek to know?
  Great without aim, and base against conviction,
    Still sowing, and still reaping what you sow,
    A harvest whereof even the seed is woe;
  Stubborn caprice, taking the name of will;
    Vice, swift to enter, to depart how slow;
  Despair that will not die, and cannot kill,
And empty toys to mock the empty brain they fill!"

On another of Hamlet's themes this is said:

" What were the world without thee? a long sleep
    Untenanted by dreams; a narrow tomb
  Wherein, the worm's reversion, we should creep
    Like worms, impatient, eager of our doom.
    The sun would rise, but only to illume
  Blank Horror—Nature, effigy of dearth,
    The wombless daughter of creation's womb,
  With dewless eyes would sad bewail her birth,
Cursing the espoused vow which gave her to the earth.

" But Love's mysterious sympathies pervade
    Creation, with strange impulses imbued;
  Which, if the soul be yet unquench'd, are made,
    Spite of the heart's inconstant habitude,
    To turn the bitter to maturest good;
  So that, whate'er remain to tempt desire
    Is from our wither'd hopes themselves, renew'd
  To worthier growth, as a fast-fading fire
Doth, by dead branches fed, a livelier strength acquire."

The first stanza is worthy of praise, although the imagery is painful, and also in some slight degree coarse; but very true and noble is the thought embodied in the opening lines of the succeeding passage. This stanza is probably reminiscent—the simile with which it closes is apt and new.

Of music Whitehead speaks thus :

"O Music ! in thy more impassioned sway
　　Thou mak'st me wild, e'en till my ravish'd brain,
Into the heaven of transports borne away,
　　Knows its own griefs no longer ; and the pain
　　It nourish'd till existence grew the bane
Of time, is eas'd of its most weary load,
　　And the soul trembles from the breast again, ·
Call'd by thy blithe strain from its dark abode,
Where, as it seem'd, it lay almost unseen of God !

"But if thy mood be of a sadder measure,
　　Thou dost my heart in deeper anguish steep ;
And all the past, foregone, or vanish'd pleasure,
　　Before me doth in sad procession creep ;
　　And I could dash me on the earth and weep,
But that mine eyes forbid the burning tears ;
　　Or yield a life I can no longer keep,
　To fill with sorry hope's dissembling fears
A calendar of woe, made up of days and years."

Hope which we bless, and Hatred with which we frequently vainly strive, Wisdom which we are taught to reverence, and Love which we are elsewhere told is our greatest earthly possession, are all referred to in these lines; but unhappily the beauty of the passage is somewhat marred by the bitter morbidity which is far too apparent at its close :

"Beware of Folly, she is wondrous wise ;
　　Beware of Wisdom, she is half a fool ;

Of Love beware, so blind with Argus' eyes;
  Of Hate, so passing hot, so lasting cool;
  Of all that work by word, or prate by rule;
Of speculation built upon desert;
  Of Hope, the brittle reed in Fortune's pool,
Which our clear-imag'd Heaven doth invert;
What granted prayer could now re-form thee as thou wert?

" Let be the baser drudgery of life
  To those who toil for plenty, or increase;
  'Twixt knaves and fools what look ye for but strife?
  'Twixt fate and thee let fruitless discord cease;
  For life is but a flaw'd and blotted lease;
And 'twixt thyself and all the world preserve
  An arm'd neutrality, a barren peace;
Lean not to one, nor from the other swerve,
Thy way is straight;—proceed with an ungalled nerve."

How vivid is the description of Time and Change!

" Lost—we ourselves seek our own miseries:
  Unconsciously above itself, the mind
Lends its immortal yearnings to the eyes,
  And with a treacherous fondness, undesign'd,
  Still makes the beauty which it cannot find.
Ah me ! the sad mutation is not slow,
  And reason errs, but is not ever blind;
For blest or curst did never mortal grow,
But time and change in league together made him so.

" Change, change, for ever change—the eternal chime
  Rings in our startled ears with eager knell,
Mocking the solemn audit of old Time
  With busy interruption ;—we rebel,
  Revolt, and yet are reconcil'd too well;

4

> "For he doth rivet all things, or estrange,
>   And to his undisputed will compel ;
> Even Nature's uniformity is change ;
> The unbounded universe is his permitted range."

¶ Hardly anything could be more beautiful than the short description given in the following stanza of a sweet summer evening in the country. The poet expresses well, by a beautiful simile, the stillness of such a scene—a stillness which almost all of us have frequently felt, and have oftentimes vainly striven to translate into words. The lines are almost as perfect a presentment of the scene described as Wordsworth's sonnet beginning—

> "It is a beauteous evening, calm and free."

> "How still ! as though Silence herself were dead,
>   And her wan ghost were floating in the air :
> The moon glides o'er the heaven with printless tread,
>   And to her far-off frontier doth repair ;
>   O'er-wearied lids are closing everywhere ;—
> All living things that own the touch of sleep
>   Are beckon'd as the wasting moments wear,
> Till one by one, in valley, or from steep,
> Unto their several homes they, and their shadows, creep."

Our poet has this felicitous line on a familiar subject :

> "The Gospel of the stars, great Nature's Holy Writ."

These impressive lines deal with one of the greatest themes of literature and life :

> "And if ye needs must moralise, behold
>   Diligent Death, unseen of man, employ'd

Prowling with full-fed leisure through the fold,
Each stride an ample grave of yet untroubled mould.

" For sometimes doffing his superfluous state,
    In realms below our lower hemisphere
Bridle and bit he flings aside elate,
    And casts his crown away, and brandish'd spear,
    And leaves his pallid steed in mid career,
Which, joyous of the unincumbered rein,
    Neighs madly through the echoing meadows drear;
Bites the vague air, and bounds along the plain,
With fire-shot eyes surcharg'd, and wild abandon'd mane.

" Come then, O Death ! for thou art welcome ever,
    Whether thou come, with darkling brow austere,
To crush out life with lingering, slow endeavour ;
    Or like young Cupid, crown'd with stars appear,
    Beside thee Psyche, in thy hand a spear,
Tipp'd with a beam of heaven's interior light,
    Still blessed be the hour that brings thee here,
And I will hail thine unaccustom'd sight,
And follow thee with joy where'er thy steps invite."

" For still to be, and be o'erthrown by sorrow,
    To wrestle with our weakness from our birth,
And all the strength we know constrain'd to borrow,
    Antæus-like, from the reluctant earth,
    If this be life, then of how little worth !—
Receiv'd in thy dominion, Death, we fling
    Aside the harness, and disdain the girth ;
No sorrow there—no grief—no suffering—
Peace, peace, 'tis much for man—O Death ! where is thy
        sting ?

The Solitary closes with the following beautiful
description of dawn, while the saddened and hopeless

4—2

man—one of those whose "heart cannot break"—
returns once more to his diurnal penance :

> "But soft a motion trembles in the sky,
>   And with a timid streak of dubious glow,
>   Curdles the east, and from his terrace high,
>   The glad procession of the light doth go :
>   Clear, and more clear, all neighbouring objects grow,
>   Wrought from the sable texture of the dark,
>   And now a fresh chill air begins to blow,
>   And now springs up the voluntary lark,
> And the sun appears, Heaven's glorious hierarch !

> "Another day breaks forth—another day—
>   Then let me close this ineffectual strain,
>   From painful, passive torture call'd away,
>   To quick reality of active pain.
>   Enough, enough, the rest is on the chain :—
>   Return'd to do diurnal penance still,
>   To the last dregs the bitter cup to drain,
>   The gloomy circuit of my fate fulfil,
> This is my measur'd task—this the Almighty's will !

The next poem in the volume is the *Story of Jasper
Brooke.* This poem is the reverse of the *Solitary,*
being full of incident rather than reflection.

The scene of the story is laid in the reign of one of
the Henrys. Its plot is as follows. A father of
ample wealth forms the project of marrying his son
Philip to the daughter of a neighbour equally well
furnished with worldly goods. He accordingly sum-
mons this son, and in a few jesting words lays his
project before him. The son is thrown by the com-
munication into a state which is described as neither
wonder nor surprise, and equivocatingly responds to

his father's appeal, by saying that the maiden selected for him is too worthy for his poor deserts. The father sneeringly insinuates that the son loves a poor girl named Julia, whose parent had claimed for her, some time previous to his death, the protection of his mercantile connection with Jasper Brooke. Philip, in the most humble manner, conveys to his father the startling intelligence that he and this Julia are already wedded. The father in a paroxysm of rage bids him begone. Jasper then conceives the infamous project of inducing the old family servant, Kirke, by the promise of a large pecuniary bribe, to commit perjury. Acting on Kirke's information, the son is arrested and conveyed to prison. Before the examination the old servant is filled with compunction at the part he has to play, and earnestly begs that his master will relieve him from his promise; but this Jasper absolutely refuses to do. When the case is called for trial, Jasper hypocritically murmurs a few commonplaces as to his wish to have died before things had come to such a pass, and refers the Judge to his old servant, who (having been sworn) proceeds to tell how various valuable jewels had been stolen ; how his master had in the first instance impeached his own honesty; how, troubled and miserable, he had eagerly watched, and how (agonizing discovery!) he had found Master Philip (whom as a child he had dangled on his knee) filching the jewels ; how, when he told his master this, he was wroth with him for traducing his ancient name of spotless purity ; and how, finally, he was only convinced of the justice of the charge by himself beholding the jewels in his son's wrenched trunk.

The Judge, on hearing this extraordinary statement, is deeply distressed, and urges the father to be more lenient, saying that justice would be enhanced by mercy. At last, however, the Judge commits Philip for trial, and in a powerful passage Whitehead describes how the two old men, Jasper and Kirke, leave the court, each well satisfied with his share in the villainy—the one that he has at least obtained revenge, the other that, the unpleasant and dirty work of his perjury being done, he will obtain a rich golden reward; and Whitehead parenthetically remarks, that the two passions which never grow cold in men of whatever age are the love of revenge and the lust for money.

Philip is of course committed to prison, his girl-wife, Julia, being permitted to be with him. A very touching and pathetic description is given of their intercourse in the prison. Julia is full of sadness and anguish; sometimes awakening to the fact that friends could assist her beloved one, and importuning him to tell her where she might find some of the many possessed of influence, who would come forward to swear Kirke's statements untrue, in order to save him. Philip, brave youth, with all dignity and composure, seeks tenderly to soothe Julia, whilst himself hopeless of rescue from his impending fate. But when Julia becomes more than usually hysterical in her entreaties he is sometimes unmanned. Then he feels bitterly

the poignant grief of having been the cause of bringing on her this sorrow. From his father he expects
nothing ; sometimes, however, he experiences a strange
sort of satisfaction in sheltering, if it be but for a few
moments or hours, the maiden he loves, and doing so
as her husband.

Little or nothing is said in the poem of a formal
conviction. But it is presumed that the law will
speedily take its course, and that Philip will be executed. The lovers eventually sink to rest in each
other's arms ; and even the gaoler, entering the cell to
remove Julia, is so touched with the pathos of their
situation, that he forbears to awaken them. In a few
words of soliloquy he says that he has seen many
prisoners and many ways of taking approaching death,
but never did he see any one with composure like this.
The young prisoner must be innocent, and the bell
shall awaken him to misery—not he.

Meanwhile Jasper invites Kirke to make merry
with him, and they sit down to a sumptuous feast.
Jasper presses Kirke to eat. The servant is almost
totally unable to do so, but he drinks deeply of
the wine. Its influence begins to creep over him
powerfully, and he loses discretion. Presently, he
darkly hints to his lord, but in a sort of half-jest,
that he, Jasper, had made away with Uberti (Julia's
father) by foul play; asks whether he died rich, and
whether these goblets from which they are now drain-
ing their wine were his. Jasper indignantly orders
him " to take his cheer and stint his prate." Shortly

after they part for the night, and, sobered by Jasper's anger, old Kirke retires tremblingly and for the last time to his accustomed bed, fearful lest Jasper, in wrath for his folly when overcome with wine, should kill him during the night.

Jasper is visited by a direful dream. His past life comes before him in all its hideousness, and also in all its joyousness. He thinks of his marriage morn; of his wife's trustful love; he thinks of her death-bed, and of the pain which he caused to her pious soul. He remembers his deed of darkness to Uberti. When in the morning the old crone who waits on him finds him, she imagines him dead, and rushes for Kirke. Together, however, they revive him, and his first cry to Kirke is to rush to the prison, proclaim that they had sworn a lie, and stay the execution of his son. Kirke asks whether this will save *their* lives?—exclaiming that he in dreams saw them both hanging on the gallows tree. Jasper says that *he* may be saved; as for himself, his stone has only to be engraved. He tells him also to send a scrivener, and hints that if he does his will in these respects he shall not have cause to repent it. Kirke hastens to the gaol; but he returns an altered man; and the scrivener is more aghast at his appearance than when he hears Jasper's tale of infamy and guilt. And Kirke comes not alone. Julia's sorrows have overwhelmed her reason, and she—now an idiot—comes with him. Jasper swoons when he sees her—his dream was not more dreadful than this. When he revives, Kirke, who evidently believes the truth of his statement, tells the father that Philip died " before his hour," and that he has brought his wife for a fresh dowry—that the law is on their track, and that he must bid him farewell.

Jasper commands the scrivener so to make his will as to leave all his money for masses for his soul· Graves, the scrivener, beseeches him to remember the girl. But the end hastens on. The leech comes ; but all his skill is in vain, and Jasper dies raving. When the scrivener and leech, awe-stricken, leave the death-chamber, they behold a hideous thing on the staircase beneath them ! It is Kirke, hanging dead from a noose which he himself has made.

This is how the poem of *Jasper Brooke* opens. The lines quoted below show that Whitehead had a large command over the octosyllabic measure, and could write excellent descriptive verse :

> " It was a dark and ancient room
>   In which old Jasper sat alone ;
>   Within, the sun had never shone :
>   But Jasper was cheerful amid the gloom,
>   As a light that burneth in a tomb.
>   ' Ha ! ha !' he chuckled, and rubb'd his hands ;
>   ' The sunshine that the ripple bears
>   Casteth its colour on the sands,
>   As yellow as harvest ears ;
>   And why are we young, or why are we old,
>   If we see not our sunshine turn to gold ?' "

How fine is the following passage, in which, after Philip's temporizing reply to his father's request to

woo the maid chosen for him by the latter, old Jasper
goes at once to the root of the difficulty, and sneeringly taunts him with a love for Julia.

> "'Hear me: Twelve years my memory dates,
> Since the good ship, from Genoa's port,
> (Would it had been the tempest's sport,
> Wreck'd in the fell Gibraltar straits!)
> Sail'd hither, bringing with her one,
> By woe and bankruptcy undone.
> Carlo Uberti was his name.
> He sought me; urg'd a piteous claim
> Of former merchandise consign'd;
> (Weak fool! to think within his mind,
> Who eats the fruit must love the rind.)
> *I* was the fool.   His story wrought
> Upon my heart—his child he brought—
> A little tender, touching thing,
> A summer cheek, an eye of spring.
> What more to move me *could* he bring?
> My house receiv'd him and his child;
> The father wept, the daughter smil'd;
> Thus, like a fool, was I beguil'd.
> He died.   What more?   The child remains;
> The child whom I have fostered still;
> And how does she requite my pains,
> My care repay, my hopes fulfil?
> And thou, would'st thou, of simple wit,
> Lure a poor sparrow to the sill,
> And frame a cage, and cherish it,
> As though its russet feathers vied
> With birds, the sun's adopted pride,
> Of scarlet plumage, golden-dyed?
> Thou lov'st this Julia; spare the lie
> That rises in thee to deny,
> What thy cheek tells me, and thine eye.'"

Then follows Philip's confession. Jasper in fierce wrath bids Philip begone, and forthwith takes measures for his unnatural and terrible revenge. He persuades, as we have seen, the old servant, Kirke, to bear false witness against his son; but when this old man relents, we find that the implacable Jasper is compelled to use persuasion rather than force to attain his ends. This is the vivid passage in which it is done:

> " ' Yet Kirke, good Kirke,'—but Jasper's eye
> And teeth tight-clench'd with malice fell,
> Suit not with soft persuasion well ;—
> ' Hast thou not promis'd ? would'st begone
> From what we have struck hands upon ?'
> But Kirke took up his former strain :
> ' The little lad; I see him now ;
> How did he tend me—soothe my pain,
> And bring me cooling drink, and how
> For hours and hours watch by my side—
> Would 'twere God's pleasure I had died !
> I have done sin for you, but this——'

> " ' The holy book hath had thy kiss,'
> Urg'd Jasper ; ' and to be forsworn,
> Better that thou had'st ne'er been born.
> Thou'rt outcast by thine own consent :
> An oath when broken is not sprent ;
> But with a curse of Heaven re-knit ;
> For angels have attested it. ,
> Dost thou forget ; dost thou regard
> What I have pledg'd—that rich reward
> Which hath been, during fifty years,
> The texture of thy hopes and fears,
> Which makes thee lord of time, with power,

> Blithe, sprightly as a paramour,
> To turn to pleasure every hour?"

Philip is brought before the Justice, and thus the old servant tells his plausible, though perjured tale:

> "Then Kirke heaves up his voice to tell
> A tale which he had conn'd too well;
> No lesson had he wont to spell,
> Which, when 'twas learn'd and turned to deed,
> Gain'd brave broad pieces for its meed.
> ' May't please you, my good master here,—
> When I have serv'd this fifty year,
> Had lost—mislaid at first he thought—
> Treasures from foreign countries brought.
> He ask'd knew I of these things aught?
> God's mercy! *I /* I do protest
> Methought my master spoke in jest.
> A rope of pearls; a Venice chain
> Which on a king's breast might have lain;
> A golden cup a king might drain.
> He questioned me of these—alack!
> No wish of mine could fetch them back,
> Unless I owned a magic ring,
> The lost, or like the lost, to bring
> Safe, by a genie, as they sing.
> I watch'd, as Master Brooke beseech'd;
> My honesty in part impeach'd,
> My duty, my fidelity,
> Quicken'd my sense, sharpen'd my eye;
> And what at length did it descry?
> That I should live to see so clear!—
> That I should live to tell it here!
> Heaven aid me as I hope to thrive!
> Young Master Philip, as I live,
> Have I not sworn it? and 'tis truth—
> True as the creed—I saw the youth,

Myself behind the arras hid,
Saw him creep past me where I stood,
And softly raise the casket-lid,
Wherein lay, by the Holy Rood !
A ruby, red as fairies' blood,
Telling whose worth, belief would fail,
Pric'd at its carats by the tale,
Committed to the goldsmith's scale.
This did I see him filch ; he fled,
I following, fill'd with grief and dread.
And to his chamber did he go,
And in his trunk the gem bestow.
Now when I told this work of woe
To Master Brooke, as duty bade,
Beshrew me, he was well nigh mad ;—
Call'd me opprobrious names and swore
I did belie the youth, traduce
The virtuous mother who him bore ;
Curs'd me and the pernicious use
He had put me to ; in fine, we clomb
Like wretches to a midnight tomb,
Trembling, to Master Philip's room ;
And there the wrench'd trunk render'd up
The ruby, chain, and pearls and cup.' "

Philip is completely overwhelmed by this cruelly false, yet seemingly probable testimony against him. His first thoughts are to proclaim it all an infamous lie ; but he glances at his father, and the diabolical aspect of his face causes his resolution to falter.

" So he said nothing ; but sank down
A leaden grief from sole to crown,
Into the anguish of a swoon.

" ' He stands committed !' This—no more
The Justice said, and to a door

> Points Kirke and Jasper and—'tis o'er,
> And thence the two old men depart
> By a by-passage, light of heart ;
> One, that revenge is on its way,
> And one that he hath earn'd his pay.
> Of the two hideous passions say,
> Thou who canst human hearts unfold,
> Which sooner will itself allay,
> The thirst of blood, or thirst of gold ?
> Neither is quench'd as men grow old."

The extremely fine, though terribly painful lines quoted above, show how powerfully Whitehead could analyze human passions.

Philip has one solace in his crushing sorrow—Julia is with him ; a single ray of sunshine to mitigate the darkness of impending doom.

> " And his young wife his prison shares ;
>   Now stilly lying where he lies,
>   Her own soft mingling with his prayers ;
>   Now, bearing in her voice Despair's,
>   Whom she awakens with her cries.
>   She will go somewhere ; she will raise—
>   It hath been done so many ways,
>   So many times,—friends who shall speak
>   Truth in such cadence, as shall wreak
>   Remorse on sin ; dread as the sound
>   Of trumpets when the angels blow,
>   Who dash the guilty to the ground,
>   Plant triumph on the guiltless brow,
>   And make earth just again : but how ?
>   Ah ! dreams dissolving into pain !
>   Thrust back to consciousness again,
>   How wild her projects, and how vain !

A huddled creature on his breast,
With a strange quietude of brain,
Which seeming to solicit rest,
Is torpid madness at the best—
She lies and murmurs as she lies,
Words of inquiry and surmise ;
Consoling flatteries soft and low,
Then piteous sentences of woe,
In loose uncertain ebb and flow.
Yet, be they words of joy or grief,
Love speaks them well doth Philip know.
'Tis to his spirit a relief
On his last day, now waxing brief,
As a warm bird in a lorn nest
To hold his widow in his breast."

This is the description of the feast to which Jasper
invites Kirke :

" Kirke twitch'd him by the sleeve :—' Old lad,
Thou com'st in time to be made glad ;
Sit down ; art hungry ? and prepare
To let thy spirit dance in air.
I have wine here so ripe and rare,
That in a trice the leaden soul,
Groping in darkness like a mole,
Touch'd by the blessing springs to light,
And mounts to heaven, as of right :—
Down—we will have a merry night.'
They sit : but Kirke, though press'd to eat,
Tastes sparingly the luscious meat,
And kneaded bread of whitest wheat ;
But lifts his cup full oft, and drinks
Till his eyes sparkle through his winks.
' 'Tis good : I trace it as it sinks,
And note it prancing through my veins,

> Like a gay troop through narrow lanes.
> Ha ! Ha !'
> 　　　　　' Yet, eat, good Kirke.'
> 　　　　　　　　　　' I can't ;
> This is the minister I want,
> Heart-cheering wine : my throat is tight,
> As though bound by a silken cord,
> The self-same cord which, on that night,
> Sent old Uberti to the Lord.
> Did he die rich ? was this his gear ?
> These goblets that do service here ?'

> " ' Peace, fool !' cried Jasper, ' take thy cheer,
> And stint thy prate : the past retriev'd,
> Is a new missal interleav'd
> With an old sermon : let it pass.
> Why is flesh liken'd unto grass,
> But that it is cut down ?'
> 　　　　　　　　　——' Aye, true,
> And turn'd into beast's profit, too.'

> " ' How say'st thou ?'—the white anger came
> On Jasper's cheek, quenching the flame ;—
> A moment—and the wolf is tame."

Here is Jasper's dream :

> " Lo ! 'tis his marriage morn ; his bride,
> His other life, sits by his side,
> A joy, a comfort, and a pride ;
> Relinquish'd to his love, and blest
> To think her heart by one possest,
> Who is her synonyme of best.

> " Again that sacred feeling fills
> His soul, and through his being thrills,
> Of tenderness that would secure
> The bliss of one so good and pure,

That feeling which would not endure.
And now he sees her still as good,
A fading form of womanhood ;
A casket fill'd with holy grief,
A frost-wrung flower that leaf by leaf
Tends to the ground : a pious shrine,
Wrought by a sinner, yet, divine.
Sees her he had made worthy heaven,
And to the heavenly gate had driven,
Upon her dying bed, and hears
Her parting voice, and sees her tears,
And joins her last, low, lingering prayer——

" How ! 'tis Uberti he sees there,
  Pleading for mercy in such tones
  As freeze the marrow in the bones ;
  Yet own no potency, to work
  In him or his accomplice Kirke,
  Who clings about the dying man,
  And does what share of death he can.

" Horror ! o'erlaid by the strong dream,
  Old Jasper gasps, but cannot scream :
  The past is on ; writhe as thou wilt,
  Thou canst not loose the serpent—guilt. "

This is what follows, Jasper to Kirke :

" ' Away,' cried Jasper, ' hence—away ;
  'Tis vain for thee to talk, thy words
  Are human, and thy voice affords
  A comfort ; yet speed hence, and stay
  The death which now is on its way.
  Proclaim all we have sworn, a lie.'

" ' And shall we save our lives thereby ?'
  Cried Kirke. ' I saw both you and me
  Hanging upon the gallows tree ;

> This, in the darkness, did I see.
> Shall we escape?'
>   '*Thou* may'st be saved;
> My stone waits but to be engrav'd;
> 'Tis hewn and shap'd: my life is nought:
> Stay! let a scrivener be brought:
> Thou dost my bidding? be but true;
> My will shall leave no cause to rue.'
> Kirke did not hasten thence—he flew.

> " But he returns a different man;
> Never was wretch so wild and wan.
> The scrivener who first doth scan
> His visage is more struck with dread,
> Than when, remov'd unto his bed,
> Jasper confess'd his guilt, and bade
> His deposition quick be made.

> " But Kirke comes not alone; he brings
> A wayward thing who mows and sings,
> Peers through his fingers, and is pleas'd,
> Then pouts, and will not be appeas'd.
> Jasper beholds and swoons—I wis,
> His dream was not more dread than this."

The poem proceeds thus:

> " Soft! he revives. ' Now hear me, Brooke,
> Said Kirke, and on his bosom strook,
> 'I saw him, and the sight hath dried
> My blood, and now what may betide
> I care not :—he is dead and gone;
> Be *this* engraven on thy stone.
> Poor knave! he died before his hour;
> I bring his wife for a fresh dower.
> The law comes for us; I can smell
> The dogs are nigh, and hear their yell;
> I go my journey—so farewell!'

"He goes, and the poor witless girl
  Draws up her lip in a proud curl,
  And says, ' Well done !' and with mock ire,
  Commands the scrivener to admire,
  Then pours such tales into his ear,
  As almost craze the listener."

Jasper continues :—

"All—all—in masses for my soul ;
  Dost hear me, Graves ?   I say the whole :
  Straight pen it down, let it be sign'd :
  O ! what a weight is on my mind !'
  Then Graves draws nigh—'Good sir, my speech
  A moment would your ear beseech—
  The girl'—here Julia, nodding, smil'd—
  'Spoke of the father of her child.'
  'Do what thou wilt—do what thou wilt—
  O God ! what way to lessen guilt !
  I tell thee, man, I must not die ;
  It is my flesh that fails, not I.' "

The poem closes in the following manner—was ever
the terrible retribution which iniquity consciously
indulged in inevitably brings with it more clearly
depicted than here ?

"The leech is come, but strives in vain
  To soothe the fever of the brain.
  Jasper dies raving :—close the scene—
  'Tis fearful to behold, I ween,
  But now he lies, as calm, as mild,
  As silent as a sleeping child.

"Now when the scrivener and the leech,
  Awe-stricken, leave the place of death,

> What is the hideous thing that each
> Beholds, down-looking far beneath ?
> The two descend, holding their breath,
> Fearing, from death above they go,
> To meet him once again below.
> Nor are they wrong ; 'tis even so.
> Kirke in a noose his hands had made,
> Hangs from the lowest balustrade :—
> His journey had not been delay'd."

I have said that the poem closes, and so in a sense it does, where the description of the main incident ends. There still remains, however, a few lines, which form a sort of epilogue ; and in which Whitehead, with a touch of something akin to the quiet art of Turgenieff, tells us how Philip long years after became a prosperous merchant and succoured the poor.

Although it will be seen that I have quoted extensively from *The Story of Jasper Brooke*, its striking passages are by no means exhausted. Here is one remarkable phrase which Jasper in wrath makes use of to Philip, referring to the latter's marriage :

> " ' First to do ill, and next to rue,
> Is to tie knots in censure's thong,
> Then beg exemption from its smart.' "

The passage in which the Justice recommends Jasper to consider mercy in Philip's case is powerfully expressed. Throughout the whole poem there is hardly a superfluous word, or an instance of literary " padding."

In the *Illuminated Magazine*, edited by Douglas Jerrold, and published in 1845, two* acknowledged contributions by Whitehead appear, and perhaps a few scraps beside to which his name is not signed. *The Story of Jasper Brooke* appeared here in the first instance, illustrated with two woodcuts by the well-known Kenny Meadows. The first of these represents Jasper, the tall old man of the Mephistophelean caste of countenance, with a pointed velvet skull-cup on his head, dressed in the picturesque costume of his period, and seated easily in a carved high-backed chair, engaged in making the suggestion of marriage to his son Philip, who stands demurely by the table. The second illustration represents the feast prepared for Jasper and Kirke. Kirke has just given utterance to the splenetic outburst in which he reminds Jasper of his former crimes. The artist depicts the master in a menacing attitude over the servant, who grovels at his feet.

The next poem in Whitehead's volume is entitled *The Death of Chatterton.* It is in many respects a powerful one. This is how Whitehead describes Chatterton's dejected attitude:

> "Hands clench'd, eyes closed, he sits, but not in sleep,
> Hands never wont to pray, or eyes to weep."

Whitehead appears to have been drawn to Chatterton, not only by the exceedingly interesting character of

---

* The other acknowledged poem being *The Wife's Tragedy,* dealt with elsewhere.

the boy-poet (which never fails to fascinate men of genius, and even those of that exceedingly large class who, possessing literary sentiments and feelings, are not by any means men of genius), but also by an interest of a more personal kind. Some of the passages in this poem have an autobiographical character. The poet is ever mentally associating his much loved and deeply mourned brother with Chatterton. This feeling is observable in the following passage :

> "Blest boy, whose doom, when I was young as thou,
> Drew my rash love towards thee, and controll'd
> My better reason; why is it that now
> Thou risest like a vision as of old ;
> And bringest with thee one of dearer name,
> More hapless—dying ere he spoke to fame ?"

If we are to trust Whitehead's judgment, this brother must have been a man of genius; at least, Whitehead's sentiment respecting him is not unlike that of the Laureate towards Arthur Hallam. Here again he expresses the feeling to which I have referred above in yet more poetical—even passionate language :

> "Ye come together—yet ye stand apart ;
> And like as brothers twins of heaven ye seem,
> And mingled love and sorrow fill my heart ;—
> Ye vanish—for ye met but in a dream.
> I wake !—alike except in death, farewell !
> One in my mind—one in my heart—to dwell."

In our examination of Whitehead's poems we next come to the *Ode to a River*. This poem shows a capacity for revelling in the delights of inanimate nature. It has that peculiar note of pleasure which might reasonably be expected from one of a poetic temperament, who had been, as Keats says, " Long in city pent."

> " Bright glittering river, that dost run,
>   From thy cool crystal chamber freed,
>   A green-hair'd darling of the sun,
>   Through glowing plain, and scented mead ;
>   With silent motion flowing still,
>   Thou calm'st the west-wind to thy will,
>   And woo'st the summer for thy bride,
> Who, with her hoarded lap, is smiling by thy side.
>
> " In thy translucent wave is seen
>   The restless sunbeam glancing bright,
>   And flowers hang o'er thy margin green,
>   Like gems of many-coloured light ;
>   And where the deepest shade is spread,
>   Birds sing above thine umber'd head ;
>   Each swells his overflowing throat,
> And makes thy waters thrill with his redundant note.
>
> " But when upon the mountain top,
>   The clouds shall lay their burden down,
>   And linger darkly where they drop,
>   Until the imprison'd winds are blown ;
>   With headlong strength's resistless force,
>   The rushing torrent tears thy source ;—
>   Down, down its loaded weight is driven ;
> Thy bed is chok'd with earth, and tree-trunks thunder-riven."

The Riddle of Life is a somewhat unpleasant poem, because it seems to indicate that in this life evil

triumphs over good. It is only another attempt of
the darkly struggling heart to penetrate the mysteries
of existence. These shoutings at soundless caverns
for echoes are peculiar to passionate natures. Here
are some extracts:

> " Now then, thou sage philosopher,
>   If to the infant we recur,
>   And trace him through each onward stage,
>   To the long journey's end of age;
>   What by philosophy is found
>   That reason may admit ? expound—
>   Tell me, was this unsullied child
>   From infancy to age beguil'd ?
>   Cozen'd by counters falsely play'd
>   And to his dying hour betray'd ;
>   The book of virtue interleav'd,
>   And by the gloss of vice deceiv'd ?
>   Was this, or that, or what you will,
>   The active cause, the impulse still ?
>   Say, is there some external sin,
>   That works into the heart within ;
>   Did outward influence control,
>   Or was the bias in the bowl ?
>   Why ponder ? thou perhaps canst show
>   More than to me was given to know ;
>   Thou may'st unwind the stubborn mesh
>   That holds alike the soul and flesh ;
>   Thou may'st with nicest skill define
>   What error is, and what design ;
>   And how, when virtues stagnant brood,
>   Evil is form'd from weaker good,
>   As petrified by water, wood.
>
> " Enough : the problem is advanc'd,
>   Solve me this riddle, if thou canst."

Next follow Whitehead's sonnets.   The second is as
under :

> " As yonder lamp in my vacated room
>   With arduous flame disputes the darksome night,
>   And can, with its involuntary light,
>   But lifeless things that near it stand, illume ;
>   Yet all the while it doth itself consume ;
>   And, ere the sun begin its heavenly height
>   With courier beams that meet the shepherd's sight,
>   There, whence its life arose, shall be its tomb.
>   So wastes my light away.   Perforce confin'd
>   To common things, a limit to its sphere,
>   It shines on worthless trifles undesign'd,
>   With fainter ray each hour imprison'd here.
>   Alas ! to know that the consuming mind
>   Shall leave its lamp cold, ere the sun appear !"

This sonnet appears in *Sonnets of Three Centuries*,
edited by Mr. Hall Caine. It is, however, altered in many
particulars, and I find from that editor, on inquiry,
that the version given there was repeated to him from
memory by the late Dante Gabriel Rossetti, who had
not read the sonnet in Whitehead's poems for more
than twenty years. The sonnet has gained vastly by
passing through the medium of Rossetti's mind, and
now possesses in the version above mentioned, quoted
on page 12, much of the resonant force of which the
author of *The House of Life* is so great a master.

Here is the fourth sonnet :

> " My gentle friend, last refuge of a soul
>   From which the world too soon hath turn'd away,
>   Take thy long silent lute, and softly play
>   Some air which childhood from oblivion stole ;

> That heavenly dew shall melt without control,
> My sullen griefs, that rule with stubborn sway;
> That strain all harsher feelings shall allay,
> And fuse my heart into one tender whole.
> Then pause upon the strings, and with thy voice
> Lure from the silent deep a radiant form
> Of earlier days and happier hours the choice,
> Ere yet my troubled spirit felt the storm;
> And having call'd it into being, cease:
> And crown it with a smile and name it Peace."

There is much truth in the following sonnet. It shows that whatever Whitehead's faults of life may have been, he at least *knew* what was right in conduct:

> " When first my heart by sorrow was o'ertaken,
> And every blossom of my youth destroy'd;
> Wherefore, thought I, should hope my breast avoid,
> And why my heart of the fresh Spring forsaken?
> Then old philosophy did I awaken,
> And moral truths by error unalloy'd,
> And ancient maxims, evergreens, employ'd,
> To guard my heart, that should no more be shaken.
> O vanity! the worst that e'er befel!
> What use, with ceaseless labour, to commit
> A golden bucket to an empty well,
> Or for Heaven's wisdom seek in human wit?
> I planted strength that flourish'd not, and why?
> The fount that should have water'd it was dry."

The seventh sonnet, which is the last I shall quote, although not comparable with that given in *Sonnets of Three Centuries*, has many qualities of symbolic and literal beauty, and it shows Whitehead in his brighter mood:

> " Methought, upon a sullen ocean toss'd,
>   The batter'd hull of an old vessel lay,
>   Drifting to rearward darkness far away ;
>   Till presently, a gallant shallop cross'd
>   The horizon's line, and at a moment's cost,
>   Shot to the wreck with streaming pennons gay ;
>   Some left it, and were sav'd, while others, gray
>   With sorrow, clung to ruin, and were lost.
>   'Tis good, quoth I, awaking, as the bell
>   Fill'd with a merry peal the morning clear,
>   This vanish'd dream of mine should surely tell
>   The fortunes of the old and coming year.
>   Our joys are on another voyage bound,
>   And with the last year's wreck our sorrows drown'd."

Evening is a pretty, reflective poem. In it there occurs the following good phrase :

> " And night is floating on the lake."

Ophelia—A Dirge, is a graceful poem, but does not contain anything specially remarkable. It is, however, not wanting in the pathos necessary to the subject.

Ippolito—A Chimera in Rhyme, is a wild and weird tale of Venetian life and sorcery in the Middle Ages. It has the peculiarity of not having malice involved in it.

Ippolito is represented as a young man surrounded by the adjuncts of wealth and refinement, who had been dabbling in the secret arts. He conceives the monstrous idea of testing these arts even upon that being he loves the most. Beneath her star he takes up a toad and the roots of a mandrake, puts them into a box, and drops honey-dew upon them in a way

which is described with great minuteness. He expects
that when the toad dies, his lady will die also; and
she does. Then he has recourse to magic, to bring
her back to life, and dropping the dead toad into one
of the canals, he goes through certain formulas, such
as scattering a powder over the withered mandrake.
In due course the lady is presumed to return to life,
but it is simply a fiendish personation of her, for by-
and-by, when Ippolito's senses begin to assert themselves, he involuntarily breathes a prayer, beginning—

and
> " Holy One, Thy servant hear;"

> " The fiend hath heard the holy word;
> The fiend hath heard the name abhorred;
> Faint and fading more and more,
> Without a look, without a sound,
> It passed away from the steadfast floor,
> And silence closed around."

Ippolito (remorseful as to the result of his sorcery)
dies also, and is buried by his lady's side.

Unlike Keats's *La Belle Dame Sans Merci*, and
Rossetti's *Sister Helen*, or his *Rose Mary*, there is, as
I have said before, no guilt involved in the poem,
except that embraced by the monstrous idea which
has taken possession of Ippolito's mind.

Ippolito has, like Faust, become so devoted to the
secret arts that he is their slave. The poem is most
fittingly termed " a chimera." It is not at all on a level
with the author's realistic work, yet it exhibits a great
deal of imagination, and a tendency to the mystic

which is strange in one who has elsewhere shown such
a hold of fact.

The following extract shows Ippolito at the commencement of his proceedings :

> " ' This is the night—the very night—
> Have I not read the stars aright ?'
> With an eye of fear and a brow of pain,
> Ippolito gaz'd at his books again,
> And clos'd them—'twas in vain !

> " Two vessels stood on the table ;—
> Ippolito to him the vessels drew ;
> One was fill'd with honey-dew,
> One with hemlock sable.
> Steadily as he was able,
> Of poison he poured a single drop,
> On the honey-dew it fell,
> Still as water in a well,
> And it floated on the top.

> " ' Hast thou not bitten the moon-grown plant ?'
> Ippolito lifted the cover of lead,
> The toad was shrunk with eager want,
> For it never would be fed.
> It lifted its eyes like a human thing ;—
> ' Poor wretch !' he mutter'd, ' it pines and pines
> And cries to my soul with its piteous signs ;
> Eftsoons,'—and with a hasty fling,
> Down he shut the box of lead,
> ' To-night it will be dead !'

> " ' Every token tells me true :
> The poison rests on the honey-dew,
> And the toad is dying too.
> I took it as it sat alone,

> Drawing the coldness out of a stone,
> And I plucked the shrieking mandrake's root,
> And the plant beneath its shiny foot.
> Of all the stars that in Heaven are,
> Was it not under the very star?
> And know I not, by that star in the sky,
> That it dies that she must die?' "

Ippolito muses on life in the following magnificent passage:

> " Ippolito gnash'd his teeth with rage:
> ' Well, there is neither youth nor age,
> Which child or grandson ever wore,
> That human power may not restore !'
> And he smil'd, and the pale fire burnt in his eye,
> ' What is life but a mockery ?

> " ' Paint me a picture—happiness
> Shall be the unexhausted theme,
> Nor be the shadows more or less,
> Nor the tints brighter than they seem :
> Is it not a sorry dream ?
> A vision fancy hath endow'd,
> A day-dream painted on a cloud !
> Draw ye these colours from the sky,
> From fountains of the orient day,
> Behold ! the very flood is dry,
> Not faster, but as soon as they.
> To-morrow shall those tints renew,
> Will it re-touch these colours too ?

> " ' Paint me a torrent in its pride,
> Seething in its tempestuous stress,
> And call it life ;—and paint beside,
> A feather borne upon the tide,
> And call that feather—Happiness !' "

Ippolito goes to visit his betrothed.   Her loveliness
and death are thus described:

> " Ippolito knelt beside the girl :
> Oh ! how beautiful she was !
> Though her eye was the blue of glass,
> Though her brow was the white of pearl ;
> On her shoulders her golden hair
> Had fallen in many a waving curl,
> And her small cold hands so fair,
> Were palm to palm on her breast in prayer.

> " ' Wilt thou not be mine, my bride,
> Though death our bosoms may divide,
> Or whatever else betide ?
> Wheresoe'er our bodies are,
> Soul to soul and heart to heart,
> Dearest, we must never part.'

> " Gently he press'd his lips to hers,
> The breath beneath them scarcely stirs,
> Softly and gently his hand he press'd
> On her soft and gentle breast ;
> And every throb in strength decreas'd :—
> Gracious Heaven ! hath it ceased ?

> " Perchance, before her inward eye,
> Her happy youth was passing by,
> Or whence that short but heavy sigh ?
> 'Twas but a momentary check
> To hopes that other mansions seek,
> 'Twas the last billow o'er the wreck,
> Ere the horizon's gilded streak.
> She felt her arms around his neck,
> And drew his lips unto her cheek,
> And in his bosom, like a bride,
> Laid her head at peace, and died."

It is now time for Ippolito to set his charm to work. We are told how he does so in the following lines :

> "Ippolito lifted the cover of lead ;
> Forty hours the toad had been dead,
> The wither'd mandrake was its bed.
> 'Thou hast serv'd thy turn full well ;
> Thou told'st me what the stars could tell.'
> From the casement he let it fall,
> Far below in the canal ;—
> He listen'd as it fell.
> Next with anxious care he drew
> The vessel fill'd with honey-dew :
> The poison-drop had fallen through,
> Down the crystal clear, and lay
> Like earth beneath the liquid day.
>
> "Ippolito a powder threw,
> Swiftly into the honey-dew :
> It creams, it scintillates, it glows ;
> Crimson, orange, umber, blue,
> Pure vivid sparkless rose.
>
> "Ippolito smote his hands with glee :
> 'Auspicious sign ! my thanks to thee,
> That bring'st such tidings unto me.
> My Isabella, rest awhile,
> No taint of death shall thee defile :
> Like a pestilential air,
> Traversing a plain of snow,
> Gathering pureness it shall go
> O'er thy bosom fair.
> Soon, O Nature ! in thy name,
> My Isabella will I claim.'"

Ippolito's disappointment is narrated, and the poem thus closes :

> " The sun has risen from his bed :—
>   Ippolito is cold and dead.
>   Look ye to that vault of death ?
>   No mystic power of mortal breath
>   That virgin hath disquieted,
>   Since with holy chant and prayer,
>   Her earthly part hath rested there.
>   Nor is Ippolito denied,
>   To lie close resting by his bride.
>   Peace be with the hapless pair,
>   And the joys of Heaven beside."

There is peculiar appropriateness in the scene of this poem being laid in Venice.

Whitehead's poems have this appropriate motto from Lord Bacon affixed to them :

" Yet, even if you listen to David's harp, you shall hear as many hearse-like airs as carols."

The poetical works are well arranged. First, as we have seen, there is a powerful reflective poem ; then we find the realistic and general work ; and lastly we have an important example of the mystic mood.

The volume concludes with the drama entitled *The Cavalier.* The plot of this play is as follows, its date being presumably shortly after the Restoration. Captain Hargrave, a brave soldier, had fought during the Civil War on behalf of the King, and from the time when as a youth he had known his first battle at Edgehill, until his cause was completely

6

overwhelmed at Naseby, he had conducted himself valiantly. But for so doing, as may readily be supposed, his ancestral estate had been confiscated by the Roundheads, and through some strange misadventure of justice it had not been restored to him when the second Charles returned to his throne. This circumstance caused him to remain poor; and accordingly, with his beautiful young wife and his children, he repaired to London, to importune the Council, and, if need be, even the King himself, to restore to him what was rightfully his. During his sojourn in London he stayed in the house of one Maynard—an honest merchant who had married his sister—and for some reason not specifically stated, he usually sent his wife to make application to the Council instead of going personally.

All his efforts seem, however, to have been fruitless, and the play opens in a room in Maynard's house, where Hargrave is telling Maynard and his sister that it is no longer right for him to continue to accept their generous and lavish hospitality, which had extended even to the use of their purse, seeing that he has little further hope of being able to requite them. He sees that by his sword alone can he in the future hope for success; and, in short, he wishes to quit their dwelling at once. From this step they are all doing their best to dissuade him, when a letter is brought in addressed to Captain Hargrave, which proves to be from the Lord Moreton, couched in the most friendly terms, hinting that all his strong influence will be used in his favour, and containing an invitation to meet him " at the Dolphin Tavern over against Paul's." Hargrave and his friends are delighted at the receipt of this letter, as they remember that Hargrave had in one of the battles saved the life of the Earl of Belmont, of whom Lord Moreton is the only son.

The second scene represents a room in the Dolphin Tavern, whither Hargrave has immediately repaired. Here he finds Lord Moreton, and his lordship's friend, Beauchamp, awaiting him. Lord Moreton, who is a young man, makes use of a few friendly commonplaces to Hargrave, and introducing him to his friend, remarks how hard a case it is that so worthy a Cavalier should be thus deprived of his rights. He trusts, however, that ere long justice may be done. He urges Hargrave to accept his purse as a gift, and when the latter demurs, he almost forces him to take it as a loan, protesting that Hargrave is too proud. Telling Hargrave that he (Lord Moreton) must at once go to obtain the influence of a certain powerful Duke in his favour, and apologizing for so speedily quitting him, he leaves him a little while with Beauchamp. This, as but too soon appears, has been a mere ruse; for Beauchamp immediately begins to unfold to Hargrave an infamous scheme, clearly hinting that if he (Hargrave) will permit his wife to minister to Lord Moreton's passion, he will reap most material pecuniary advantages. Hargrave is filled with indignation, and, on Lord Moreton's return, thrusts back the purse, and threatens that if he does not at once leave the house, he cannot be answerable for the consequences.

In the next scene Hargrave, weary with grief and wild with anger, returns to Maynard's dwelling to find his wife waiting for him in joyful expectation. There are powerful elements here. We have the contrast between two persons bound by the closest ties, loving one another dearly, having no concealments or reservations, yet the wife is pained because for the first time the husband cannot bring himself to speak; and the husband, on his part, is grieved because his wife seems to misconstrue his silence. Thus there very nearly arises a serious misunderstanding through no fault of either. At length, however, enough is explained.

In the following scene we find that Hargrave has determined to make one final effort to obtain his rights, and for this purpose determines once more to send his wife to the Council. She departs on this errand—certainly an extraordinary, if not an unnatural one, in view of the fact that Hargrave knew that Lord Moreton had previously practised against her honour. Time elapses. She does not return; and Hargrave, filled with anxiety, rushes to the house of Lord Moreton, and with drawn sword demands to know where his wife is. It should, perhaps, be said that before he appears on this errand, we are distinctly given to understand, from a hurried conversation between Beauchamp and a creature of Lord Moreton's named Madam de Grave, that the nobleman(?) had compelled Mrs. Hargrave by force to enter his house. Beauchamp puts Hargrave off with sneering and lying words, and so the scene closes.

The succeeding scene again occurs in Maynard's house, where in a bitter and somewhat unwarrantable vein, Hargrave speaks doubtingly of his wife's fidelity. She has not yet returned, and he presumes that she has wantonly left him for Lord Moreton. Presently, when all is bitterness and gloom, Mrs. Hargrave bursts suddenly into the apartment. Being somewhat calmed, she slowly, and with many pauses most natural under the circumstances, narrates her seizure by Lord Moreton's hirelings; how Lord Moreton himself presently approached her, and repeatedly strove to violate her honour. At length he had almost effected his purpose, when, in desperation, she perceived a knife lying close at hand. She seized it, and killed him.

This tragic recital is scarcely concluded when Beauchamp, with officers of justice, bursts into the room, and crying out that this woman has murdered Lord Moreton, seizes Mrs. Hargrave. Her husband and the Maynards soothe and console her, telling her that she will soon be released, and she is led away.

Once more we see a chamber in Maynard's house. Hargrave is anxiously awaiting tidings of his wife's trial. Maynard enters, and tenderly breaks to him the dreadful news that she is condemned. It is the old story—a trumped-up tale and perjured witnesses. The fabrication in this instance being that Mrs. Hargrave had already had a *liaison* with Lord Moreton, and that she had killed him owing to his refusal to give her some jewels she wished to possess. The friends are in agony, but Hargrave, controlling himself as much as possible, seeks an interview with his wife.

Shortly after his departure, Madam de Grave appears, and earnestly begging to see him, is in his absence met by the Maynards. To them, with deep contrition of heart, she tells that so great are the pangs of conscience that she is unable longer to conceal her share in the infamous plot which has resulted in Mrs. Hargrave's condemnation. She beseeches them to go at once, state the true facts of the case, and stay the execution of the sentence; a request which it is needless to say they accede to with alacrity.

The last scene is in some respects the most beautiful. Mrs. Hargrave is discovered lying on a couch at the back of the stage. Her husband enters the cell, and their discourse is most touching. At length Maynard joyfully arrives, makes known the happy change of events, and tells how he has obtained a respite preparatory to the King's pardon.

The Cavalier is written throughout in blank verse, and with the single exception of the letter from Lord Moreton to Hargrave, there is no prose dialogue whatever. The verse is always melodious and correct, but there is sometimes rather too much of a tendency to degenerate into prose diction cut into lengths. This is perhaps, however, more owing to Whitehead's desire to avoid theatrical bombast, and to make his characters speak about the subjects which would naturally occupy their talk in real life, rather than from any weakness in the lines themselves. There is also an absence of the striking phrases which are so prominent elsewhere in Whitehead's writings.

Here, however, is an exception. Hargrave says that a temporary alleviation of grief is—

> " Like the beam shot from a clouded moon,
>   Borrowed—and spent on darkness."

The following extract from the first scene is interesting, and I quote the last scene in its entirety as a favourable specimen of Whitehead's dramatic powers.

Here is the extract from the first scene : '

Mrs. M. Dear brother, be persuaded. Let not pride,
The weakness of great natures, and of mean ones
The poor disguise, find entrance in your bosom,
Displacing worthier inmates. Still be just
To us who love you, and your own noble heart :
We know what you would say ; leave it unsaid,
And what you really think us, show indeed,
By liberal acquiescence.
Har. My dear sister,—
And Maynard, trusty and most trusted friend,
Lend me a moment's patience. Full two years
Have we been shelter'd by your roof, partaken
Your hospitable board, shar'd your free purse,
And for all benefits, of word, or deed,
Or of those nameless courtesies that make

The vital air of friendship, have been still
Your grateful debtors : well, but hear me, Maynard,
I have beseech'd, nay, have besieg'd the Council,
That they would lend an ear to my just claims ;
I would recover my estate,—'tis mine
As truly as the King's crown his,—by blood ;
Blood which was shed, and freely, in his cause.
My claims are not allow'd ; well, what remains ?
I cannot stay with you : too long already
Have I been wrapp'd in a deceitful hope,
Which is now worn to a shred : my sword alone
Must help me now, and it points out a road
To honourable service.
 May. When we see
The road you speak of, will I stay you ?   No.
Like a tir'd host, I'll show you to the door,
Aye, hold the stirrup for you, and with smiles
Bid you good speed.   Look you, proud Captain Hargrave ;—
Seated once more in your estate, which yet
I must believe you will be, and once more
First of the shire, with your broad lands before you,
O'er which the crow flies wearily to roost
On your old tree-tops, you may hug your pride
As closely as you will, but here you shall not.
 Har. Maynard, it is not pride.
 May. I'll warrant now,
Should fortune suddenly with one hand raise you,
And with the other thrust me to the earth,—
And should your sister here, and I, come to you,
With piteous tale of bankruptcy and ruin,
You would receive us with cold scorn—nay, bid us
Trace back the path we came.
 Har. You do not think so :
You know me better, Maynard.
 Mrs. M. He but jests——
Forgive him, brother.

May. What, then, you would house us ?
You'd entertain us for a month, a year,
Would you ?—a longer time, perhaps ?
    Har. For ever,—
Or were I not the vilest slave alive.
What ! could I see my sister and yourself
In want, and I in want of heart to serve you,—
To bid you welcome to my house and lands,
And ask you share them ?   Sir, you wrong me.
    May. Well, then :
What pride is this that takes not, but must give ;
And asking sufferance for the thing it is,
Denies it to another ?   Come, no more——
I shall be angry else.

This extract may not show Whitehead's dramatic powers at their highest point, but it at least proves his command over his materials, and his capacity for expressing in the dramatic mould an unoriginal, even commonplace, situation.

The following is the second scene of Act III., and concludes the play. Few would be willing to deny its powerful character, a power which grows more intense towards the close.   How fine are the words of the heroic wife when dissuading from self-destruction :

(Mrs. Hargrave discovered lying on a couch at the back of the stage.)

Enter HARGRAVE.

Har. She sleeps.   Now, mercy, with thy sacred balm,
Anoint her soul, and the sweet dew of peace
Drop on her heart, that she may glow of Heaven,
Ere Heaven receive her pure and gentle spirit.

(*Mrs. Hargrave rises, and, perceiving her husband, approaches
him.*)

 Mrs. H. I have wish'd to see you, Henry; they have
  made me
Guiltier than truth could make me—they have sought
My life, and they will take my life, by means
That even murder's self would shudder at.
One fear, and only one, remains : can you
Believe me the vile wretch they falsely make me?
 Har. I have deserv'd this at your hands, and feel
The deep reproach. Oh, Margaret, Margaret,
My words are words that have no space to hold
The feelings that oppress me. Could my soul speak,
You had not ask'd that question.
 Mrs. H. It has spoken.
Thank God for that. Forgive me—I am happy.
 Har. Can you be happy in an hour like this?
 Mrs. H. I could—but to leave you and the dear children—
This is death's bitterness.
 Har. They are protected.
 Mrs. H. And you, dear Henry?
 Har. Heaven will not desert me.
 Mrs. H. In whom I trust. Oh, Henry, I have pray'd,
And have not pray'd in vain. No heart so weak,
But Heaven can fill it with an angel's strength :
That strength, my husband, is effus'd from prayer.
The world, which once, I fear, we lov'd too well,
Thought of too much—applied ourselves too long
In vain to satisfy, is pass'd away :
Like a thin shadow—which it is—'tis vanish'd,
Melted, and all my hopes are gone before me,
To the one kingdom.
 Har. Why, 'tis well—'tis well—
You have done with a most worthless world—'tis well—
And through the wide and ever-open gate

Of death, would pass to glory—but *the* death,—
You have not thought of that—the ignominy—
The hideous shame, whose engines cauterise
Our name for ever: that might be escap'd.
Might it not be escap'd?   I would out-tire
A thousand years in prison, so that this
Dishonour might be spar'd.
   Mrs. Har. Do not talk thus :
Pray for me, rather, that my nature fail not
In the last dreadful moment.
   Har. I cannot.
The time is near at hand, and I must speak.
This shall not be ; I should go mad to know it—
I must not see you perish on the scaffold,
A public spectacle of shame—a show
For myriads to gaze upon with horror.
   Mrs. Har. Speak not thus wildly to me—it must be—
My life is forfeit to the laws, and I
Must pay the penalty.
   Har. Yes, but how ? but how ?
Forestall the act—anticipate the doom,—
We have the precious means in our hands.
   Mrs. Har. What means are these ?
   Har. Here !   (*Produces a phial.*)   Let us die together.
   Mrs. Har. Oh, weak, rash man ! what is a shameful death,
If this is glorious ?   Because the night is dark,
Who calls the lightning ?   Do you wish to die
Because you fear to live, and yet would rush
Into a world of never-ending life,
And endless woe to those that come unsought.
Promise me this—swear to live—you will live.
We are not as ourselves, but as our keepers
In trust for others, dearer than ourselves,
And for their sake——
   Har. You torture me in vain.
I cannot bear the thought—must not endure it.

You plead as ever, like yourself and virtue,
But now your words rebound from my full heart,
And fall unheeded.
    Mrs. Har. Yet reflect, reflect—
The power that has permitted the event
Forecasts the issue.   Trust that—mistrust yourself.
    May. (*without.*) Where are they?   Conduct me to them
    instantly.
    Har. They come to take their last farewell of you :
The time's at hand, and they will bear you hence
To instant execution.   I will not live   .
To see it.

      (*Hargrave is about to take the poison, when Mrs. Hargrave,
      with a shriek, snatches it from his hand.*)

          Enter MAYNARD, *followed by his wife.*

    May. I have such tidings for you.
    Mrs. Har. Oh, speak them—speak them !
    May. The woman has confess'd—Beauchamp's secur'd—
A respite has been granted—the King's pardon
Will follow it betimes.

        (*Hargrave drops upon his knees.*)

    Mrs. H. (*after a pause.*) Oh, my friend—
Your timely news has saved two lives—perhaps,
Two souls—but that must not be dwelt on now,
My husband !
    Har. Margaret !   [*They embrace.*
    Mrs. Har. Let none with impious doubt,
Suggest to Providence the way to guide him,
Who, when he least perceives, and would defy her,
Is then most prompt to serve him.

In Duncombe's *British Theatre* there is an acting
edition of *The Cavalier.*   Duncombe's volume is without date, but the copy at the British Museum bears

the British Museum mark, 7 June, 1852. The edition of *The Cavalier* therein is stated to be the "only edition correctly marked by permission from the prompter's box"; to which is added a description of the costumes, cast of the characters, the whole of the stage business, situations, entrances, exits, properties and directions, as performed at the London theatres. It is also stated to be "embellished" with an illustration "by Mr. Findlay, from a drawing taken expressly in the theatre." This, however, is neither specially remarkable nor attractive.

The character of Hargrave was played by the elder Vandenhoff, the actor of classical parts; and Miss Ellen Tree, the tragedienne, appeared as Mrs. Hargrave. Mr. J. Vining was also in the cast, as was likewise Mr. Elton—I presume the same Elton to whose family Charles Dickens was so kind after the actor's death by drowning.

Although, as I have before said, there is considerable force and pathos in the closing scene of *The Cavalier*, there is no doubt that in such a case poetic justice demanded that in order to complete a picture of misfortune, every piece of good fortune should have come to the hero and heroine too late. This would have intensified the feeling of sympathy and regret for their wrongs ; and it was thus that the play originally ended. Whitehead, however, in deference to popular clamour, changed the catastrophe. Thus a fine poetic close was sensibly marred.

Whitehead nevertheless retained the altered version,

and it appears both in Duncombe's *British Theatre*
and in the collected edition of the poetical works,
published in 1849.   There can be little doubt that,
with all its faults, *The Cavalier* entitles Whitehead to
recognition as a writer of poetical drama.

CHAPTER III.

CHARLES WHITEHEAD wrote, probably in conjunction with his brother Alfred, and published anonymously in 1834, *The Autobiography of a Notorious Legal Functionary*, with fourteen illustrations from designs by the well-known caricaturist, Kenny Meadows. Such is the title on the title-page; but on the half-title-page it is simply termed *The Autobiography of Jack Ketch.* This is the only book by Whitehead which appeared without his name. Perhaps his reason for anonymity is to be found in the character of its contents; perhaps in the fact that, having produced in the same year *The Lives and Exploits of English Highwaymen, Pirates and Robbers*, in two volumes, he did not wish to be further identified by name at so short an interval with subjects of such doubtful savour. It is significant, also, that notwithstanding all Whitehead's love of literary extravagance, he never seems to have appended his name to *Jack Ketch*, though the work ran through many editions.

It is supposed to be the history of the functionary whose name it bears, before he assumes his office. As we gather from the title, it is in the autobiographical form, and in order to account for the diction being more brilliant and the orthography more correct than we should naturally expect from the person who appears to speak, Whitehead has prefixed the following " Advertisement :"

" It may be deemed a pleasing evidence of candour to confess that, in accordance with a modern usage adopted by other great authors, our autobiographer has called in the aid of an obscure man of letters, for the purpose of adjusting his somewhat capricious orthography—of clipping his vernacular tongue, so that it may speak with fluency and correctness—and of applying salutary bandages to Priscian's head.

" He has also employed him to stick a flower here and there, throughout the volume ; and to throw in the required amount of moral reflection.

" He has been further advised to announce the publication of his more mature experience, under the unambitious title of *The Ketch Papers*, should the public receive with due favour the performance which he now tremblingly commits to its merciful consideration."

One would almost have expected from the title of the book that its subject-matter would have either been treated in a light humourous manner, or from the standpoint of broad farce. It is hardly conceivable that any writer would produce in a serious mood a volume loaded with such painful and often loathsome details as a book dealing in sober earnest with the hangman's life, especially in the older days, must necessarily contain. But this work is a strange combination. Much of it is written in the lively, frolicsome vein just alluded to, with a good deal of melodramatic hysteria; but there is not a little that is quite tragical in its terrible and natural earnestness. This is to be noticed in portions of the narrative of *Jack Ketch* proper, but pre-eminently in the incidental episode entitled *The Confession of James Wilson*, which contains, despite its being at times far too terrible, the finest writing in the book.

The Ketch Papers never seem to have been published, at least there is no record of their existence in the catalogue of the British Museum.

Mr. John Ketch, according to this veracious autobiography, was born in the charming neighbourhood of a narrow lane in the almost pathetically appropriate vicinity of Newgate. When one thinks of the sweet character this neighbourhood possesses even now, we can readily mirror to ourselves the Elysium it would be then. His father's " vocation, or rather vacation," was that of a waiter. His mother was nominally a washerwoman, and we are told that from behind these two " masked batteries, these two defenders of our small garrison were enabled to make such reprisals on their common enemy—the world—as permitted them to display as respectable an appearance in the court as any of the few other inhabitants of that colony could contrive to establish."

From the foregoing remarks it will be seen that the book opens with playful humour and with little coarseness. Any discerning reader may also catch the note on which Dickens afterwards produced such wonderful effects. Years go on, and John is already a stirring little boy, when one morning his mother receives an intimation that his father has at length been caught in the pursuit of his true calling, or, as Whitehead wittily puts it, "in the act of investing himself with the authority of a distraining broker without any legal warrant for such an investment." Themis was inexorable, and he paid the usual penalty enforced in those days, and that speedily. Jack presently gets admission to the parish school, and fills up the intervals of learning by endeavouring to acquire the initiatory gradations of the noble art of picking pockets. His schoolmaster at the parish school is a man named Misty, "a tall, thin, placid creature," and it is remarkable that his character, as sketched in the book, bears, as will be seen by my reference to it in a previous chapter, distinct points of resemblance to that of Charles Whitehead himself. He is a marked personality in the book, and meets and converses with Ketch long after a change of fortune had caused him to cease to be a scholastic drudge.

Ketch's uncle is the hangman; and upon his mother's being obliged to take a lengthened voyage abroad at Government expense, he went to live with this relative. By-and-by, however, there ensued in the avuncular household a connubial quarrel, and in consequence of it John goes to an attorney's office, where as a junior he is also to reside. Snavel, the attorney, proves an unscrupulous practitioner, and Ketch is not slow in acquiring the more disreputable of his attainments. On his attempting to decamp with a client's money, Ketch and another clerk, Wisp, prevent his doing so until they have extorted black-mail.

Ketch soon commences a career of petty larceny, thus enabling Whitehead to show his intimate knowledge of the life of the lower classes in London. Ketch marries a sweet young girl, who soon dies, in a great measure owing to his unconscious cruelty, want of sympathy, and misapprehension of her character. It is noteworthy that, at this point in the narrative, Whitehead makes Ketch exhibit emotions and express sentiments altogether more noble than we conceive the mind of such a man capable of, and for a while the style of writing ceases entirely to be farcical and becomes genuinely pathetic. It does not continue so, however, but gradually grows pregnant once more with too much false melodrama. I have been in great doubt as to whether to quote the following passage. It has reference to the death of Ketch's uncle, and exemplifies in a marvellous manner Whitehead's grim humour and also his remarkable dramatic instinct. Indeed, the embryo hangman's admiration of the " new tie " is matchless from a certain point of view. I cannot, however, but entertain doubts as to whether a writer is justified in making a humorous use of such a situation. Ketch has been summoned to his uncle's house, and entering hurriedly, wonders for what he can be wanted. He is told to go upstairs into a certain room. The extract must now speak for itself:

7—2

" Here the mystery was at an end. Suspended from a beam by a brand new rope, which he had exhibited to me on the Saturday evening as the particular line he had selected for the suspension of Wilmot,* hung my imprudent, and, perhaps, culpably rash uncle ; and at the corner of his left ear stuck out a knot which for intricacy of tie and ingenuity of construction, rivalled that which is termed, *par excellence,* a true-lover's knot. The chair by which he had raised himself to a line with the fatal noose, had either fallen or had been kicked from beneath his feet ; and methought, as he hung, surely never had twisted hemp borne so interesting an appendix. He looked like a pair of sugar nippers ; but alas ! unlike in this,—that he was never more to nip the sweets of existence in this sublunary world.

" I cut him down ; but life had, I dare say, been long extinct ; and to endeavour to recall him to this lower world, would have been not only a fruitless and unprofitable, but also an absurd, task :—for the debt of Nature once satisfied is not easily renewable,—the old lady bearing an antipathy to such proceedings, similar to that of Falstaff,—who ' liked not that paying back.'

" In default of any available elixir, therefore, I was fain to set my ingenuity at work to discover some probable or plausible reasons for the commission of so unexpected a climax to my uncle's period of sojourn in the flesh, and was baffled and perplexed at all points. Could any consideration in which Wilmot was included—any unaccountable tenderness on that score, have superinduced this paltry evasion of his professional duties ? Impossible ! the whole tenor of his life forbade the humiliating conclusion. Could the memory of his wife so distract his sea of troubles as to cause him to run into this unfriendly harbour ? If so, he

---

* The criminal who was to suffer that morning.

deserved the rope's-end to which he had subjected himself, as a hopeless and pusillanimous lubber. No; it was clearly an unsuccessful experiment. I examined the knot again and again; it was a new tie; simple, and yet how complex! admirable for its completeness, and yet, in its negligence, how picturesque! Tyburn had never witnessed such a tie; nor had Newgate hitherto glanced at such a noose. I preserved it as an invaluable work of art. I admired the design while its execution I deplored."

Writing like this is certainly open to the charge of excess; nay more, even to that of irreverence, using the word in its broadest sense, and there is too much self-consciousness in it, but it is nevertheless, dramatically, very striking.

Jack desires to succeed his uncle in his office, and with this view he writes an eloquent letter to the Sheriff. The Sheriff appoints an interview, and with much trepidation of spirit Jack goes. This is the account of that interview:

" ' Can you hang?'

" ' I can, sir; I studied under my late uncle, by whom I was considered——'

" ' Silence! Are you fully alive to the particular duties which the important office you will occupy calls upon you to discharge? Hold your tongue, and don't interrupt me. Do you know that you may be required to hang your own father, mother, grandfather, grandmother, — nay, every relative you have in the world; and that you will be called upon to swear that you will do these things if occasion demands?'

" I answered that I was perfectly aware of these contingencies, and quite willing to take the required oath.

"'Good,' said the ordinary. 'Are you aware,' he continued, 'of the responsibility and the respectability of the office?'

"I looked blank at this question. Was Kilderkin serious? He was.

"'Consider,' said he encouragingly,—'consider for a moment. You are performing an operation properly belonging to the sheriff—you are the representative of the sheriff —you are equal with the sheriff.'

"'Equal with the sheriff?' cried Hopkins, turning suddenly round; 'nay, Mr. Kilderkin, not exactly so, surely.' Kilderkin nodded his head.

"Hopkins scratched his. 'Eh?' said he, 'do you class us together? Do we go abreast like horses in a curricle, *passibus equis,* as we used to say at Merchant Taylors'?'

"'*Passibus asinis,*' cried the ordinary; 'stuff—nonsense —fudge. I say, Mr. Hopkins, that for the time, mark me, for the time, Mr. Ketch fills your situation. He is your *locum tenens*—he does your work. *Qui facit per alium, facit per se*—he who does a thing through another, does it virtually himself. If you pick a man's pocket with a dead man's fingers, I'll warrant you won't get dummy to hold up his hand in the dock: *you* suffer in *propriâ personâ.*' Here Kilderkin chuckled amazingly, while a no less amazing gravity drew down the visage of Hopkins.

"'Do you understand all that I have said to you?' resumed the ordinary; 'do you subscribe to it; are you willing to undertake the situation, and to perform everything that shall be required of you, proper and peculiar to it?'

"'I expressed my readiness to do all these things, and manifested my gratitude by many broken sentences of thankfulness and respect, and slidings of the foot behind me; and every other ceremony proper to the occasion.

"'Very good,' said Kilderkin, 'very good. Now, then,

take one word of advice. Never hang the wrong man—
never fail to hang the right one ; and never hang yourself,
as your poor simple uncle did. And now,' and he rose and
approached Hopkins, 'I think we may say that this young
man may take it for granted that he is to succeed his kinsman in his duties, and that he may prepare to get his hand
in, at all events, forthwith.'

" 'I think so,' said Hopkins. 'You may prepare, young
man, to get your hand in forthwith ; and in due time you
will be sworn into your office.'

" Again I mumbled the same sentiments of gratitude and
respect, and with many profound bows retired from their
presence."

Jack Ketch was first published by Edward Churton,
of 26, Holles Street, Cavendish Square, one of the
co-publishers of the *Highwaymen*, but from some
cause or another the third edition, appearing in 1838,
and of which I possess a copy, was published by J.
Chidley, of 123, Aldersgate Street. Perhaps Mr.
Churton found that his library subscribers no longer
liked his connection with so "notorious " a work. The
justice of this supposition is further strengthened by
the fact that an edition of the *Highwaymen* was
published in 1842 by Bohn. Anyhow, Mr. Churton's
firm was still in existence in 1838, for a list of his
books appears at the end of the *Jack Ketch* edition of
that year.

I have thought it best to deal separately with *The
Confession of James Wilson*, both because of its being
entirely distinct from the rest of the book, and also
because it is incomparably the finest thing in it. It is

introduced by Whitehead as a manuscript which has
been given by a criminal, before he ascended the
scaffold, to Ketch's uncle, who requested Ketch to read
it to him.

It is the history of a very sad, crime-stained life,
and is supposed to be an account of the criminal's
career, written by himself the night before he suffered,
in the hope that by writing it he might, in some degree,
lessen his load of guilt—a load which to him had been
life-long. It may perhaps be well here to state that
though this episode is unquestionably one of the
finest single things in the book, it is not so because the
story itself or the characters present notable points
of novelty, but because of the literary workmanship,
which is singularly powerful. It is hardly too much
to say that the story is one of the most realistic products which Whitehead has given us, even if it were
rash to affirm that it is one of the most extraordinary
products of its kind in our literature. The analysis of
emotion is thrilling in its detail, and the descriptive
passages are quite the finest of their kind in Whitehead.

I shall endeavour briefly to give a summary of the
tale ; but in such a case it is very difficult—indeed, impossible—to convey any idea of the force and vitality
of diction which gives to the tale its chief interest.

James Wilson is the son of a poor country clergyman. He is an only child, and his mother has died in
his early childhood. His boyhood is spent among the
ennobling influences appertaining to a quiet rural exist-

ence. His father constantly endeavours to instil into his mind religious and moral principles. By-and-by a sister of his mother's dies, leaving an only daughter of about his own age. This girl, named Lucy Cowley, is possessed of a small competence, and it was her mother's last wish that she should go to reside with Wilson's father. The inmates of the little household soon begin to discover that this addition to their small circle is a very pleasant one, and James, who had been formerly rather backward in his studies, and has been of an untractable disposition, becomes softened by his gentle companion's influence. Of course, the familiar result ensues, and the older members of the household begin already to speak among themselves of a union in the far future.

As time passes, it happens that the clergyman has occasion to go to London, and while there, casually meets with a former college companion who is possessed of ample means. This gentleman has a son whom he is anxious to place for two or three years with a clergyman in order to prepare him for the University, and he proposes to place him under his friend's care. Very naturally, Wilson's father is willing to accede to this proposal, and returns to his country home accompanied by the youth, whose name is Beaumont. Beaumont is about a year older than James, and in the sketch of his personality Whitehead gives us a beautiful study of a frank, noble, high-spirited lad, as generous as he is gifted. He is one whom it is impossible to know without loving, and James himself becomes sincerely attached to him, and strange as it may seem, ever remains so. Francis Beaumont has greater ability than James Wilson, and is also handsomer. His superiority in the former of these respects is so marked, that almost unconsciously even Wilson's father would remind his son of it indirectly; and on one occasion he congratulates him on his progress in study, and adds that he is not as far behind his friend Frank " as might be expected." These remarks have a distinct effect on the peculiarly morbid vindictiveness of the boy's nature, and at length, when he begins to perceive that even Lucy's girlish affection has gone forth to Beaumont and been reciprocated, he broods constantly over his wrongs, and entertains vague thoughts of vengeance. And yet he loves Beaumont.

One day he is so overcome by suspicion and jealousy as to listen secretly at a door and overhear a conversation between Beaumont and Lucy, in which they speak of their mutual love and their future marriage. Lucy also ridicules James's personal defects. A little while afterwards James meets Beaumont in the orchard and accuses him of listening to what " that girl " had said concerning himself. A quarrel ensues, Beaumont accusing James of eavesdropping, and they almost come to blows. Presently Beaumont enters James's room and offers a full and manly apology. But this has come too late as far as James is concerned. He begs that their friendship may be considered at an end. So they part. Beaumont is to go the same afternoon to visit some friends at a neighbouring country town, and, not expecting to return until late, he obtains the key of the door, so as to avoid keeping any of the family out of bed on his account. James is now maddened by revenge, and, urged by some half-determined idea, he resolves to meet Beaumont as he returns.

The following extract tells what immediately ensues :—

"It was a beautiful moonlight midsummer night. I raised the window cautiously, and looked out. All was silent. The roof of a wash-house rose within a foot of my window, grown over with stone-crop and aged moss : it was a safe venture for the feet. I got out, and thence descended into the garden by a ladder, which I had placed against the tiles during the afternoon. But I had forgotten to close my window, and climbed up again for that purpose. Within my chamber all was stillness and peace : it was full of the moonlight, and every object around was distinctly visible. There was my Bible lying upon the drawers by my bedside—oh! should I return? should I delay my purpose? should I cast it from me for ever, and step once more into the pale of heavenly forgiveness? My head swam round, and my eyes were dizzy and full of a watery humour; —they were not tears. Eternity hung upon that moment. I closed the window, and descended into the garden. A few minutes' hasty walk, and I had crossed the orchard, and getting over a ditch, and proceeding along a field-path, I found myself in the highroad.

" What had I come forth at this hour of the night to do? What was I about to become? Who was I? These questions whirled through my brain as I reeled along like a drunken man ; but I dare not, or could not, answer them to myself. And now my mind misgave me, and my knees smote together with dreadful violence. When I think upon

that hour I almost pity myself, for then indeed I was a
wretched creature. I had left my father's house at dead of
night, liable to be discovered, and yet afraid to return;
something commanded me to proceed, and I wrung my
hands together, and moaned in the direful agony of my
spirit. At this moment the sound of coach wheels arrested
my attention. I had just time to conceal myself behind a
hedge when the London mail drove rapidly past, and the
sound of the horn announced its approach to our village.
A thought struck me—should I hasten to London ?—fly at
once and for ever from a place where nothing but mortification and misery awaited me, and, seeking for employment
in some obscure corner of the metropolis, endeavour to
procure a living for myself, and become a respectable and a
happy man? Alas ! I had but a few shillings about me;
and, utterly without recommendations or knowledge of mankind, how should I fare in a place like London? Besides,
should I leave the field to Beaumont? Should I relinquish
Lucy, whom I had sworn to obtain ? abandon my father,
whose declining years I had promised to watch over and
protect? 'No, no,' I muttered, and my self-possession
returned; 'I will not verify their opinion of me at home—
I will not turn out the fool they think me. Beaumont
shall not live to exult over my downfall; and my father
shall, perhaps, live long enough to know that he has been
the unconscious instrument of embittering the youth, and
blighting the aspirations of his son. I can forgive him and
Lucy; but Beaumont——' I started, for a well-known
whistle reached my ear. Beaumont was returning, evidently
in high spirits, whistling a tune which I knew to be a
favourite."

This familiar sound, which indicated Beaumont's
approach, had the effect of rousing into uncontrollable
fierceness Wilson's rage against him. He seized a

sharp flint and struck him violently. Beaumont was much injured, but succeeded in rising and struggling forward a few paces. He said a few words of mingled pity and reproach to Wilson. Wilson, after giving him the first blow, had, by a strange revulsion of feeling, run towards him murmuring that he did not know what he had done. But instead of being made penitent by hearing Beaumont's words, his former feelings returned, and he sought to stab him with an old knife he had found the previous afternoon. There was a brief but desperate struggle. Beaumont, with the fearful energy which contends for life, tried to parry the thrusts of his adversary, and for a little while succeeded in doing so with his hands. At length, however, the fatal thrust was given, and he fell dead.

Terrible now is Wilson's agony. With a loud cry he flings his weapon from him, and, distracted, is overwhelmed with the thought of what he has done. But even in such straits of mind the instinct of self-preservation makes itself felt ; and acting according to its dictates, Wilson rifles Beaumont's pockets of what they contain, and flinging a heavy purse into a neighbouring pond, so that the motive of the crime might be supposed to be robbery, he creeps stealthily back to the house.

I have thus endeavoured to give some idea of this part of the story. The incident as told by Whitehead is intensely real. We seem to see the very scene enacted before us. But his account has many elements of the terrible and ghastly, and whilst thus in style very fine, is almost too horrible for quotation. The horror of the succeeding hours of that night Wilson never could forget. At first, as forsooth his vengeance (?) was satisfied, he began to reflect on his amiable class-mate whom he had formerly loved, and even now loves as a brother. But soon come more ignoble thoughts ; he is concerned for his personal safety, and wonders how he can avoid suspicion, fearing that his very looks will betray him. The morning comes. Lying in agony on his bed, he has seen the " grey night wear away," and hears the first twitter of the birds among the boughs, and perceives the first " streak of morning " tinge the eastern clouds. (Whitehead, with the true knowledge of the contrast which would be most striking here, has represented the dawn of a glorious day.) Presently Wilson hears the man-servant go forth, and knows that ere long the murder will be discovered. His surmises are correct. Soon he hears the sound of excited voices, then footsteps, and well he knows what dread burden is being carried into the house. Very shortly afterwards his father seeks to awaken him (for he has feigned deep sleep), and in great distress brings him the direful tidings. Wilson is filled with emotion, an emotion which his father naturally misconstrues.

Beaumont looks beautiful in death. They have covered his wounds and strewn flowers on his corpse. Wilson is deeply and sincerely affected, and sits down by the body of his former comrade. Lucy and his father leave the room, and, perhaps scarce conscious of what he is doing, he takes the hand of his " injured friend." Suddenly some blood exudes from the wound, and with a loud cry he faints.

When he once more becomes conscious, he finds his father and the housekeeper near him, and the former tenderly reproves him for overmuch sorrow. He is filled with fear which almost amounts to superstition. He resolves to devote his life to repentance, is over-whelmed with remorse, and remains almost incessantly watching the corpse until the funeral is over. The murdered boy's father, who has been summoned, conceives such a favourable impression of his character from his conduct, that, before leaving, he places a twenty-pound note in his hand. A day or two afterwards, Wilson's father informs him that a man has been arrested on suspicion of having committed the murder. James is filled with renewed anguish at his words, and becomes so ill that he is carried to bed with a strong tendency to fever. This, however, he overcomes with a great effort, as he fears the disclosures of delirium. By-and-by James learns that the man has been released through want of sufficient evidence, and something prompts him to go at once to him and give him the twenty pounds as a small recompense for the loss of character he must sustain. The man, whose name is Williams, is some-what astonished at this unexpected generosity, and for a moment looks suspicious, but the shade of doubt appears to pass away, and they part.

Years roll on. Beaumont's murder ceases even in this quiet country place to be the perpetual theme of conversation. Wilson has never been the same since, but his former hopes have revived, and he is presently to marry Lucy.

On the night preceding his marriage he has a dream, a dream which has visited him often, and in which every circumstance of the never-to-be-forgotten event which has embittered all his life is enacted over again, with, perchance, increased horror. He awakes, "feverish and unrefreshed," and with the undefinable dread which sometimes remains with him for months, and then only leaves him to return with even greater force. The subsequent portion of the narrative is one of the very finest in Whitehead. It narrates how Wilson, terrified lest his friends should perceive his strange demeanour, had to feign previous sickness as an excuse for it; how very soon he recovered his composure, and marvelled at his previous fears; how his bride was calm and apparently happy; how by-and-by, when the nuptial procession set out on its way to the church, the villagers thronged round, anxious to testify to the general rejoicing, and to show that the two persons most nearly concerned were the chief favourites of the place; how many a blessing and good wish were heard by James, and each one of them "fell like a curse" on his soul. During these moments his thoughts are all of Beaumont. He reflects on the main cause of his former hatred to him, and recollects that it was in reality the fear lest Beaumont, not himself, should marry Lucy. His is the triumph; he has won the day; but what has he lost?

Lucy and himself are now in the church, and he suddenly remembers that he must pass near Beaumont's tomb, and that the very echoes of his footsteps will vibrate through the ashes of his murdered companion.

"As we knelt before the altar, my feet were resting on the gravestone; and as my father proceeded with the service, and I looked up to make the responses, my eyes fell upon the Ten Commandments, nor had I power to avert them. As I gazed, were my eyes dazzled? Was it strong imagination? No, no, there was the terrible sixth commandment, 'Thou shalt do no murder.' A vivid and close fire burnt along each letter of each word, and gradually brought the divine prohibition before me, so that I might have touched it with my hand. It was no human power that supported me till the conclusion of the ceremony, when with a heavy groan I fell back senseless."

At length they restore him to consciousness, and he finds himself surrounded by solicitous friends concerned at his sudden illness. But they do not guess his secret. How can they? He has kept it so well. How bitterly he feels the mockery implied in this phrase:

"I attempted to rise, but something held me back: I looked down; I had been lying on the grave of Beaumont. Was it an angel of heaven that whispered to me at that moment in mercy to my wretchedness? I bowed my head, and breathed a prayer—a short prayer to my poor friend; and I knew that from that hour forgiveness would be extended to me, and that he would intercede for me, and that I should at length find pardon from above."

He arose far more calm and tranquil than he had

felt for years, and vowed that for Beaumont's sake he would make his young wife as happy as such a man as he was could.

"'Poor Beaumont!' sighed my father, as we prepared to leave the church. He had been musing over the short and simple inscription. Lucy sighed also, and her hand was pressed against my arm involuntarily. 'Poor Beaumont!' I repeated to myself; 'happy—happy—thrice happy—lamented with sincerity—mourned by the wise and good, and dying ere sin or sorrow could mar or obscure that noble heart!' Could I have exchanged my fate with his? but no, I wished not that. Had I but died, and were he living to enjoy the happiness which he might have deserved, and which I could never hope to attain in this world! But let me draw my narrative to a close; for the night wears apace, and my strength is almost spent."

All this is the very highest style of art. The passages descriptive of the marriage ceremony are truly magnificent in their intensity and imaginative ardour.

During seven years all went well. James was comparatively happy, and his father still lived to rejoice in the innocent pleasures of his grandchildren. He was growing old, however, and one day, finding himself ill, he knew that he was dying. His son was alone with him at his bedside, and the father, in pathetic tones, thanked him for having been throughout life a dutiful son, and told him that he had never given his father a moment's uneasiness. Very naturally the son experienced deep agony of mind on hearing this. His conscience could not bear the strain of so much undeserved eulogy. He felt that he must now reveal to his father the secret of his crime. He began to do so, but the thought of embittering his father's last moments caused him to pause. Perceiving his reticence, his father begged to hear what it was that preyed upon him, and referred to the " foolish quarrel " James had had with Beaumont the day before the latter's murder. James, horror-stricken, ejaculated an inquiry as to when he had heard of this. His father told him that the housekeeper had overheard them, and told him years ago, but that he had never mentioned the fact, lest it should grieve his son. But while in the very act of saying this, something in James's look told him the sequel of the quarrel. He strove to speak, but fell back dead.

.I have dwelt too long already on this episode in the book, and will not attempt to recount Wilson's subsequent agony of mind, an agony of mind which he had to bear alone ; nor the humiliating interview which he soon after had with Williams, whose silence he was forced to buy in an ignominious manner. I will hasten on to the last incident in this direful history.

One fine summer evening Wilson's children had, as usual, been playing in the fields, and on their return were eagerly conversing among themselves, when their father entered the room. More with a view to divert his thoughts than for any real interest in the matter, he desired them to tell him the subject of discussion, when his eldest boy came forward and showed him an old rusty knife which he said they had found "in the hedge of the orchard field." It was the knife with which their father had murdered Beaumont so many years before. Great was Wilson's anguish at beholding this evidence of his guilt, and he was hardly able to ask his children to go to their mother; but at length, with a great effort, he did so. He felt as if he were going mad. His wife entered the room, and inquired whether anything had occurred. He replied in the negative, but asked her to take the children to bed. She perceived that something was greatly amiss, and left him for awhile to his own distempered musing, and he heard her whispering to the children to ascend the stairs softly, as their father was very ill. By-and-by she re-enters the room, and then her husband makes the terrible disclosure.

She becomes insensible, and for hours remains in this condition; and when at length she recovers consciousness, she spurns her husband from her. He entreats her to have pity on him, but in vain, and for three days he tends her, but all his endeavours to shake her obduracy are fruitless. On the night of the third day he goes downstairs, and the old evil thoughts which he had once encouraged return to tempt him; and, alas! he yields to them. Next morning he rises early, and drawing a phial from his pocket which he had carried for years, " lest it should be required in a case of sudden emergency," he pours its contents into a warm drink which he has prepared. This he takes to his wife, but as usual she refuses anything from his hands. In this instance, however, he insists, and she obeys. He knows little more until his youngest child enters an upper room where he is, and tells him that her mother is very ill. He enters his wife's room, and finds her dying. She speaks pitying words to him, words of forgiveness. Ah, how he regrets that these words had not been spoken sooner! She dies, and he disappears, hardly knowing for what purpose, for the gift of life is to him no longer worth possessing. The next morning he is found by one of his own men, and given up to justice. The closing lines of the confession are very pathetic, and exemplify clearly what would, in the imagined situation, be naturally the reflections of a man of this character at such a moment.

There can be no doubt that *The Confession of James Wilson*, as a whole, is exceedingly fine, not so much, as I have said, from any points of novelty in the characters themselves, or in the situations depicted, as from the brilliant workmanship and the thrilling analysis of emotion. Wilson is not by nature a bad man. He has been betrayed into one bad action, and that deed, once committed, entails the rest. I think it was, however, an artistic mistake on Whitehead's part to make Wilson poison his wife. We can bring ourselves to extenuate the boyish crime, but we can hardly forgive the outrage on our sympathies caused by the later atrocity. Had Whitehead permitted Mrs. Wilson to live on after a knowledge of her husband's crime, the vestige of former love and a regard for her children would have been sufficient to deter her from bringing him to justice, and the mingled emotions of their future intercourse would have enabled White- head to employ one of his finest gifts—the gift of creating and describing varied impulses and moods of mind. But even as it stands, *The Confession*, in its entirety, is almost, if not quite, equal to Victor Hugo's *Last Day of a Condemned Man.*

Whitehead published in 1834—although I am in- clined to believe he may have written it many years earlier—a book entitled *Lives and Exploits of English Highwaymen, Pirates, and Robbers.* On the title- page we are informed that the contents of the book are "drawn from the earliest and most authentic sources, and brought down to the present time; with sixteen engravings by Messrs. Bagg." Considering the direful and awe-inspiring character of the narra- tives, it is truly dreadful to reflect that there were materials for them down to 1834. The present writer does not remember 1834, but he knows many per- sons who do, and as he has never heard from them such terrifying details as are here given, he would fain believe that the statement that his great book was brought down to date was made by that important personage "C. Whitehead, Esq.," in order, if possible, to heighten the gloomy and tragical character of the communications he is about to make to his readers.

The following are some specimens of the contents of the book. It were well to state that Whitehead is far too gallant to exclude ladies from this category of eminent persons, and not to be outdone by him in this respect, I shall deal with them first. I presume they belong to the last-named class on the title-page, for they can hardly be called highway*men*, and I never yet heard of a female pirate, unless it be a young lady novelist who pirates from a more ingenious romancer the salient features of one of his plots.

Eighteen pages are taken up in the first volume with an account of the "German Princess." This madam was born at Canterbury in a humble station, but through her pre-eminent amatory abilities, and the amazing faculties she possessed of getting scot-free from her numerous lovers when she had fleeced them, she lived for a long period in great affluence. She was at length hanged.

Ann Harris was an exceedingly juvenile young lady when she matriculated at the college of crime, and in three years she was "thrice a hempen widow." A remarkable story is told about her, which, if true, goes to prove that she was endowed with much originality of invention and fertility of resource. One day she resolved to commit an extensive robbery, but before doing so, called on a physician who kept a private lunatic asylum, representing herself as an unfortunate matron whose husband she much feared was becoming mentally deranged, and would soon require to be placed under restraint. His principal hallucination was that his wife owed him money in payment of goods supplied to her. She heard what the doctor had to say, and, agreeing if necessary to place her husband under his care, went her way. In the afternoon of the same day she went to the shop of a large mercer and bought very extensively from him. She then agreed with him that he should return with her in her coach to her residence in order to receive payment; but instead of driving to where she lived, the carriage was driven to the lunatic asylum mentioned above. Here, at a sign from her, several lusty men seized the unfortunate mercer and *nolens volens* dragged him inside. In a few lachry-mose words she explained the situation to the physician, who listened to her with a willing ear. The doctor immediately proceeded to examine his patient, and said that he, poor gentleman, was very bad indeed; the more so as he, on being accused of lunacy, and being still held with anything but a fairy touch by the strong men, bellowed for his money or his goods, in addition to, it is needless to say, stoutly asserting his sanity.

In short, Madam Harris's little stratagem succeeded to admiration, and on her retirement from the scene, the doctor gave the most drastic instructions as to the mode of treatment and regimen to be given to the patient, the principal feature of the dietary being weak barley-water until his mind was restored. Ann Harris had, however, the grace, as soon as she had got a sufficient distance away with her booty, to write to the mercer's wife, telling her of her husband's deplorable plight, and politely requesting her to release him.

It is always sad to record the early end of genius, but truth compels me to state that according to this admirable book an ungrateful State soon deprived Ann Harris of her existence.

Now for the gentlemen. William Cady is a young man who begins life as a physician, and cures his uncle of an exposthume by making him laugh; and Mr. Charles Whitehead very gravely instances several reliable examples of similar cures which are on record, the most striking one being that of a reverend and puissant cardinal who, being in *articulo mortis* with the same complaint, was cured by seeing his favourite monkey dancing on his state bed crowned with his stately nightcap.

Very speedily, however, Mr. William Cady grows weary of the tame duties of an ordinary physician, and feels that there is no scope for his abilities in that walk of life. Accordingly, he takes to the road, and having robbed Viscount Dundee, he is fain, in order to escape the consequences from a non-appreciative world, to hide his brilliant light under the dark habit of a friar at the English seminary of Douay. Here he speedily acquires a pre-eminent measure of the odour of sanctity, and becomes the fashionable confessor of the young ladies of that town. At length one day, by the gentle persuasion of a loaded pistol held to the head of his fair penitents, he extorts from them an adhesion to one of the first principles of Communism, at least a century before that word came to be used by a world ever dull to accept any new doctrine, however good. In brief, after making them share with him their goods, he decamped. Needless to say, he also was hanged.

We do not hear of Patrick O'Brian, the next worthy of whom I shall speak, that he had the nine lives which appertain to the Kilkenny cats of his native isle, but we are certainly led to suppose that he had two. For it is told of him that being hanged for the first time he entered on his second life, took once more to the road with great success, and did not close his career till another and more efficacious application of the hempen rope was vouchsafed him.

This work of Whitehead of which I have been speaking originally came out in two volumes, published by Messrs. Bull and Churton, Holles Street. The copy in the British Museum is now in one volume, but with two distinct title-pages. The first, illustrated, bearing date 1833, the other 1834. The preface is amusing, and shows decided marks of juvenility. It strives to prove that it were not well to think of this book simply as one from which to receive a certain kind of entertainment. It asserts that by thus holding the mirror up to vice, it will advocate virtue in the strongest possible manner, and it ends with the moral reflection from Dr. Paley, that even were expediency our sole guide, it alone would tell us that honesty is not only the best but the *sole* policy. The book, notwithstanding its somewhat ludicrous character, exemplifies clearly the dreadful barbarity of the times when events such as it chronicles were possible. The volume is almost destitute of literary merit, and frequently the style is so bad that with every allowance for the conditions under which it was produced (being, no doubt, task work) we could reasonably expect better things from the man who afterwards wrote *Richard Savage.*

Whitehead wrote and published, somewhere about 1838, *Victoria Victrix*, and the *Athenæum* on the 4th of August of that year reviews it. It terms the production "a little gay pamphlet," and calls it a song suited to the times. It also playfully rallies the minstrel for prophesying. The hope which the following lines express has, however, been realized more fully than is the usual fate of such predictions :—

"Hark ! stealing softly upward, float around
    Dissolving strains, that the rapt soul enthral ;
  Ne'er issued from the crystal urn of sound
    Sweeter, or at the sea-nymph's festival,
    Arose from pearl shells in Nereus' hall.
Italian and Teutonic airs too long
    Have charmed our English Muse ; she will recall—
She *has* recalled at length her native song,
And bids us to forget her self-inflicted wrong.

    *   *   *   *   *   *

" But oh ! shall Poetry revive once more ?
    (Would that some loftier voice her cause would plead !)
  Will not thy hand, thy youthful hand restore
    Her glories, and award her honour'd meed ?

    *   *   *   *   *   *

" But thou shalt flourish : if my hopes be true,
    Thy sons no longer upon chance shall wait,
  Or humbly still at Fortune's threshold sue
    For alms that never come, or come too late.
    The penalty of daring to be great

Has been too often paid ! by fortune thrust
  With spurns from her inhospitable gate,
In whom should outraged Genius place his trust ?
In whom but thee, young Queen, the gentle and the just."

    *   *   *   *   *   *

The poem is in the Spenserian stanza, but how different is it from *The Solitary! That* is not seldom despairing, but] always impressive. *This*, a lively utterance filled with the evanescent sentiments of a particular period — sentiments, though the feelings which produce them ever remain in a rightly constituted citizen, yet the mood in which they are here expressed is not often indulged.

Mr. Bentley, Whitehead's subsequent publisher, advertises in the number of the *Athenæum* previous to that in which the notice mentioned above appears. It is not stated, however, by whom *Victoria Victrix* was published, nor is it included in Mr. Bentley's list.

The Memoirs of Joseph Grimaldi, the celebrated clown, were edited by Charles Dickens, or, as he preferred to style himself on the title-page, " Boz ;" and in some subsequent editions Whitehead seems to have been concerned. In the British Museum catalogue, the first edition of this work with which he seems to have anything to do is dated 1846, and is there stated to be " revised by Charles Whitehead." From the same source I learn that the next edition of the book in which he was concerned is dated 1853, and is stated in the catalogue to be " revised by Charles Whitehead, with notes and additions." There is also a further edition, similar in all respects to the last-named, illustrated by George Cruikshank. It was published by Messrs. George Routledge and Sons.

To the *Grimaldi Memoirs,* which at the British Museum have been re-bound with an outer cover of sober green, very different from the flaring one on which is portrayed a comical portrait of the hero, which still remains as the inner cover, Whitehead contributes some interesting notes elucidatory of the subject, but nothing of any special importance.

The *Grimaldi Memoirs* may certainly be accepted as one of the remaining evidences of Whitehead's friendly intercourse with the young novelist who was then rising into fame—Charles Dickens.

CHAPTER IV.

WHITEHEAD AS A WRITER OF SKETCHES.

Smiles and Tears; or, The Romance of Life, was published by Mr. Bentley in 1847. The work is in three volumes, and it is perhaps worthy of remark that it has no dedication or preface, but is introduced simply by a few lines of what is termed "Advertisement," dated London, 8th April of the above-mentioned year. The volumes are clearly a compilation from fugitive sources, and they must be judged as such. Nevertheless, the style and workmanship evince cleverness throughout. It would appear from Mr. George Hodder's *Memories of My Time* (Tinsleys', 1870) that the first sketch in the book, entitled *Passages in the Life of Francis Loosefish, Esq.*, was originally called *Passages in the Life of Jonathan Loosefish, Esq.* Again, the last story, entitled *The Stockbroker*, has clearly been reprinted, with a few verbal alterations, from *Heads of the People; or, Portraits of the English*, a miscellany of tales and sketches, contributed by Thackeray, Leigh Hunt, R. H. Horne, Samuel Lover, Douglas Jerrold, and other writers of distinction.

It is somewhat remarkable that Whitehead has not included his other contribution to *Heads of the People—Tavern Heads—*in *Smiles and Tears.* This was probably because to his mature judgment, despite its cleverness, it appeared at times rather coarse.

The stories and sketches, composing *Smiles and Tears,* are in three different forms of composition. First, the rollicking farce as seen in *Loosefish,* the thing which comes straight out of the comedy of the Wycherly and Farquhar period, with a complete absence, however, of the grossness which disfigures these authors and the general literature of their epoch. Second, a sombre type of story, which occasionally drops into a style that is sometimes reminiscent of Edgar Allan Poe, but without his morbidness. The story of *Edward Saville* belongs to this class. While making this general remark, I would not wish to affirm that Whitehead borrowed from Poe, or that Poe drew any of his inspiration from Whitehead. Third, quietly humourous sketches, cast in the mould of Leigh Hunt. *Confessions of a Lazy Man* is one such. *Some Passages in the Life of Francis Loosefish, Esq.,* is a series of mad harum-scarum adventures invented to illustrate the career of an adventurer. From this sketch I give the following representative extract, which will sufficiently illustrate the character of the whole :—

"And now Magson's bill was falling due. The days of

grace had commenced, the day after to-morrow, and presentation must ensue.   Sooth to say, it was hardly convenient to me to meet this bill ; the alternative, therefore, must be to run away from it.   How did I curse the foolish delicacy that had withheld me from writing to my uncle Grindley, explaining my connubial intentions and soliciting fifty pounds to enable me to carry into effect that desirable arrangement.   I had felt, however, that an abrupt intimation of that nature might prove fatal to my cousin Ellen, whose love for me was altogether of a romantic character.   Magson, then, must be once more applied to.   I must raise ten pounds under pretence of taking up the bill, and then start into the country, and rely upon splendid eloquence, embellished by the most persuasive, and, if necessary, pathetic diction.   Some affected purists would, I know, condemn this step as rash and unadvised.   I can only say that it is frequently resorted to by persons of the highest respectability.

" The very first thing on the following morning I found myself at Magson's door.   As I entered, the odour of coffee was pleasingly fragrant, and the girl was just bringing in the hot rolls.

" ' Magson,' said I, shaking him heartily by the hand, ' I am come to breakfast with you ; your bill falls due to-morrow.   I can't wait half an hour—must conduct Charlotte to the morning concert : we are to be married, you dog, on Tuesday next.'

" ' Well, that is *most* extraordinary,' said Magson ; ' the very day on which *I* am to be married.'

" ' You—you going to be married !'   And I gazed at the old-fashioned juvenile with astonishment.   ' Well, but let me tell you.   Ten pounds——'

" ' Two years ago,' interrupted Magson, making an arch in the centre-piece of a hot roll, ' I went into the country on a month's leave.   There I met a young lady and her excellent parent, with whom I became acquainted.   I renewed the intimacy last year, when I paid my addresses to the young lady, which were rejected. But this year, on renewing my proposals, the old gentleman gave his consent, stating that he believed his daughter's objection to me had been weakened, an attachment she had formerly conceived for some worthless spendthrift of a nephew of his having subsided.'

" ' Well, my dear fellow, I give you joy,' said I, not paying much attention to this narrative. "But, touching business, I want you to lend me ten pounds for a day or two, to enable me to meet your bill. I must not appear to want money, you know, until I get my wife's property.'

"'Impossible, Loosefish, impossible!' cried Magson, setting down his coffee-cup. 'Didn't you tell me that the bill should be taken up ? It *must* be taken up. Your father-in-law, Mr. ——'

" 'Trotter,' said I.

" 'Mr. Trotter will lend you fifty pounds instantly.' (Poor short-sighted wretch, how little he knew Trotter !)

" ' Besides,' he continued, ' I want every farthing I can lay my hands upon at this moment. I must cut a dash for a month or two. I told the old fellow I had six hundred a-year in the Mint, and, you know, I only get a hundred and fifty. The girl has lots.'

"Here was a sordid villain ! At that moment I could have drugged his coffee with hellebore.

" 'And so you won't lend me the ten pounds ? Very well, Mr. Magson.'

" ' I can't,' he replied ; ' and I wish you'd be off now. I expect my wife, that is to be, and her father, every instant. Oh ! here they are ! Now, go, that's a good fellow.'

"Urged by curiosity, I approached the window. ' Ha ! can it be ?' cried I, in an ecstasy.

" ' Can it be ?—It is !' said Magson.

" ' My uncle and cousin,' I rejoined ; and rushing to the street-door, which I opened, I flung myself into the arms of

the old gentleman, embraced my cousin with that warmth
which is my chief and most amiable characteristic, and
drew them into the parlour.

"Magson's face, as we entered, assumed the sourness of
small beer with which thunder has been making too
free.

"'Very strange!' said he; 'a most extraordinary co-
incidence.'

"'Very,' replied the old gentleman, wiping his forehead.
'So then, nephew, you know Mr. Magson?'

"'He *was* a friend,' said I, with bitterness; 'but now—oh,
uncle! Well, how have you been?' And I drew my chair
towards my relatives, and entered into an interesting conversation.

"'Loosefish, a word with you for one moment,' cried
Magson, with an air of chagrin.

"I approached him.

"'Now, can't you be off,' said he, appealing to me. 'You
see you are not wanted; you can meet your friends some
other time.'

"I turned away from him in disgust. 'Oh! my dear
uncle,' said I, with emotion, 'what a viper you were about
to take to your bosom! Oh! my beloved cousin, how
nearly you were sacrificed! What do you think that
monster gets per annum at the Mint?'

"'Six hundred, on the rise,' said Grindley.

"'One hundred and fifty, and the salaries are about to
be reduced; and to my certain knowledge his mother keeps
a cake-shop in futile opposition to the Chelsea bun-house.'

"Magson held down his head in utter confusion, while the
head of my revered uncle appeared to be twisting round on
a pivot with inconceivable rapidity, so instantaneously did
his eyes glare upon every article in the room.

"'Let us retire from the odious wretch!' said Ellen, with
a thrill of horror.

"'Nay, hear me,' cried the crest-fallen culprit. 'It is

true I have been guilty of duplicity, but let me plead my love
for——'

"I generously rushed between Magson and the incensed
parent, and caught the descending walking-stick ere it clave
open the skull of the former.

"'Leave him to his conscience,' said I, with dignity; and
I drew my cousin's arm between my own. 'Adieu, sir!'
and we marched in triumph from the forlorn villain."

Edward Saville is a story of love, jealousy, and
madness. Saville is a young man of violent temper
and unbending will, and the sequel will show that he
was slow to forgive and relentless in his hatred.

At the age of twenty-three he became his own
master, and followed a course of pleasure frequently
pursued by young men in his situation, partly, as he
himself tells us (for the tale is couched in the autobiographical form), to relieve a feeling of loneliness.
One evening he was at the theatre, and the friend who
accompanied him directed his attention to a very lovely
girl, who, with her mother, occupied the next box.
He was smitten by her beauty, and the usual result—
at least in stories of this class—followed. When the
play was over, he watched her to her home. At length
he obtained an introduction to the family, and upon
personal acquaintance he was more fascinated than
ever by the object of his devotion. Her name was
Isabella Denham, the daughter of an officer killed in
the Peninsular War.

They were at length married, and for four years
knew no diminution in their happiness. A son had
been born, and that circumstance had augmented their

felicity. One day, by the merest chance, Edward Saville encountered in the street a young man named Hastings. They had been schoolfellows at Eton, and at college their intimacy had become friendship, but, as frequently happens, they had not met for several years. Next day Hastings dined with his friend, and very soon became a most frequent visitor. He was one of those men often to be met with, who, living for pleasure, had no apparent vice. He was living, more-over, on expectancy, and consequently had little ready money; and Edward Saville went so far as to help him in a pecuniary sense. By-and-by Edward Saville became much engaged with some troublesome business connected with his estate, to conclude which it was necessary that he should visit his property. He ex-pected to be absent about six weeks, and as the London season was at its height, he deemed it cruel to tear away his wife from the conventional round of festivity in which she was then taking even more pleasure than formerly. Begging Hastings to look in now and then, and see that his wife was not lonely or out of spirits, Edward Saville left for the country. He was detained more than two months, but at length, finding himself released from an irksome attendance on very unpleasant business, he returned " with all the ardour of a lover " to his home. Hearing his step, his little boy went to greet him, but his child's mother was not there. Pre-sently his housekeeper entered and he knew the worst: his wife had forsaken him for Hastings.

Overcome by this terrible blow, his reason for two

years was dethroned, but at length he awoke from what he fitly termed this "long, long, hideous dream." Slowly he recovered strength both of mind and body, and at length he was restored to his house. But the memory of his wrong remained with him, and when he strove to banish it, the endeavour almost distracted him ; accordingly, whether for good or evil it is not necessary here to say, he encouraged feelings of revenge. He had never had sufficient firmness to see his child since his recovery, but one evening, hearing the boy asking of one of the servants who " that white-haired gentleman " was [his hair had become grey through grief], and " why he lived in the house ?" he sent for him. He found him much grown, and a fine boy. At first the child did not know him, but at length was induced to overcome his shyness sufficiently to sit on his father's knee. His parent, putting back the hair from his forehead, asked him if he would not give him a kiss. But when the child lifted his face to do so, and looked at his father, the glance recalled to the latter with such painful fidelity the son's unworthy mother, as to cause a sudden faintness to overcome him. He was thankful to permit the servant to remove his poor child from his sight ; and he did not see him again.

Edward Saville was never weary of tracking the destroyer of his peace, and the unhappy participator in the betrayer's guilt and infamy. He sought them in Paris, but found they had returned to London. Here, however, for a while he seemed to be baffled, for all his endeavours to circumvent Hastings in his old haunts were fruitless. But one day when walking down a wretched street in the vicinity of Clare Market, he encountered a degraded creature issuing from a low tavern. None but Edward Saville could have recognised who it was, but *he* did so instantly. The man strove to escape, but Saville struggled to capture him, and very soon, with "savage triumph," dashed him to the ground. Saville, however, was in his turn seized by several of the by-standers, who, regardless of his entreaties and ravings, held him firmly until the other had escaped. This encounter made Saville ill once more, but in a month he was well again. With much difficulty he at length discovered the public-house from which Hastings had emerged, and from the landlord he obtained every particular he needed. Hastings had changed his name to Harris, and existed, rather than lived, in a small room in a filthy court near at hand. Easily Edward Saville found the place; he ascended the stairs and burst suddenly into the room. A man and a woman occupied it. They were not Harris and his unhappy companion. Saville demanded to know where Harris was. No sooner had he spoken than he heard a shriek from a sadly too well known voice, and a woman dropped to the ground in a fit. Saville again fiercely demanded to know where Harris was. "He is there," gasped the man, pointing towards a bed, on which Saville, for the first time, perceived a shrouded corpse lying. Hastings had indeed escaped him.

The injured husband, at the advice of his physician, settled a competence upon his former wife, and hoping that the worst had passed, and that time and occupation would do much to relieve his state of mind, he resolved to strive to forget what was irremediable. One day he was told that a woman desired to see him. Imagining that she was one who came perchance to crave for money, he ordered her to be admitted. A woman, meanly dressed, appeared, whose countenance was concealed. Moving towards him, she sank on her knees; her lips quivered, she would have spoken had she had power, but with a groan she fell senseless upon the floor. It was his wife! Summoning his housekeeper, he ordered that she should take care of the poor creature, and let her want nothing, but remain in his house till she recovered and other arrangements could be made.

Some days afterwards his housekeeper informed him that her charge was dying. He bade her take his child to the sick-room, saying that doubtless its occupant would wish to see him; and then he heard for the first time that the mother had seen the boy every day since her strange return; and that, moreover, she had seen him many times during the last two years, when he, the father, was mad. In extenuation of this breach of trust, the housekeeper told him how her former mistress had come, and falling at her feet, had implored her permission to see the child. This she could not refuse.

That afternoon Edward Saville went towards the lodging which Hastings had formerly occupied. The

woman of the house told him a sad tale. It appeared
that Hastings had fallen into a life of the lowest debauchery, and had constantly ill-used his companion,
striking her, and telling her "to go to her Mr. Saville."
The people in the house were very conscious of her
obedience and gentleness amid these trials, and
esteemed and admired her much, supposing her the
wife of the man who maltreated her—an impression
Saville did not disturb.

Feelings of forgiveness began to steal into his bosom
as he thought of the happy, beautiful, and innocent
girl he had met at first—how she had never received
a single glance of unkindness from him ; and to think
that she "had become the slave, the drudge—the
spurned and beaten drudge—of a cruel miscreant."
The thought was too horrible ! In this mood of mind
he returned to his home. The rest of the story will
be best told by the following extract :

"I had scarcely entered my own house, when Mrs. Martin
sought me.

" 'For mercy's sake, sir,' she said, in agitation, ' come and
take your last leave of my mistress. She is dying, and has
prayed to see you once more !'

"I followed her in silence. I met Herbert [his physician]
at the door of the room.

" 'I am glad you are come,' said he. He was in tears.

" 'I am too weak, Herbert ; am I not ?'

"He pressed my hand. 'No, no !' and he left me. I
entered the room, and sat down by her side. She spoke
not for some minutes.

" 'I wished to see you once more, Mr. Saville,' she said at
length, in a low tone, and without raising her eyes to my

face, ' to implore, not your pardon, for that I dare not expect, but that you will not curse my memory when I am gone. You would not, Edward,——' and she tremblingly touched my hand as it lay upon the bed,—"if you knew all, or if I could tell you all.'

" I answered something, but I know not what.

" 'I have been guilty,' she resumed, ' but I did not meditate guilt. Heaven is my witness that I speak the truth. I was betrayed, and the rest was fear, and frenzy, and despair !'

" I could conceive that now. I could believe it. I did believe it; and I was human. I took both her hands in mine.

" 'Look at me, Isabella ! look in my face !'

" She did so, but with hesitation ; and as she did so she started.

" ' Nay, we are both altered; but other miseries might have done this. I forgive you from my heart and from my soul. As we first met, so shall we now part. All shall be forgotten,—all *is* forgiven. May God bless you !'

"Those words had killed her. Her eyes dwelt upon me for one moment with their first sweetness in them ; a sigh, and earth alone remained !"

There is considerable power in the tale of which I have just given a résumé. The theme is an unpleasant, even a painful one, and it is questionable whether the portrayal of such feelings as those of Edward Saville after his wife's misconduct are likely to be productive of good, or—to put the objection in another form, for the benefit of those who deny the didactic functions of romance—whether such delineation is good art. The scene wherein the sinful mother supplicates a menial on her knees for a sight of her child, is finely conceived and brilliantly brought out, and is, perhaps, the finest thing, as a unit, in the tale.

Confessions of a Lazy Man is a piece of playfully insincere writing : writing, indeed, with no pretence to sincerity.   From the following clever passage the tone of this, and of many similar articles, may be gathered :

"I am not inclined to place much faith in the sincerity of Thomson's laziness.   He has the credit of having been the laziest of men, but I do not think that he deserves it. There were, I doubt not, Thomson's seasons of activity. His 'Castle of Indolence' is not a sincere or a well-imagined poem, *I* could have suggested; but, no matter, I will not boast of my perfections.   The persons introduced into that poem always appeared to me rather bustling people than otherwise.   Eating peaches from a tree with one's hands supporting the skirts of one's coat, as Thomson did, was an awkward and laborious process.   Have them plucked for you, say I.   Nor is the popular anecdote related of the bard a whit more in his favour.   It is recorded that a gentleman calling upon Thomson found him in bed, and foolishly inquired why he did not rise ?   The reply of the poet is altogether paltry and contemptible.

"'I had no motive, young man.   Could any earthly motive induce *me* to get up, unless, indeed, it involved a solemn guarantee of a softer couch in the immediate vicinity ?'

"Besides, Thomson altogether forgot (let me hope that he was too lazy) to dwell upon his motives for lying still.

"I had great faith in Mr. Coleridge.   From all I heard of that great man, I was inclined to feel a friendly interest in his welfare.   I would have extended my hand to him, had he been lying in an adjacent bed.   He has himself told us that he composed his fine fragment of 'Kubla Khan' in his sleep, thereby causing the claims of occupation to give place to the demands of repose. I can picture to myself the venerable poet and philosopher in his study. My mind will only permit me to conceive him perusing the shortest, and therefore the most exquisite, pieces of our approved authors. A paper, perhaps, of the 'Idler,' or the 'Lounger,' the least long of Horace's Odes, or Anacreon's; elegies, epigrams, an occasional Idyll—it should be called an Idle—of Theocritus, or the 'Ode to Tranquillity,' by his friend Mr. Wordsworth.

"For my own part, I glory in what fools consider my shame. I have almost discovered the perpetual immobility. The revolution of the earth is motion enough for me, and for any reasonable man, can anyone conceive a more lamentable figure than a bustling impertinent, busy in other people's affairs or his own, and laughed at for his pains, or baffled in his projects? Who cuts the more philosophical figure of the two, the locomotive blockhead who bursts into a bedroom to apprise the sleeper that his house was on fire; or the disturbed sage, who, calmly addressing himself again to sleep, remarked, that when it reached the first floor it was time enough to rise?

"What young man ever left the University with more gratifying credentials than those conveyed in the following concise summary of his merits by one of the Fellows of the College, 'Sir, he had nothing to do, *and he did it.*'"

As a whole, *Smiles and Tears* is not a book upon which can be founded a claim on behalf of Whitehead's genius; that claim must rest on other work. But though the volumes are by no means equal to his best, indeed, are perhaps his worst work in book form, they are by no means contemptible.

Among Whitehead's miscellaneous contributions to periodical literature not included in *Smiles and Tears* is, as I have said, one paper contributed to *Heads of the*

People; or, Portraits of the English, a highly amusing and most cleverly written miscellany. "The Heads," or character portraits, were all by that admirable illustrator, Kenny Meadows, many, indeed, being worthy of the highest praise. The Miscellany appeared in 1839-1841 in two volumes, the publisher being Mr. Robert Tyas, Cheapside. It was subsequently reprinted in one volume, the publisher then being Mr. David Bryce, 48, Paternoster Row. This later edition (of which I possess a copy) is without date.

Whitehead's only contribution, with the exception of a brief one entitled *The Stockbroker*, is called *Tavern Heads*. It is a light rambling paper, sometimes coarse in a slight degree, but always vivacious, descriptive of tavern life in London, with racy sketches of different types of revellers, and here and there snatches of original humorous verse. It often exhibits clever writing, but it is not comparable with the author's higher works. In common also with a great deal of Whitehead's other writing, it leaves an impression on the mind that he was deeply impregnated with the Cockney character. The pictorial illustrations are not very refined, but two of them, " The Parlour Orator," and " The Last Go," are most exquisitely humorous.

Whitehead was an early contributor to *Bentley's Miscellany*, for the first half-yearly volume of this magazine, which closes with the preface signed "Boz," dated London, June, 1837, contains *Edward Saville*, and a poem entitled *The Youth's New Vade Mecum*. The latter opens with a most humorous letter from

Whitehead to the editor of *Bentley's Miscellany*, Charles Dickens. The letter states (by a transparent fiction) that the enclosed poem is by an intimate friend, now a "sexagenarian sire." He goes on to say that the love of such a parent is the concentrated essence of the love of mother, grandmother, aunt, great-aunt, uncle, and great-uncle, besides that of all conceivable agèd relatives, all fused into one.

The subject of the poem is advice to his son by this father who married so late in life. The poem is characterized by a good deal of vivacity throughout, and as I have given no other specimen of Whitehead's vein of humorous verse, I now append the following example :

> "My son, whose infant head I now survey,
>   Guiltless of hair, whilst mine, alas ! is grey,—
>   Whose feeble wailings through my bosom thrill,
>   And cause my heart to shake my very frill,—
>   Incline thine ear, quick summon all thy thought,
>   And take this wisdom which my love has brought :
>   Perpend these precepts ; sift, compare, combine ;
>   And be my brain's results transferr'd to thine.
>
> "Soon as thy judgment shall grow ripe and strong,
>   Learn to distinguish between right and wrong :
>   Yet ponder with deliberation slow,
>   Whether thy judgment be yet ripe or no ;
>   For wrong, when look'd at in a different light,
>   Behold ! is oft discover'd to be right,
>   And vice versâ—(such the schoolmen's phrase)—
>   Right becomes wrong, so devious Reason's maze !
>
> "Take only the best authors' mental food,
>   For too much reading is by no means good ;

And, since opinions are not all correct,
Thy books thyself must for thyself select.
Accumulate ideas : yet despise
Reputed wisdom,—folly oft is wise ;
And wisdom, if the mass be not kept cool,
Mothers, and is the father of, a fool.

"Be virtuous and be happy : good ! but, stop,—
They sow the seed who never reap the crop ;
For virtue oft, which men so much exact,
Like ancient china, is more precious crack'd :
And happiness, forsooth, not over-nice,
Sometimes enjoys a pot and pipe with vice.

" Get rich ; 'tis well for mind and body's health :
But never, never be the slave of wealth.
The gain of riches is the spirit's loss ;
And, oh ! my son, remember gold is dross.

" Be honest,—not as fools or bigots rave :
Your honest man is often half a knave.
Let justice guide you ; but still bear in mind
The goddess may mislead,—for she is blind.

" Hygeia's dictates let me now declare,
For health must be your most especial care.
Rise early, but beware the matin chill ;
'Tis fresh, but fatal,—healthy, but may kill ;
Nor leave thy couch, nor break the bonds of sleep,
Till morning's beams from out the ocean leap ;
Lest, crawling, groping, stumbling on the stair,
Your head descend, your heels aspire in the air ;
As down the flight your body swiftly steals,
Useless to know your head has sav'd your heels,
Prone on your face with dislocated neck,
You find that slumber which you sought to check.

" Early to bed, but not till nature call.
  Be moderate at meals, nor drink at all,
  Save when with friends you toast the faithful lass,
  And raise the sparkling, oft-repeated glass ;
  Then, graver cares and worthless scruples sunk,
  Drink with the best, my son,—but ne'er get drunk.'

" Bathe in cold water : cautious, and yet bold,
  Dive,—but the water must not be too cold :
  And still take care lest as you gaily swim,
  Cramp should distort and dislocate each limb.
  When such the case, howe'er thy fancy urge,
  Postpone the bracing pastime, and emerge.
  Dangers on land as well as water teem,
  But now the bank is safer than the stream.

" Say you should chance be ill (for, after all,
  Men are but men on this terrestrial ball);
  Should sickness with her frightful train invade,
  Lose not a moment, but apply for aid.—
  Yet fancy oft imagined symptoms sees,
  And nervous megrim simulates disease.—
  Lo ! at your call—the cry of coward fear—
  A chemist and a cane-sucker appear :
  The one tough roots, from earth's intestines dug,
  Pounds with strong arm, dissolves the nauseous drug; '
  The other, gazing with portentous air,
  Surveys the foolish tongue that call'd him there ;
  To dulcet tones that breathe deceptive calm,
  Your cash expires in his diurnal palm,
  And, sick of physic you were forced to swill,
  Long-labelled phials indicate the bill."

To the volume comprising the six months' productions whose vitality kept alive *Bentley's Miscellany*
during the closing months of 1837, Whitehead con-

tributed *John Ward Gibson* (included in *Smiles and Tears*), and *Rather Hard to Take*, another humorous poem. The latter is descriptive of a poor artist's trouble on being asked by a family to paint their grandfather's likeness, that venerable relative being now dead, and the artist having never seen him in life. Pathetically the painter asks whether the relatives have any portrait of the dear departed, any memento, anything to recall him as he appeared in joyous existence? No! They have nothing! But stay, one of the ladies becomes possessed of a happy idea. She leaves the room, signifying the general purpose, but not the particular object, of her quest. The artist's hopes are raised; he anticipates that now he can execute his commission in such a way as to add to his fame, and, what is still more important, replenish his scanty finances. Presently the absent one returns, carrying carefully in her arms an old hat—the sole memorial. Deplorable is the consternation and agony of the unfortunate limner.

From this brief summary it will be seen that there are materials here for an amusing poem, but unfortunately the execution is not on a level with the conception.

Flora Macdonald, The Heroine of the Rebellion of 1745, is an historical article, presumably consisting of a review of a certain Mrs. Thompson's *Lives of the Jacobites*. Our author begins well in a philosophic manner, but subsequently appears to be cramped for space. It shows Whitehead as having a sincere regard and affection for all that was heroic and chivalrous in the prejudices and feelings which prompted the last struggle for the Stuarts. This article appears in *Bentley's Miscellany* for 1846.

Pizarro and his Followers is an epitome of the early part of that adventurer's career, chiefly gathered from Prescot's *History of Peru,* for which work the writer evinces a sincere admiration.

The Wooden Walls of Old England is a somewhat commonplace article of the hackneyed type.

The Insurrection in St. Petersburg in 1825, with some Account of the Conspirators, is a much more able article, giving a full account of a Russian insurrection which occurred in that year, and which was unwittingly aided by a conflict of generosity between two brothers, the elder declining to reign.

Aliwal and Sir Harry Smith (with a portrait of that officer), gives an interesting account of the battle, one of those in the Sikh War of 1845. This contribution is not signed by Whitehead, but it is noted as his in the index to *Bentley's Miscellany,* 1848. He also contributed two able articles which were signed to *Bentley's Miscellany* for the same year :—*Caricature and Caricaturists,* and a *Memoir of Captain Marryatt.* In the first named he claims for the British nation great distinction as caricaturists, but he especially deals with the life and times of James Gillray. A portrait of him, and fac-similes of several of his famous or most successful caricatures, are given. One of them appeared at the time of the threatened French invasion, and represented George III. as King of Brobdignag, looking through his telescope with amused curiosity at Gulliver (Napoleon), who was standing on the opposite cliff brandishing a little sword. This cartoon helped greatly to sustain the national spirit.

The Memoir of Captain Marryatt is a pleasant and comprehensive sketch, written very shortly after the death of that gallant officer and successful *littérateur*.

As far as I have been able to see, Whitehead ceased to contribute to *Bentley's Miscellany* after 1848. At least, I cannot find any signed contributions subsequent to that year.

A poem by Whitehead, entitled *The Wife's Tragedy*, appeared in the new series of the *Illuminated Magazine* for 1845. It is a somewhat lengthy poem for a periodical, as it extends to nearly 500 lines. The metre is a species of *ottava rima*, and the characters introduced are a young man whose name is Henry Eustace, a young lady named Louisa, whom he marries, and a girl named Julia, cousin to Louisa, who, a short while after their marriage, comes to pay them a long visit.

Henry Eustace is a young man whose father had died when he was yet a mere child. He had a good position and prospects, and we are told that consequently, when he attained to a responsible age, he added one more votary to pleasure. But by-and-by he beheld a certain maiden, and, greatly to the surprise of his "wise predicting friends," he wooed her, although she had neither "beauty, wit, nor wealth." Despite, however, her lack of what many are pleased to consider the three most desirable qualifications in a wife, she was endowed with numerous pre-eminent charms, and one of the prettiest passages in the poem is that which describes what these were.

No little rift came in the lute of their happiness, and they were married. There had been a promise long standing made between Louisa and her cousin Julia, that whichever of them should be made a matron first, the other should come to her new home for a long sojourn. Consequently an invitation was sent to Julia. Julia came; and, as we might have expected, is represented as very beautiful. She is delineated as flippant and thoughtless, although not possessed of any positively evil intentions. We are now told once more the tale which we have heard over and over again, with merely a change of names, and occasionally a slight variation of incident. The youthful husband is attracted by the loveliness of his guest, until he forgets his sense of duty so much as to reveal his feelings towards her. She puts him off, telling him she can never be his while Louisa lives. He is crushed; but presently his better nature seems to return to him, and soon entering once more into the presence of his wife, seizes her hands and kisses them. She is pleased, and, tenderly accusing him of his long absence, they are reconciled; at least, as far as that word can be used in a case where we are led to suppose that the wife was totally unaware of her husband's defalcation from duty.

This unsatisfactory story ends in an unsatisfactory

manner, as the last few lines would seem to indicate that Louisa had, if possible, greater trials before her than those through which she had just passed. Viewed from a critical standpoint, this tale is very far from being equal to Whitehead's best productions, either in its conception or execution. Compared with *Jasper Brooke*, it is indeed weak. Here are some illustrative extracts. The poem opens with the lines which follow:

> "A youthful couple at the altar stood,
>   And in hushed order, ranged on either side
>   Were relatives, the nearest of their blood
>   And friends, by feelings of the heart allied;
>   And, as the rite proceeded, all of good
>   That might befall the bridegroom and the bride
>   Was wished by these, and wafted thence on high
>   With many a prayer not in the Liturgy."

The next stanza I quote, describes, not without vigour, the youthful pleasures amidst the meshes of which Henry Eustace had been entangled:

> "And all delights that youthful passions seek
>   And think they find, were his, such vain delights
>   As on the mind the body's vices wreak,
>   And make their very shames their parasites;
>   Suggesting manhood in a hollow cheek,
>   True wisdom in well-nurtured appetites,
>   Deep knowledge of the world in scenes that make
>   The soul sick, and the heart of memory ache."

But the writer—rather unreasonably, considering the manner of young man his subject is represented as having been—soon tells us in the following words how

Eustace became deeply attached to a maiden possessing all the virtues and charms except that of loveliness :

> " There was a maiden whom, as though to chide
>   The rashness of his wise predicting friends,
>   Eustace beheld, wooing her for his bride ;
>   And they who charged him with ambitious ends,
>   And talked of his hereditary pride,
>   Now deemed him mad, or made him frank amends.
>   Certain, the girl had gained his heart by stealth,
>   For she had neither beauty, wit, nor wealth.

> " She was not beautiful : yet how to trace
>   Worthier perfections which my power defy :
>   That decency of mien transcending grace ;
>   That gentleness, which was veiled dignity ;
>   That sweet serenity of air and face,
>   Which of her inward heaven was the sky ;
>   That purity of a plain heart, made wise
>   By nature beaming from her Sabbath eyes."

Julia's loveliness is well described in this stanza :

> " She came : in truth there was rare beauty here.
>   Behold the dark complexion of the south,
>   The broad black eye as moonlit water clear,
>   The arch audacity of the rich mouth,
>   Whose lips capricious, playfully severe,
>   Now staid as age, now flexible as youth,
>   Aye-varied loveliness, had still their cue
>   From one who all their fascination knew."

The revulsion of feeling caused by Julia's refusal of his unworthy proposals brings back to him by-and-by fond memories of his wife. He seems to see her, and he can no longer resist his impulse to go at once into her presence. The poem closes with these two stanzas :

" O, Earth and Heaven conjoined, in thought abused !
    He could not bear the sight, but rose and seized
    With quivering limbs, teeth clenched, and eyes suffused,
    Her hands and kissed them—and the girl was pleased,
    And his long absence tenderly accused,
    But spoke dear nothings, that his heart was eased ;
    Then laid his throbbing temples on her breast,
    And fondly dreamed he as herself was blest.

" A little while—a little longer while—
    Be blest ; for O, what meets thee, or awaits—
    How Hell this instant his infernal guile,
    About to be triumphant, celebrates ;
    How, to engrave thy name, the lifted style
    Prepares, in that dark book which men called Fate's,
    Thou knowest not : be blessed then, and be blind :—
    Sweet flower ! guilt casts thee hence, but Heaven shall find !"

The Spanish Marriage—A Dramatic Story, was contributed by Charles Whitehead to the *Victorian Monthly Magazine* (Melbourne), July, 1859. It is stated to be a dramatic story in three parts, but of these only the first appears in the above-mentioned magazine of that date, and as no more copies of it are in the British Museum, it is not improbable that the magazine was discontinued before any further numbers were issued. The magazine was even then in its infancy, the first number having been issued in June, 1859.

The period of the story is 1567, and the plot of the drama is as follows:

Don Charles, son of Philip II. of Spain, loves, and is affianced to, Elizabeth of Valois. Philip, his father, who is a widower, has been secretly paying suit to Elizabeth, Queen of England, and has been rejected by her, when he turns his eyes to France, and addresses with success his son's betrothed. From what cause the lady's infidelity arises does not appear, but she is married to her regal suitor, and the portion of the play which is published deals with the son's anger at his desertion, with the father's suspicion of his son's disloyalty, and the disclosure that despite the lady's kingly alliance, she has been unable entirely to overcome her former affection for the prince. The character of Don Charles, though exhibiting a moroseness perhaps natural under his somewhat trying circumstances, is cast in an heroic mould. That of Elizabeth exhibits purity and sweetness, and lends itself to the inference that the author meant to extenuate her offence by subsequent disclosures. The character of the King is vindictive, treacherous, and cruel, capable of any unnatural persecution of his own flesh and blood to appease his passions.

Philip, indeed, as depicted by Whitehead, bears a certain affinity to the King Claudius in *Hamlet;* and this perhaps suggests a parallel of some closeness. Don Charles, both in natural bias of mind and in his bearing towards the King who has wronged him, is not wholly unlike Hamlet; while Elizabeth stands between the elder and younger man pretty much as Gertrude docs in Shakespeare's far greater play. The atmosphere of these earlier scenes, the first of which I am about to quote, is not unlike that of the first scenes in *Hamlet*, less, of course, the incalculable difference that will suggest itself to every mind:

SCENE I.

The exterior of a Cathedral at the back of the stage. Enter from the door Charles and Posa, who descend the steps and advance hurriedly to the front of the stage.

Charles. These impious marriage rites ! Oh holy nature,
How art thou now profaned !
    Posa.   But yet, my lord,
Permit the friend who ventured to dissuade you
From being present at this ceremony,
To urge the danger of a seeming scorn
Cast on the king by your abrupt departure,
Before the benediction had been given.
    Charles. The benediction ! frightful mockery !
Had I stayed longer, Henry, I had rushed
To the high altar, and in tones to thrill
The ashes of the dead beneath my feet,
Proclaimed the scene a most unrighteous lie.
    Posa. Let me implore be calm.
    Charles.   Be calm ! and love ?
You know she was affianced unto me ;
She knows it too ; letters have passed between us,
Our portraits been exchanged.—You know the king
Made overtures to Elizabeth, Queen of England,
Who said her hand was otherwise engaged
In grasping tight the sceptre. Thwarted there,
This father casts his eye tow'rds France and sees
His son's betroth'd—thence, and now, weds her. Shame

On royal contract oaths !   I am a slave,
A thing for men to whet their wits upon,
To have suffered this.
   Posa.   I grieve for all the wrongs,
Scorns and indignities which——
   Charles.   From my birth,
Forget not that !—
   Posa.   The king has heaped upon you
But he is absolute, and waves his will
O'er every head at pleasure.   Hear me now :
There is no being on the earth so helpless
As a king's son and heir ; he's sought and flattered
And lov'd for that which may be, not which is ;
All in expectancy, and meanwhile nothing—
(*Aside*)   He does not listen.
   Charles.   Stay, they are about
To leave the church ; the sacrifice is ended :
Stand close : you shall see pomp and majesty,
A king and queen, pass by—a stately sight !
You would not think, sir, that the king bears with him
A perjured heart—the queen a blighted one.
(*The doors of the Cathedral are thrown open, and a marriage
    procession comes slowly forth and passes out.*)
Didst thou behold ? all is accomplished now,
And nought remains for me but to begone.
After to-day I must not see her more.
Must not ? who shall prevent me but the king,
Who knows not what a heaven shines through her eyes
Into my soul ?   Oh thou hast triumphed o'er me,
Thou ruthless father, and I must submit,
In meek endurance of thy sharpest taunts,
So I may live here in her presence.

The following scene between Philip and one of his
courtiers and confederates has something in common

with the scene between Claudius and Hamlet's schoolfellows, Rosencrantz and Guildenstern:

A Chamber in the Palace.

Enter PHILIP *and* GOMEZ.

Philip. You know I trust you—place full faith in you ?
Gomez. That knowledge quickens all my forces in me
To show myself your servant, and to merit
Your instant confidence.
Philip.   I can believe it.
'Tis three weeks since our proxy, Alva, brought
Our to-day's queen to Spain.   Four days ago—
(Didst mark his sudden flight out of the church ?)
You hinted something touching the prince and—well ?
Gomez. My gracious lord,
I spake but as my duty prompted me.
Philip. I know: you said so—my own doubts had travelled
The ways of yours before them.   Do not speak yet.
Gomez, all private feelings in this case
(Even had I stronger warrant of suspicion
Than yet I dare to dream of) shall be thrust
Out of my heart, or into it so deep
That their persuasions be not heard.   Attend—
It is a fearful, a most dangerous thing
For subjects, howsoe'er in place exalted,
To peer and play the spy upon a prince ;
To tread upon his shadow when he walks,
Make tiptoe steps into his steps, and then
Vanish to some convenient refuge, where
Both eye and ear can be employed.
Gomez.   Your highness !
Philip. But still more fearful, still more dangerous, when
The lynx becomes a jackal which would lure
The lion to his prey—that prey a son.

Gomez. Your highness misconceives my honest purpose,
Which my too active fears perhaps suggested :
I sought to warn your grace, who even now
Were pleased to speak of your precedent doubts.
  Philip. And if I did—what then ?   Yours were projected
Into my ear before you knew of mine.
Now Gomez, mark !   If I do not commend
(As how should I do that ?) the officious zeal
With which yourself, and, I suspect, your wife,
Have plunged into this perilous matter, still
I think your love and loyalty have been
The incitements to it—and I grant you pardon :
And now what you have gathered with such pains
Must be more fully told me, and confirm'd
By such addition as your vigilance—
Your wife's, too, brought to aid—may haply furnish.
  Gomez. It shall be done.
  Philip.   Yet further : howsoe'er
I move in this, what I design to do,
What I may do, shall be made known to you ;
Your counsel may direct me.   But, I warn you,
By the love I bear you, by the pregnant hate,
Pregnant with ruin if thou be not faithful,
Whate'er I meditate, design, or do,
Be silence thy good angel ; be thou secret
As the deep dungeon, or the deeper grave
To which thou goest if thou be not so.
  Gomez. I am entirely yours, my lord ; so wholly,
That graves and dungeons of your highness' pointing
Affright me not.   I am not wont to make
My tongue the herald of my thoughts.
  Philip.   You are not,
'Tis therefore that I trust you ; presently
Attend me ; I would spell the inmost soul
Of my rash son.   I bring the queen with me,
You know my object—note him.

Gomez.   And the queen ?
Philip. Go to : have you two eyes ?   In a short space
Attend my pleasure in the antechamber.

         [*Exit* PHILIP.

Better, however, than either of the foregoing scenes,
more dramatic, exhibiting more subtlety of character,
more by-play of passion, disclosing more perfidy on the
part of Philip, and more cynical scorn on the part of
Don Charles, with simple, girlish, self-betraying affection on the part of Elizabeth, is the following scene, in
which the king and Gomez set traps to catch the
prince, pretty much as Hamlet and Horatio set traps
to catch Claudius :

Elizabeth.   Doubt it not ;
If you but understood the prince's nature—
Nay,—but you do not smile :—I am strange to Spain—
Rather I mean,—oh, pardon my rash boldness !
If you had studied it——
  Philip.   As you have done——
  Elizabeth. If envious courtiers had not interposed——
  Gomez (*hastily*). Madam—the king——
  Elizabeth.   Well, sir, is here ; and here
Is the king's son ; and you are here.   What then ?
May I not speak ? (*To* GOMEZ) Forgive my childish haste.
  Philip. We see your gen'rous ardour, and approve it :
But if you can restrain it for a while—
(*To* CHARLES) Have you e'er thought of marriage ?   You are
   silent,
Must I repeat the question ?
  Charles.   Once, my lord,
You know I did ; now, 'tis no thought of mine.
  Philip. But if I could demand the hand for you
Of a princess, as young and fair as—(*glancing at the queen*)—

Charles.   Who ?
Philip. As young imagination might depict,
Were there no pattern.   She is one whose beauty
Is nature's copy of her inward graces.
Elizabeth. Who is the lady whom your majesty
With such unwonted earnestness commends ?
Philip. First, how our son inclines to this proposal
We would fain hear.
Charles.   My duty made no question,
I would in all humility submit
My own unworthiness.   Such paragons
Are not for one who has been long a shame
To you and to himself opprobrious.
Philip. Let the past trip to rearward, and accept
My present love.   You turn away, Don Charles,
You need some better spirit to direct you ;
You are still wayward, unamenable
To the behests of reason and of duty.
Charles. I am sorry for it.
Philip.   .   Sorrow leads to mending,
And I would have you mend.
Charles.   And so I shall.
This fatherly solicitude, expressed
So sensibly, must cause a change in me.
I feel it work already.   Pr'ythee, your Grace,
Who is the fair princess you have selected
To help my reformation ?
Philip.   Were you worthy,
As I now see you are not——
Elizabeth.   Oh, my lord,
Touch not his pride too nearly ; pardon me,
This is not gracious in you.
Philip.   Were you worthy,
As now I see you are not, to espouse her,
Her name and title had been told.   But now——

Charles. That princess, ages since drown'd with Atlantes,
What was her name—her title?
    Philip.   Would you mock me?
    Charles. I would I knew the lady's name;—perchance
Elizabeth of England?

(PHILIP *rising hastily, all rise.*)

    Philip.   Trifling babbler!
I am not angry with you, but lament
A weakness of the brain which, day by day,
Seems to increase. I can but grieve for you.
    Charles. Not love me, as you promised?
    Philip (*to* GOMEZ).   Come with me.
                [*Exeunt* PHILIP *and* GOMEZ.

The final scene of the first part is enacted in a
garden avenue. Philip enters, followed by Gomez,
and later in the scene Elizabeth appears. Philip is
now more than ever certain that Elizabeth is loved by
his son, and seems to be firmly convinced, though
without any real reason, that Charles not only loved
Elizabeth before she married, but that their love, however pure then, has become guilty now. Philip seems
pleased to see his son suffer mental anguish. This is
how Part I. closes—Philip speaks to his wife:

Philip. Elizabeth of Valois, mine own wife—
Mine—mine—what do I seek? what do I see?
A brow, as 'twere, the rainbow to those eyes
That never more should weep—clear cloudless eyes
And blushes made for Love to light his torch by,
You are my beautiful—how? silent still?
    Elizabeth. Your gaze confuses me.
    Philip.   Does it affright you?

Elizabeth. My lord will suffer me to leave him now.

[*Exit.*

Philip. Oh God ! she loves him—everything denotes it.
The tongue may lie, but looks give up the truth.
Said I too much ?   Will she suspect ?   No matter.
And *thou* would'st shake the tree, and crush thyself
With the fruit that falls from it ? forbear ! 'twere pity
Two should be sped at once—but if—but if—
Not zig-zag, but straight lightning.

[*Exit.*

The " Duke of Alva " is ranged among the *dramatis personæ*, but no dialogue is assigned to him in the first part, the only one which I have been able to see.   There are in this work several striking passages which recall the power of phraseology evinced in Whitehead's earlier poems.   Here is a notable instance of what I refer to :

" What do I see ?
A brow, as 'twere, the rainbow to those eyes
That never more should weep—clear cloudless eyes
And blushes made for Love to light his torch by."

The principal objection which can be urged against the work is the absence of local colour, and to one who has lived in the country in which the scene is laid this deficiency is very marked ; but it could hardly be expected that Whitehead, unacquainted with the country, could give this local colouring, when, as every one knows who has tried to do so, it is most difficult to impart it in a realistic and truthful manner.   On the whole, therefore, it may fairly be said that Whitehead did well in not attempting to describe or to give local allusions concerning a country he did not know.

Readers of modern English poetry are tired of tawdry second-hand descriptions of Spanish life and scenes. It is a pity, however, that Whitehead had not lived in Spain for awhile. He might have given us as realistic and true a picture of how men and women lived and loved in the Spain of that epoch as Longfellow gives of the Spain of a later day in his *Spanish Student.*

Altogether this fragment of a play seems to me a powerful one, more pictorial, more human, than *The Cavalier,* while the dialogue is more forcible and sinewy.

We meet with Whitehead as a poet on the first known occasion of his becoming an author; we meet with him again here in the same capacity after eight-and-twenty years have checkered his career; and one cannot help thinking with something akin to emotion of the gravely different feelings with which he must have written at these widely separated periods.

We imagine with what proud hopes the young and highly-gifted man in the full fervour of early manhood published not only his first long poem, but his most important poetical work; a poem of whose power he must have been conscious. One reflects with what hopelessness the weary, toil-worn man, over whom the sorrows of fifty-five hard years had passed, saw the publication of his last signed work. For he must have said to himself that if the efforts of his best years had only resulted in disappointment, neglect, poverty, and at length banishment from the world's metropolis of literature, how could he expect that this drama, the labour of his declining days, published in a country, however friendly, still in all probability alien to his sympathies, and therefore unlikely to appreciate his best work, could retrieve his position ?

CHAPTER V.

In his preface to the *Earl of Essex*, Whitehead apologizes in the following terms for touching so delicate and difficult a theme:

"The subject I have chosen is a great one; and, to do it full justice, might task faculties far greater than I have to employ.

"'The words that Bacon and brave Ralegh spake,' are not easily imitable; and it were indeed 'conjuration and mighty magic,' whereby the illustrious personages who present themselves in these volumes should be worthily evoked. One has already been called up by a mighty magician who, in the vigorous delineation of historical character, stands second only to Shakespeare. 'Wherefore, then, did you rashly make choice of such a theme?' I cannot reply. But let not my silence be my own condemnation."

As will be seen from the above, the work is an historical one. It has an affinity to the historical romances of Scott, but differs from that novelist's mode of treating history in some important particulars. We must remember that Scott's sympathies were with the age of chivalry, an age which had hardly ceased to exist at the epoch during which the incidents narrated in the *Earl of Essex* were supposed to take place, and that Whitehead's mind, on the other hand, belonged in its characteristic features to the Bohemia of a later age.

The romance deals almost entirely with the notable points of the career of the Earl of Essex subsequent to the rebellion of Tyrone, and principally concerns itself with depicting the inner life of Essex, Ralegh, Bacon, and Queen Elizabeth during the closing years of that sovereign's reign. Although the scenes are necessarily heightened in a romantic manner, and a number of characters foreign to authentic records introduced for the purpose of picturesqueness and variety, yet in the main the proprieties of history are carefully preserved. Occasionally, and probably also for the sake of picturesqueness, Whitehead even varies the spelling of proper names, calling Sir Ferdinand Gorge "Sir Ferdinando Gorges," and Blunt "Blount." In his *Life of Ralegh*, the above-mentioned knight appears likewise as "Gorges."

Naturally, in a romance of this sort, the chief interest centres in the author's views of the historical personages dealt with. Whitehead puts the following estimate of Essex into the mouth of one of the minor personages:

"'Had my Lord of Essex,' thought Cuffe, as he went his way on his mission to Bacon, 'had yonder feverish being my cool brains in his skull, to qualify his hot ones—he might yet arrive at a greatness of which he never dreamed.

11—2

Or had I his hot brains in my skull, to give action to the
torpid mass that slumbers there, I might conduct myself to
greatness of which I have dreamed often.   Towards this,
Master Bacon plods.   And for lack of that vital heat in his
brain-pan, which, with nought beside, makes men mad, but
seasoned with what is called prudence, makes them great—
for lack of this, perchance, Master Bacon, with all his
wisdom, will plod in vain.   In sooth, then, what is coolest
in my brain, shall be levelled at what is hottest in the brain
of Essex, as air at fire, which coolly blows it into a blaze.
It shall go hard, but we burn out a path between us, o'er
which we may walk abreast.' "

Whitehead thinks, concerning Ralegh, that he never
courted public opinion, but did what he deemed right,
and left the result to time.   Essex, he avers, ever did
what he could to conciliate public favour and commend himself to it, and would generally sink any
principle, however important in his own judgment, in
order to flatter or pander to the popular taste.
Characters so radically opposed very speedily come
into collision, and the following is the first scene in
which they appear together :

" ' My Lord of Essex,' resumed Ralegh, ' I have heard
that high words passed between you and Sir Robert Cecil
at the council-table to-day.   I am here to offer my services
as mediator betwixt ye.'

" Essex heard him in evident wonder.   ' You !—come as
mediator !   Grace of God !   Sir Walter Ralegh !—you !'—
and he broke into a short quiet laugh.   ' Of this world's
marvels——'

" ' This is not one,' said Ralegh, quietly finishing the sentence. ' Is this the first time I have been here on a work like

this ?   Have I not closed your two hands in one, ere now ? Who but I made peace between your lordship and the Earl of Nottingham ?   What marvel in this ?   Why, sir,' and Ralegh smiled good-humouredly as he said it, 'I am the great peacemaker.'

"Essex smiled not in return.   On the contrary, his face became clouded with rising displeasure.

" ' You moved on the part of my Lord of Nottingham, by command of the Queen,' said he ; ' and in the former case at the request of Sir Robert Cecil ?'

" ' I grant that.'

" ' May I ask, then,' continued Essex, ' whether, upon the present occasion, you are sent by the Secretary ?'

" ' My Lord of Essex,' returned Ralegh, with some warmth, 'I am not one to be sent anywhere, or to any man, or by any man, and this you know right well.   I brook no sending but from the Queen.   Sir Robert Cecil knows not of my coming.'

" ' Then, wherefore do you come ?' asked Essex, with affected indifference, raising his brows.

" ' It is ill, and of bad example, at the least,' returned Ralegh, 'in these times generally, but in particular at this time, that there should be open division between yourself and Cecil.   It may, as I conceive, breed danger to the State.'

" ' Is not your concern for the State somewhat of the youngest ?' asked Essex, with a sneer.   ' When, Sir Walter, was it born ?'

" ' About the time that you were,' returned Ralegh ; ' when I first drew sword against the Queen's enemies.'

" ' Is it not, then, somewhat of the idlest ?' pursued Essex. ' You are not a Privy Councillor.'

" Ralegh arose from his seat.   ' Is not this talk somewhat of the idlest, my Lord of Essex ?' he inquired, with a frown. ' I am not a Privy Councillor, but I have assisted at councils when sworn heads lacked brains.'

"'Which you have brought with you, doubtless?' said Essex.

"'Yes,' answered Ralegh promptly. 'Enough of this. One word, and I am gone. Do you reject the offices I have proffered?'

"'I do.'

"'You seek no reconciliation with Sir Robert Cecil?'

"'I do not. I scorn, and I defy him.'

"'It suffices,' said Ralegh, proceeding towards the door.

"'Stay,' exclaimed Essex; 'a few words of our own differences.'

"As Ralegh returned into the middle of the room, Essex came forward and met him, so that they stood face to face, scarce a foot's length between them.

"'Sir Walter Ralegh,' said Essex, with unusual calmness—for when addressing an enemy, or one whom he supposed to be an enemy, his anger commonly endured no check from his reason—'I know you love me not.'

"'You know it. I will not gainsay it,' replied Ralegh. 'I have no cause to love you.'

"'Let that be. You have no cause to hate me.'

"'I bear a good memory, my lord,' said Ralegh; 'but I do not hate you."

"'What less than hatred could have prompted you to stab my reputation in the back?' cried Essex vehemently; 'with gibes and jeers to scoff at my proceedings in Ireland, and this to our gracious Queen? By Heaven! Sir Walter Ralegh; by Heaven!'

"'By Heaven! I understand you not,' broke in Ralegh. 'What mean you? If ever I spoke a word——'

"'Oh! you can speak words enow, sir,' exclaimed Essex.

"'I can, sir,' replied Ralegh, recovering his coolness, which he had well-nigh lost; 'and I can justify them. I spoke not in my life a word yet I dare not justify. Thus much I tell you. If ever word dropt from my lips of your conduct in Ireland, it was in answer to questions urged by the Queen's grace, which I, her servant, was bound to answer, touching points, too, upon which I am competent to speak. But gibe and jeer! that, on my soul, did I never.'

" ' I have proof that you have wronged me to the Queen,' said Essex.

" ' You lend too ready an ear to base poor villains,' returned Ralegh, 'who abuse it grievously. Their proof, my lord, were, like their courage, most absent when most wanted.'

" ' That we shall see,' rejoined Essex. ' In my letters to the Queen, from Ireland, I have charged you, Ralegh, with what I have this minute spoken to your teeth. That touches you, I perceive. I am frank with you.'

"It was more than a minute ere Ralegh replied. No motion of the man betrayed the wrath that boiled within him. His eye, nevertheless, which in his calmest mood men in general almost feared to look upon, shone out, disclosing with a glance of fire all that was passing inwardly.

" ' Years gone, my Lord of Essex,' he said at length, ' I had brought you to a quick reckoning for this.'

" ' A quick reckoning! This to me!' cried Essex, stepping back, and laying his hand upon the hilt of his rapier. ' Cannot it be told now? What hinders?'

" ' What must serve for both—my discretion,' said Ralegh.

" ' You keep your temper well, sir,' observed Essex scornfully.

" ' I do; but know you not, the sword is as keen in its scabbard as when it is drawn? Having taken thought, I thank you, my Lord of Essex. It is you, I find, who can stab reputations in the back. But I am now in the Queen's hands. If you seek your proof from her, and if you find it,' stepping up to Essex, and tapping his sword-hilt gently with his finger, ' then, my lord, we will come to a short and to a sure reckoning.'

" With this he turned upon his heel, and taking his hat, left his antagonist without further word."

Most readers will agree with me in thinking that this is a well described and vivid scene.

The Queen Elizabeth of Whitehead is an impetuous and somewhat arrogant lady, tempered, however, with occasional promptings of a gentle disposition such as are not usually associated with that Sovereign. It is true that in the fine scene I am about to quote these softer qualities are not apparent; but they neverthe-less exist in Whitehead's delineation of the Virgin Queen, as a subsequent extract will show.

" ' Had you not all you required,' returned the Queen, ' when you proceeded to Ireland ? Did you not engage, with the force you carried with you, to destroy this rebel Tyrone —long ere this to destroy him ?'

" ' I deny it not,' said Essex.

" ' Where, then, is performance ?' cried the Queen. ' The rude raw levies of the rebel flout us—nay, by God's right arm ! fight us, beat us. The head of Tyrone waggles with laughter, which months since should have been sheared from his shoulders.'

" ' I spoke rashly, and like a fool, when I engaged so much to your majesty,' returned Essex. ' I knew God's justice never fails in this world, and that He was with us ; but I forgot that His ways are not our ways ; nor His time our time ; and that when He pleases to work by us, He makes us His instruments, not His ministers ; His limited slaves, not His discretionary servants. Sickness has wasted your majesty's troops ; death has been busy with them. I pro-vided not against that.'

" ' Now, by God's justice, of which you speak, Essex, you make me mad,' exclaimed the Queen vehemently. ' Why had you not led them against the rebel ere sickness wasted or death smote them? This truce—this dishonourable truce !'

" 'Dishonourable, madam !' cried the Earl. ' Heaven forbid his Queen should be dishonoured by Essex. That truce.was made but to gain time.'

" ' Gain time !' echoed the Queen contemptuously. ' Why had you not gained Tyrone, and brained him? A truce to gain time ! What terms are made with rebels? When rebellion stalks, all the time between the avenging sword and its punishment is disgrace. Go to ; I thought I sent a soldier to Ireland, but I find I despatched a scrivener.'

" 'Let me be judged,' cried Essex, in scarce smothered tones of anger, ' by those who have carried arms, by those who have led an army into the field.'

" 'You have been, my Lord of Essex, judged and con-demned,' said the Queen.

" ' By Ralegh, doubtless,' exclaimed the Earl quickly.

" ' Oh, sir !' said the Queen, stepping up to him, ' once more harping on Sir Walter Ralegh ? We read your letters, my Lord of Essex, in which you touched our honour nearly, as flinging upon us a suspicion that we harboured about our person calumnious tale-bearers and sycophants. You pointed at Ralegh therein. By our sacred honour as a Queen, as gallant a gentleman and as faithful a servant as ever prince had.'

" ' He hath practised against me,' said Essex.

" ' Do I speak twice ? I tell thee, thou temerarious and froward youth, he hath not. He is no practiser, as thou art, who wouldst this moment, if thou couldst, destroy him. 'Tis fitting he should know of this.' The Queen walked to the door, which she flung back, ' Send hither Sir Walter Ralegh.'

" ' I bring him hither to shame you,' said the Queen, re-turning. ' Had you taken pattern by him, ungovernable boy,

you had not stood before me now for censure and for punishment.'

"The last words were scarcely spoken, when Sir Walter
Ralegh entered.   Essex gnawed his lip, and frowned darkly
upon his rival, whose face, however, was directed towards
the Queen.

"'By Heaven! this is not to be borne,' muttered the Earl.
'Chid like a whipped schoolboy, and in his hearing.   But,
time—time—oh, hasten it, Queen Elizabeth!'

"The thought that came into his brain, at that moment,
gave him ease.   His brow cleared again.

"'Soh! Sir Walter,' cried the Queen, 'we have sent for
you in good time, Sir Walter; come forward and answer to
us.   Do you know that you have been busy with the reputation of this our faithful cousin and servant, Robert Earl of
Essex—this patient, but, chief of all, this obedient subject?
Do you know that you have slandered him to our ear during
his absence on our affairs in Ireland?'

"'Your Majesty knows, right well, I am not this thing,'
answered Ralegh, in a sonorous and deliberate voice, casting
a look of defiance at the Earl.

"'Is not the Queen of England in presence here?' exclaimed the Queen angrily.   'Bend your eye upon us, Sir
Walter, and to us direct your speech.'

"'I humbly crave your majesty's pardon,' said the knight.
'My Lord of Essex charged me with as much (I thank him),
to my face, yesterday.   To-day, as I conjecture, it has been
repeated to my sovereign, but for whose dread presence——'

"'Swords were leaping, and blood staining the floor of
our palace?' interrupted the Queen.   'I cry you mercy,
gentlemen. Peace, Ralegh, I command you. These looks and
gestures we endure not in our presence.   How, sir?—not a
word—one word, and ye speak next, both of ye, through
walls of stone.'

"'Yet must I speak, or choke,' exclaimed the Earl, strid-
ing towards Ralegh.   'Sir Walter, you know—death! why

am I thus fooled?—Do you not know you have wronged me ?'

" Elizabeth stepped between. Holding forth her right hand, the forefinger of which she shook in the Earl's face, she said : 'Robert Devereux, on your allegiance, we command you, silence. Ralegh, leave our presence instantly. From this ungovernable man you have nought to fear.'

" ' To fear, gracious madam ?' said Sir Walter. 'I have not been used to fear your majesty's enemies. My own,' he added significantly, 'I have been used to despise and to defy.'

" ' From his words, I meant, foolish caviller,' returned the Queen, ' you have nought to fear. He cannot wrong you here. I know your worth and service. Bégone. I speak not again.'

" ' I am commanded,' said Ralegh, with a deep reverence. When he again raised his eyes, and directed them sedately to the face of the Queen, not a glance or a feature disclosed even the vestige of passion. ·The Earl looked in vain for an exchange of mute defiance. The knight retired unmoved, as he had come.

" The peremptory dismissal of Ralegh, which, under a less critical aspect of his fortunes, or in a calmer condition of his mind, Essex might have regarded as an evidence of the Queen's partiality towards himself, or of an inclination to his cause, he was not, at the present moment, disposed to hold in any account. That Ralegh should have been suffered to make his appearance at all—that he should have been summoned, evidently (for so it seemed to him) to descry, that he might report, the Queen's anger against him—that he might share the triumph of his humiliation—these, and the rough fibres of feeling which instantaneously shot out of them, were damning vexations that made it the most difficult task he ever experienced to control his temper within the bounds of reason, even in the presence of his royal mistress.

" As it was, if no outbreak of fury was heard, the struggle to repress it was seen, and seen distinctly.

"'Speak, sir,' cried the Queen; 'if you have aught to say let your words come forth. Stand not thus—heaving and swelling, like—what shall we say?—like a rebel. Methinks we see before us Tyrone; or is it his ambassador we see, come to propose terms of treason?'

"'Not treason, your majesty, will I utter, but truth,' exclaimed Essex, speaking very rapidly—'but truth. You have done me wrong—shame added to wrong—why should I not say it?—shameful wrong, therefore.'

"'Take care, Essex—take care, my Lord of Essex,' said the Queen, wrath striving to put on solemnity. 'Not an inch of further ground have you. One step more, and the gulf. Your wrong—your shame—what are they?—where are they?'

"'Is it not enough,' answered Essex, 'that I stand here before you to undergo your majesty's reproof—charged with I know not what—since nothing but vague charges, or charges vaguely urged, have I yet heard—I, who have devoted my life, my fortune, my honour, ease of body, peace of mind— my whole soul, to your service—is it not enough that I bear with patience your displeasure—(oh, madam! how undeserved, let time, when Essex is no longer of it, show); but that I must be made also a spectacle to my worst enemy—a puppet for his laughter—a butt for his derision?'

"'I hope your patience may play you no jade's trick, for yet further have you to journey with her—or without her,' returned the Queen. 'Thou malapert boy, if this is bad, thou must bear more and worse.'

"'Never!' exclaimed the Earl. 'More I cannot bear, nor can you impose.'

"'We shall see that,' returned the Queen, nodding her head slowly.

"'We shall see,' repeated Essex scornfully; 'we—who are of the world—not you, who are above it—that princes can sometimes err, and may sometimes be censured for their errors.'

"So saying, he flung from her in disdain.

" 'God's death, my Lord of Essex,' cried the Queen, following him. 'Remember! See you this hand? Remember! I can chastise insolence. Your ears are red already.'

" 'Just and merciful God !' cried Essex, raising his hands towards Heaven, and then dashing them, half clenched, into his bosom, as though he would fain pluck forth his heart. 'My dearest, most honoured, most gracious mistress,' for with these soft words did he seek to soothe, to flatter his rage into needful submission, 'have me before your council—have me into your Star Chamber—let me be tried by my peers, and judged—judged—not cast without judgment. If I am guilty, censure me ; fine me ; let me be imprisoned—kill me ; but oh ! madam, damn me not thus before death, which now were most welcome. If I am proved innocent, then——' He paused.

" ' What then ?' asked the Queen.

" The thought that had suggested, or was about to prompt his words, had, it seemed, flown off. He waved his hand, and broke into a short quick laugh, tears of vexation, whether he would or no, bursting from his eyes.

" ' Then, madam, when next I take a leading-staff, I will come to your majesty to teach me how to command.'

" 'In the meanwhile,' said the Queen, very calmly, 'I will teach you how to obey.'

" It was a forced calmness, lasting no longer than till she reached the door, which she flung so violently open that it recoiled, jarring on its hinges. Twenty years seemed to have been shaken from her, as she flamed into the outer room.

" ' Come forth, sir,' she exclaimed, one arm extended backwards towards the door from which she had just emerged, her eyes glancing exultingly at the lords and gentlemen of the court, with whom the chamber was well-nigh filled. 'Noble lords and gentlemen, you are here in good time met, to see the beginning of justice. My Lord of Essex, come forth.'

"The Earl was already at the door, and now descended the steps. He was ghastly pale, as though a sudden presentiment of impending ruin possessed him, which he could neither avoid nor resist.

"'Who was that fool,' the Queen said to him in a low voice, 'who thought the lion slept, because his own eyes blinked? Come forward, Sir Richard Berkeley; fulfil your office.'

"That functionary advanced on the instant, more like a machine than a man, with so formal and measured a step, and so impassive a countenance, did he make towards the Earl. He laid his hand upon the shoulder of Essex, saying, in a cold, equal voice:

"'Robert Devereux, Earl of Essex, I arrest you in the Queen's name.'

"With a like utterance, as cold, as equal, the Queen said:

"'My Lord Keeper, the Lord of Essex stands committed to your charge, to await our pleasure.'

"The Earl turned his head with a sorrowing but reproachful look towards the spot where the Queen the moment before had stood; but she was gone. There was a short, deep, silence. Not a word—a whisper of triumph—not an eye that spoke gladness; and yet Ralegh, and Cecil, and Cobham, and the Lord Grey of Wilton were there—foes against whom he had sworn irreconcilable enmity."

This courtly quarrel is perhaps one of the most vividly described scenes in the three volumes. The characters live before our eyes. We see their excited gestures, and almost hear their wrathful tones.

One of the main features of the book deals with the relation between Bacon and Essex, and into this it will be necessary to enter at some length. Bacon's character as given by Whitehead is that of an ambitious man : a man who would not allow any friendship, however intimate or endearing, or however he might have been indebted in the past to the man to whom he owed this friendship, to stand in the way of his own self-advancement.

Let us deal with some considerations arising out of the conduct of Francis Bacon in the famous trial of the Earl of Essex : a trial which, with its surrounding incidents, occupies a great space in Whitehead's romance. In the Earl of Essex we have a man who is in a certain sense condemned beforehand by his sovereign, and that sovereign requires Bacon to engage in the trial. Bacon was the friend of Essex, and had been materially benefited by him. The question therefore arises, what course should Bacon have pursued? To assist ourselves in finding data for a correct answer, it will be needful to look at the matter in several aspects.

I.—If a true friend and just man :

(*a*) He must still have accepted the task, or have forfeited for ever all hope of worldly advancement. A monarch's request, especially if that monarch were of the House of Tudor, must be obeyed.

(*b*) He might have undertaken the task in order to keep it out of unfriendly hands. When a friend conducts a case against a prisoner, it may be safely presumed that all will be done consistent with truth to minimise the points which will tell against him, and to increase the importance of the circumstances which tell in his favour.

(*c*) Bacon might have shown in his pleading that duty went against inclination.

II.—If a disloyal friend and unjust man :

(*a*) He would show pleasure in the work.

(*b*) He would also be glad of an opportunity to throw back Essex's favours under the semblance of enforced duty.

III.—But without being a disloyal friend, or an unjust man, Bacon might have reasoned thus :

(*a*) He had received favours in his private capacity.

(*b*) He was about to impeach Essex in his public capacity.

(*c*) The two things were quite distinct.

As some of the following extracts will sufficiently show, Whitehead takes a rather unfavourable view of Bacon's conduct towards Essex. He represents him as wanting in gratitude for that nobleman's previous generosity, and that part of his speech at the trial referring directly to Essex is not what it should have been—a mournful and painful leave-taking of a friend at the command of duty.

Here is a passage describing how the Earl bore himself during his trial. Whitehead rarely gives Essex credit for possessing much self-control; but making all due allowance for this, it is nevertheless sad that a man in such favourable circumstances and of such rare abilities should have so frequently failed to exercise the cool and collected judgment which was perhaps the only quality lacking to have enabled him to be of the utmost value to his country, as well as to gratify his highest personal ambition.

"The Earl, although, indeed, there was but little of contempt in his nature, which was formed rather to resent insult, whencesoever it proceeded, than to rise superior to it, might have listened, perhaps, with some appearance of that meekness and patience which the circumstances of his present condition could hardly fail to point out to him the necessity of assuming, to Coke's insolent presentment of charges affecting himself singly; but he was ill able to rest upon his knees when Mr. Attorney, first recalling to the remembrance of the commissioners how greatly the Earl of Southampton had offended his royal mistress by marrying Mistress Vernon, the cousin of the prisoner, without having previously asked the Queen's permission—proceeded to tax Essex with partiality and injustice in permitting his affection for his friend not merely to overlook, but to disregard, at once the incompetence of Southampton for the office into which he had been thrust, and the claims of others who had a better right to it. With more difficulty, if possible, did he restrain himself when Coke, urging the preposterous number of knights created in Ireland by the Earl, scornfully reiterated an interrogation which, it was generally believed, had been put to him by the Queen at Nonsuch; namely, ere he made so many knights, why had he not built almshouses for them; and he fairly sprang to his feet, hurling a glance of fury at the impudent calumniator, when Coke, at the close of his speech, recurring to the treaty the Earl had, at a moment's thought, concluded with Tyrone, charged him with hastening back to England, as much to avoid the personal consequences to himself, if he tarried near the rebels his incapacity had strengthened, as to obtain his pardon from the Queen, ere that incapacity and those consequences became apparent.

"At the moment that Essex thus suddenly arose, a

12

female hand was, for an instant, stretched forth from between the velvet curtains behind the chair of the Lord Keeper. It touched him slightly on the shoulder, and was again withdrawn. Egerton took no seeming heed of the interruption. As though the signal had been preconcerted in anticipation of some such impatient demonstration on the part of the Earl, the Lord Keeper half-raised himself from his seat, and said:

" 'My Lord of Essex, you may continue standing ; or if you are weary, it is permitted to you to be seated. Use your pleasure. A stool hither for my Lord of Essex.'

"The command was instantly obeyed ; and Essex, trembling with anger, took a seat. There was nothing in the speech of the Solicitor-General Fleming to add fuel to his resentment, or even to keep it alive. Fleming insisted upon the unhappy events which followed the Earl's departure from Ireland—Tyrone having broken the huddled truce agreed upon between them. He concluded, but in no acrimonious spirit, by reminding the Earl that such an opportunity, as he had foregone or forfeited, of advancing his honour and establishing an illustrious reputation by the reduction of the Irish rebels, he could no more expect should ever again be presented to him, than that from off him the heavy disgrace could be removed of having pretermitted so fair an occasion.

"Affected by the solemnity of Fleming's peroration, and, perhaps, moved by a conviction of its truth, the Earl could not avoid showing deep concern in his countenance ; and it was with these altered feelings, whose shadows had been so called up into his face, that he was now to listen to Bacon, who had it in charge to conclude the accusations against him."

The extract which follows describes Bacon's speech at the trial, and the effect produced by it on Essex. Nothing could give a clearer idea of Whitehead's high opinion of Bacon as an orator than the remarks which close the passage. If the speech could influence a man such as Whitehead describes Essex to have been, and that even against his will, it must indeed have been pregnant with the highest attributes of forensic eloquence.

" His voice, nevertheless, faltered as he commenced ; and beyond a wandering consciousness that he was uttering words he had already many times rehearsed, he could hardly be said to know what he was speaking. He began by acknowledging the benefits he had received at the hands of the Earl, and he declared the gratitude they had inspired within him. The language, however conveyed, was as elegant and perspicuous as the best that was wont to proceed from his lips ; and by the time he had made an end of this, his self-possession was restored to him. He proceeded. But now, he said, he bade all present bear witness—and here he turned, and stood facing the Earl—there must be an end of the connection that had so long subsisted between them ; there must no longer be the claims of friendship on the one hand, or its duties on the other. They were, henceforth, single and separated. For his own part, from this day, he lived for the Queen, and was hers alone—wholly, entirely the servant of his gracious mistress.

" The manner in which the words, whereof the above is the substance, were spoken, was singularly inappropriate to the matter. Whether it was that Bacon, feeling or fearing a recurrence of the painful weight of obligation that had but now oppressed him, adopted a louder and more resolute tone of voice, that his emotion should not rise, or that it might not be seen—or that he was vexed into angry impatience by seeing before him (for with some the inopportune presence of a benefactor suffices to cancel all obligations) the man who had caused his pain—whether of these, is matter of conjecture.   Certain, however, it is, that instead of that mournful and tender leave-taking of a friend at the command of duty, which had been alike touching and graceful, his tone was that of a man who rebukes the generosity of his benefactor, and who throws back, even into his face, obligations of which he has long been weary.

"This prefatory matter dismissed, Bacon forthwith proceeded with the charges he had been required to urge. He recounted certain speeches disrespectful of the Queen which had been uttered by the Earl; and read portions of his letters to her, of expostulation or of complaint, couched in language to the last degree unbecoming in a subject addressing his Sovereign.   Bacon, when, in the first instance, he had sat down to frame the accusations it was his province to bring forward against the Earl, had taxed his ingenuity to devise such a form of presenting them as should satisfy the Queen, without offending or injuring Essex; but the feelings of the advocate carried him much further than he designed; and the man who had just before formally released himself from the obligations of friendship, was now with eloquent fervour inveighing against the heinous crime of ingratitude.

"There was more than one smile ere this speech was concluded.   That upon the lip of Coke was so villainously disdainful, that Bacon, had he seen, must have been struck dumb by it.   But, however it influenced others, the effect of this speech upon the Earl was of a very different nature. There was truth in it—truth told in language so forcibly significant and impressive — not an expletive word—no arrowy phrases overshooting or falling short of the mark— so admirably consequential an adjustment of one sentence to another, and yet each sentence complete in its sense, and until the next arose (it seemed so) sufficient to the end— nothing more being to be said, and yet more and more succeeding, which piled up, not extended, the accusation—that Essex, spite of himself, his pride, his self-love, his sense of wrong, his wilful shutting-to the door against conscience, felt for the time (and could not choose but feel) that he was that very monster of opprobrious turpitude which Bacon had conjured up, and shown with a full glaring ghastly light upon it—not naming it—leaving it to himself to name."

No wonder that even the prisoner at the bar, on hearing these words of brilliant pleading, felt, despite his pride, at least for a moment, that he was the " very monster of opprobrious turpitude" that he was charged with being. But despite all its excellences, this speech had one fault. The fact that Bacon, though treating so lightly in his opening words the sense of former obligations, yet dwelt so much in his peroration on ingratitude, laid his flowing periods open to derision, and his enemies were not slow to accuse him (and with considerable appearance of reason) of contemptible time-serving and hypocrisy.

I must allow Whitehead to tell in his own words the touching and impressive interview between the Earl of Essex and Francis Bacon, which follows :

" ' My most noble lord,' began Bacon, 'in the performance of a grievous command——'

" ' No more,' interrupted the Earl. ' Make of it what thou wilt, Bacon, it will not hence out of my bosom. And yet—there,' and he seized his hand, and shook it, grasping it tightly. ' Francis, I have ever honoured you for that great effluence of the Godhead which hath already, and which, I trust, in a greater measure, will yet come forth from you. O ! let not the world—the time o'ermaster you. Here is my hand ; and, by my soul, never did it more heartily press yours. I love you ; but henceforth we must be as friends who have lost each the other, but who trust to meet once more in Heaven.　Fare you well !' "

Despite the acknowledgment of the better qualities of the two men indirectly made by introducing such a scene, it must be allowed that Whitehead has frequently treated Essex rather badly, and that while he does not refuse to admit that Bacon had some virtues, he evidently does not consider him a good man.

Respecting such an important point as the conduct of Bacon towards Essex, it is well to ascertain the views of historians.　Mr. James Spedding, in his *Letters and Life of Francis Bacon* (vol. ii., p. 159), dealing with the years 1599, 1600, says, that the people of the time thought that Bacon was plotting against Essex, whereas he was really doing what he could to dissuade the Queen from bringing the Earl's case in question publicly, and to induce her to pardon him on certain conditions.　Again (vol. ii., p. 190) Mr. Spedding represents Bacon as acting a worthy part towards Essex, in endeavouring to restrain him from clandestine or treasonable proceedings.　Mr. Spedding does not appear to think that Bacon did any wrong towards Essex in his great speech at the trial.　The historian (vol. ii., p. 366) thus sums up the matter from *his* point of view :

" With the publication of the Declaration of Treasons, as now set forth, the history of the relation between Bacon and Essex may be considered as concluded and complete. For though I shall have to recur to it hereafter in connection with the 'Apology'—a work which belongs to a later period —I shall have nothing material to add, having already taken into my account the disclosures for which we are indebted to that most interesting narrative. In a note to Dr. Rawley's 'Life of Bacon,' I said that I had no fault to find with him for any part of his conduct towards Essex, and that I thought many people would agree with me when they saw the case fairly stated. Closer examination has not at all altered my opinion on either point. And if I have taken no notice of what has been said on the other side, it is because I do not wish to encumber this book with answers to objections which a competent judgment would not raise; and I cannot think that any of the objections which have been urged against Bacon's conduct in this matter would naturally suggest themselves to a reasonable person in reading the story as I have told it."

From a certain aspect, this summary is very conclusive; but it must be urged against it that Mr. Spedding seems to feel that he is as much holding a brief for Bacon, as Whitehead seems to hold a brief for Ralegh. It has been well said that truth is many-sided, and the aphorism is very applicable to this case; so much can be truly said in support of diametrically opposed opinions respecting the conduct of Bacon towards Essex. Certainly, to say that Bacon should not have taken part in the trial would be to judge him too severely, but there can be equally little doubt that the tone of his speech was sometimes needlessly inconsistent with former friendship.

The most striking feature of the novel's close is the Queen's attitude before and after the trial. Here is a fine extract, showing one of Whitehead's excellences as a writer of fiction—his power of introspective analysis of mingled feelings and emotions. In this passage the Queen refers with surprise to the fact that Essex had not solicited his life from her. She was mistaken; he had sent a message to her, and that in the manner most agreeable to her, by one whom he supposed to be a friend. It was only by the perfidious conduct of Nottingham that his wife did not fulfil her promise to Essex.

"The account they speedily brought her of the condition in which they had found their spiritual charge at once astonished, perplexed, and affected the Queen. Could it be that this man, erewhile so rash, impetuous, disdainful, could be so soon wrought to a most sincere and self-reproaching contrition? Was this feigned? Was it a cunning expedient to preserve his life? No. Over and over had he proclaimed that he was weary of his life—that the preservation of it did not consist with her majesty's safety— that he wished to die.

"There was no resisting the belief that there was no feigning here. Yet, he was an enthusiast; his mind had become weakened; he knew not what his real feelings were, and was rather prostrated than penitent. His life 'did not consist with her majesty's safety.'

"The Queen liked not that. 'Poor, fond, weak fool— that even in this most ignominious strait of fortune, canst prate of power thou hast not, and never hadst—whose treason was crushed ere it could crawl—how should I fear thee now?'

"It was not long ere her working mind made his penitence itself an argument against him. He repented of his treason, as treason, not as it had been practised against her; and he would fain make his peace with God, but cared not to offer to her the reparation of a contrite soul. This was to reproach her. There was human pride and petulance in this.

"'Lo! no traitor am I—or if—I seek no pardon from

my Sovereign. I am a martyr. Robert Devereux, thou shalt not live.'

"The Queen was inexorable.

"What of absolute power Queen Elizabeth did not possess, was rather in the theory than in the practice of the constitution. Nature had given her a most absolute will. Great as she undoubtedly was, the magnitude of her mind made her so; not a grand and sovereign authority over its operations. She seldom subjected herself or her feelings to examination.

"Yet, as the day drew nigh for the execution of Essex— of her erring and peevish favourite, whom to forgive had almost grown into a habit and a pleasure; who had once been possessed of so large a share of her affection, and whose very frailties had made him more dear to her than the virtues of 'her Philip' Sydney had ever done—she could not but reflect that, let him be the worst the good or the best could pronounce him, she herself had gone far to make him so. She had borne, nay, she had sometimes encouraged, his arrogance towards others, in the day of his pride and triumph; could she wonder at—ought she so strongly to resent—his injurious conduct towards herself? Is it not ever thus, that they who are rewarded far beyond their deserts, and not because of them, but for the love that is borne towards their possessors, wantonly turn against their benefactors, making provocation to themselves out of a juster, however niggard, reward of others' merit? Does not the spoiled child strike his mother, and take most delight in torturing her who is his fondest, although not his best friend? And, since folly should meet its punishment, is it not just that it should be so?

"Again, had she not driven, goaded him to these desperate courses for which he was about to suffer? Had she not tempted and trifled with him, by too harsh and too prolonged a show of resentment? When he would have made a submission which, until he offered it, she would have deemed sufficient, had she not exacted more and more, and more abject still, and this many times, until the man's soul became possessed with utter weariness and disgust? She could hardly deny to herself a tittle of these accusations which her mind brought against her.

"Still, to mar the salutary effects that might have proceeded from this self-questioning, true to her nature (which was likewise the nature of Essex, to which, also, he had proved too true), there arose constantly the all-prevailing plea, that he should have conceded everything; the creature of her hands, whom she had made for her pleasure, and might unmake at her discretion, he had nought to do or to desire, but to permit himself to be disposed of as she willed—the more readily, since he knew, or should have known, that her partiality for him was such, that it was not likely he would lie long under her displeasure. And now, naught of the game remained to play, but the last stake. Would he beg his life of her? He would not, as it seemed. 'Then, perverse and obstinate and sinful wretch!' (she spoke not of herself, but of Essex) 'he shall die.'

"Meanwhile, neither Cecil nor Ralegh, nor any of the reputed enemies of the Earl, were suffered to come into her presence, a circumstance from which some of his friends augured that it might be well and profitable to urge what they could in his behalf. They were speedily made to feel the mistake they had committed, in a perpetual banishment from the court. There was one nobleman, indeed, to whom she spoke unreservedly of Essex, save in relation to the feelings respecting him which perplexed her heart, and now, on the last day, agitated her inmost soul. She had never suspected the enmity of Nottingham to Essex; and since the imprisonment of the latter in the Tower, he had been in almost constant attendance upon him, and had even persuaded Essex into a belief of his friendship.

"To the Countess of Nottingham the Queen, on this

eventful day, would probably have unbosomed herself, less with a view to derive counsel or comfort from her, than from a desire to ease her heart of a load which oppressed it almost to bursting. But the Countess, some four days since, feeling unwell, had taken an airing in her coach; and afterwards waiting upon her majesty, had fallen down suddenly in a swoon, and was still confined to her apartments in the palace.

"The most abject and miserable of her subjects suffered not as did Queen Elizabeth on that day. Yet she would not relax or relent—the more inflexible as every passing hour brought on the speedy night which, rolling away, was to reveal her victim on the scaffold. At length, impatient of his obduracy—maddened to think that her mercy was scorned and despised—she sat down and signed the warrant for his execution, which, an hour afterwards, she despatched by a trusty hand to the Constable of the Tower. That fatal document is still in existence. The firmness and decision of the signature are indeed remarkable, if it be not remembered that the hand which wrote, could cancel; and that she yet hoped she might be entreated to do so.

" Scarcely was the warrant despatched, when a revulsion of feeling took place. O God! it must not be. So young to die—the son of him who had met no noble treatment from her hands—of Walter Devereux, the gallant soldier, noble in person as in honour, who, scarce a year older than was now his unhappy son, had been stretched in his grave. No warning voice called from it; no awful shadow thence, or from above, stood a pale horror in her sight; yet, for the moment, voice nor vision could more have shaken her soul. Affrighted, almost frantic, she summoned Sir Henry Cary to her presence, to whom she gave it in terrible command to hasten to the Tower and countermand the execution.

" ' Begone! I charge you; and do my bidding as you value my favour or your life. Stay! I am very foolish. How now! we have forgot ourself. It is past.'

" She walked the length of the apartment, and returned.

" 'Cary, you may go.   Tell our Constable of the Tower he shall hear from us again by twelve of the clock.   Meanwhile, as we have ordered you.'

"Cary bowed reverently; nor raised his head till the Queen had entered the ante-room of her privy-chamber; then, instead of hastening out of the palace to the Tower, in obedience to the command of his royal mistress, he struck down the gallery and made for the apartments of the Earl of Nottingham, who was, by marriage, nearly allied to him, the Countess being his sister.

" He called the Earl forth, and drawing him aside, communicated to him the Queen's change of purpose—a piece of news he had reason to believe would be most unpalatable to his brother-in-law.   Nor was he mistaken.

" The Earl, crossed, enraged, yet withal alarmed in no common degree, hastened with Cary down the gallery to a retired chamber, where, although he could not hope, and if he could, would not have dared, to dissuade the other from obeying the Queen's orders; yet, representing that there was no haste, since the countermand could derive no additional force from its early delivery, and suffer no diminution of its virtue by delay, he induced Cary to tarry awhile till he had taken counsel with Cecil how the untoward lenity of the Queen might best, if at all, be thwarted.

" He returned to Cary in a couple of hours, with a very troubled countenance, and bade him begone, telling him that the Secretary was fearful of intruding himself into the presence of the Queen, and that the matter must take its course."

It would take too much space to narrate in detail the final episodes; how the Queen again changed her mind, her misery on the day of execution, and the gloom which was cast over her remaining days.   It must be sufficient to say that these things are well told, that the work, as it approaches conclusion, increases in interest, and that passages at the end reach a high point of almost epic grandeur.

Altogether the book, though in some respects the most popular in style of Whitehead's works, is, viewed as an historical romance, not on the highest level. But it is certainly equal to the best works of such writers as G. P. R. James or Harrison Ainsworth. The period dealt with was not Whitehead's period, and therefore the book could not be Whitehead's best work.

Whitehead published in 1854 *The Life and Times of Sir Walter Ralegh*, with copious extracts from his *History of the World*. This work partakes of the character of an historical disquisition on Sir Walter Ralegh. It will therefore be best to deal with it by showing Whitehead's views on various aspects of Ralegh's individuality. It is thus that the author refers to the lineage of his subject :—

" Whilst Sir Walter was yet—not smarting under, but—smiling disdainfully at the envy and detraction that surrounded him, John Hooker,* an eminent antiquary, and related to Ralegh, in a dedication to the knight of his translation and continuation of the ' Chronicles of Ireland,' tells him that the family of Ralegh—sometimes written Rale and Ralega in ancient deeds—were settled in Devon-

---

* He was uncle of the illustrious Richard Hooker, author of the " Ecclesiastical Polity," who is commonly styled by divines and others learned in divinity, " the judicious Hooker."

shire, and in possession of the seat of Smalridge, before the
Norman Conquest, and that one of the family built a chapel
there, in gratitude 'for his deliverance on St. Leonard's
day from the Gauls, by whom he had been taken prisoner ;
and that he hung up therein, as a monument, his target.
(The records of this foundation are said to have been given
by a priest of Axminster to Sir Walter, as their most
rightful owner.)

"So much for the antiquity of the family ; but Hooker
avouches that his kinsman and friend was allied to the
Courtenays, Earls of Devon, and other illustrious houses,
nay, that he can|trace the stream of consanguinity up to
the Kings of England ; for he says, ' that one of his ancestors
in the directest line, Sir John de Ralegh, of Fardel (another
seat of their ancient inheritance, in the parish of Cornwood,
eight miles east of Plymouth), espoused the daughter of Sir
Richard d'Amerei, who married Elizabeth, daughter of Gilbert Earl of Gloucester, by Joan d'Acres, daughter of King
Edward I., which Gilbert was descended of Robert, Earl of
Gloucester, son of King Henry I.' So he goes up to the
Conqueror, adding further, ' that in like manner he may be
derived by his mother out of the same house.' "

It is quite apparent, however, from the remark
which Whitehead appends to this somewhat lengthy
statement, that in his opinion Ralegh so little regarded
his high ancestral claims as to think that their only
advantage was that they " silenced and tended to put
to shame his traducers on the score of birth ;" and in
vindication of his opinion, Whitehead quotes a long
extract from the *History of the World*, in which
Ralegh discusses in his quaint manner the claims
of descent *versus* those of personal merit.

In this connection it may be well to refer briefly to

the somewhat remarkable fact that there is diversity even in spelling the name Ralegh. Whitehead uniformly spells it without the *i*, and gives us as his warrant for so doing a facsimile of Ralegh's seal, which one would think, if it be genuine, would entirely settle the question ; and yet Hume, Southey, and innumerable writers, invariably insert the letter referred to. A very recent author, however (Sir John Pope Hennessey) omits the *i*.

Whitehead had an exalted, not to say extravagant, opinion of Ralegh's powers as a poet. Of the well-known sonnet on the " Fairy Queen," he says that it is " one of the finest in the English language, and would almost justify any hyperbole that a conjecture of future poetical greatness might raise upon it."

Whitehead says this *apropos* of the fact that Spenser is reputed to have remarked that his friend Ralegh " had a more ethereal genius than his own "—a compliment which Whitehead conceives to be flattery, notwithstanding the foregoing praise.

Another example which he gives shows Ralegh's muse in her courtly dress, but this sonnet no more than the preceding one justifies the eulogium passed upon him.

It is curious to notice that, notwithstanding all Queen Elizabeth's liking for Sir Walter Ralegh, she still felt unwilling that he should obtain what was then deemed one of the highest honours which could be conferred on a man eminent as a scholar or in literature. Perhaps the Queen thought that were he

always to obtain his desires, he would become intract-
able; a quality which no Sovereign could brook in
courtiers less than Elizabeth.

The matter is thus referred to in the book under
notice :—

"A little before Leicester's death, the University of
Oxford, like her sister, ever sagacious of a rising sun, and
with a fervid Persian disposition to worship it, which later
times have not abated, had incorporated him Master of
Arts, that he might be the more capable of becoming their
Chancellor when the office should become vacant, as it did
shortly afterwards by the death of Leicester. Elizabeth,
however, did not please that this high honour* should be
conferred upon him, and Sir Christopher Hatton was
elected."

It is very natural that there should be many opinions
as to the interesting question of Ralegh's statesman-
ship. Not only was the age in which he lived one
which could be viewed from innumerable standpoints,
but it was an age in which many problems, social and
religious, as yet unsolved, were so perplexing men's
minds and insensibly modifying their conduct as to
make it difficult—indeed, well nigh impossible—for
us to pass an impartial judgment on it. Try as we
may, we cannot, being possessed of nineteenth century

* The University of Cambridge about five-and-twenty
years afterwards elected Robert Carr, Earl of Somerset, their
Chancellor—the miscreant who a year or two subsequently
was convicted of poisoning Sir Thomas Overbury. Why
should not the highest honour a University has it in her
power to bestow be conferred upon genius or learning?

intellects, acquire the habits of thought proper to the sixteenth. Then, again, there is a special difficulty in this particular case, for Ralegh's character was many-sided. Few, however, will question Ralegh's conduct in the following instance :

"The alarm of the Spanish preparations against England being now at its height, Sir Walter, in November, 1587, was one of the Council of War appointed to consider what was best to be done in this emergency, upon which occasion he drew up a scheme of operations, which is cited as a proof of his exquisite judgment and rare abilities. This document is still in existence, and fully bears out the eulogium it has called forth ; but in his *History of the World* he has en-larged upon his favourite doctrine,* and insisted upon what he always maintained, namely—that a country is ever better defended by sea than on land—so eloquently and convinc-ingly that we only wonder some of the disputants, two years ago, had not reprinted it, when we were all to be terrified into a belief of an invasion by France."

The next extract which I shall give has reference to Essex. Referring to Leicester, he says :

"It was now that he introduced his step-son, Essex, a lad of twenty (but who had been Leicester's general of the horse), to Elizabeth. This young nobleman had, when a boy, conceived a strong aversion against the Earl, which that wily person had so effectually succeeded in removing, that

---

* What powerful and weighty language Ralegh would have used in condemnation of the scheme to do away with our natural marine defence by tunnelling under the English Channel !—H. T. M. B.

his *protegé* had imbibed from him certain rules for his conduct as a courtier which, being of high spirit, and of a frank, although by no means of a noble nature, he knew not well how to apply.   Too proud to stoop for favour, he had not the abilities to rise by desert.   Courteous and liberal to his friends, by whom he was beloved, he was the darling of the people, whom he courted ;* but he must needs play the antics of a froward, spoiled child before a Tudor, to whom Henry the Eighth has transmitted some of the tiger, and he suffered at length for his ingratitude and presumption.

It is curious to notice Whitehead's estimate of Essex in this passage, and to compare it with the more finished and elaborated portrayal of him which our author has given us in his historical romance *The Earl of Essex*.   But, both here and in that work, he has rigidly adhered to that unfavourable view of Essex's character of which I have already said enough when dealing directly with the work in question.   It is sufficient at present to remark that this paragraph, no less than that romance, testifies to Whitehead's knowledge of and insight into that period, though, as I have said, it does not show that his sympathy was with it. In contrasting Ralegh and Essex he almost invariably does so to the advantage of the former ; nevertheless his conception of Essex is a just one.   There is little doubt that one of Ralegh's chief failings was his under-estimation of what would now be termed popular

* The Lord Treasurer, Burghley, had noticed this love of popularity in Essex, and the disdain of it in Sir Walter. "Seek not to be Essex : shun to be Ralegh," he says in his precepts to his son, Sir Robert Cecil.

opinion.   Perhaps, however, this fault was more owing to the prejudices of the time in which he lived than we can ever now realize.   It is difficult not to believe that the complaisance of Essex towards the people had its origin more from a feeling that their support would facilitate his personal ambition rather than from a sincere conviction of the justice of their claims.

Concerning Sir Walter Ralegh's religious views we have the following :

" Meanwhile, what are we to think of Archbishop Abbot, who, in a letter dated February 19, 1619* (four months after Ralegh's death, and nearly five years after the publication of ' History of the World '), expressly charges him with ' questioning God's being and omnipotence, which,' his grace adds, ' that just Judge made good upon himself, in overtumbling his estate, and last of all bringing him to an execution by law '?   Must we in charity suppose that Abbot was the only man in England who did not, by this time, know the wretched falsehood of the calumny, and that Sir Henry Montague, the judge who passed sentence upon him, had released him from that aspersion ?   Was an Archbishop of Canterbury the only scholar in the nation who had not looked into so remarkable a book (more than remarkable) as the ' History of the World,' or, having done so, who had omitted to read the very first paragraph ? †"

---

* To Sir Thomas Roe, then ambassador at the Court of the Mogul.

† It is a solemn and majestic passage : " God, whom the wisest men acknowledge to be a power ineffable, and virtue infinite, a light by abundant charity invisible, and under-

It is painful to be obliged to descend from the sublimity of these closing words to deal with the subject to which reference must now be made, for it is the antipodes, so to speak, of Ralegh's character from that which formed the theme of the last extract. Here are Whitehead's words :

"Ralegh, however, has been accused by his enemies—many of whom have shown little mercy to his memory—of having exercised excessive and needless cruelty in Ireland. It is not true : this great man had not an atom of cruelty or vindictiveness in his composition ; nor has any author,

standing which itself can only comprehend—an essence eternal and spiritual, of absolute pureness and simplicity, was, and is, pleased to make Himself known by the work of the world, in the wonderful magnitude whereof (all which He embraceth, filleth, and sustaineth) we behold the image of that glory which cannot be measured, and withal that one, and yet universal nature, which cannot be defined. In the glorious lights of heaven we perceive a shadow of His divine countenance ; in His merciful provision for all that live, His manifold goodness, and, lastly, in creating and making existent the world universal by the absolute art of His own word, His power and almightiness : which power, light, virtue, wisdom, and goodness, being all but attributes of one simple essence, and one God we in all admire, and in part discern, *per speculum creaturarum*, that is, in the disposition, order and variety of celestial and terrestrial bodies —terrestrial in their strange and manifold diversities ; celestial in their beauty and magnitude—which, in their continual and contrary motions, are neither repugnant, intermixed, nor confounded. By these potent effects we approach to the knowledge of the Omnipotent Cause, and, by these motions, their Almighty Mover."

treating of military affairs, more earnestly and more eloquently, or more often, denounced the cruelty of conquerors, deplored the miseries of war, and advocated the rights and duties of mercy. He has himself said, speaking on a very different subject, ' Whosoever is the workman, it is reasonable he should give an account of his work to the workmaster ;' and since to subordinates seldom falls any portion of the honour they have been instrumental in procuring for their commander, nay, since it is dangerous to lay claim to it (we have Shakespeare's warrant for it*), let the shame of any action—if shame there be—light upon the workmaster to whom the workman renders his account."

With all Whitehead's partiality for Ralegh, he does not seek in this passage directly to combat those who accuse Ralegh of cruelty in Ireland. His language is rather that of a skilful counsel concealing a weak point in his client's case by an eloquent argument in favour of his innocence in general. This is significant. We shall by-and-by see what excellent reasons Whitehead had for adopting this course. Here is a remarkable letter. It refers to a period mentioned also in Whitehead's romance of *The Earl of Essex*, when Ralegh was in temporary disgrace. It was certainly a clever device :

"It seems clear to me that Arthur Gorges intended to do a friend's turn for Ralegh by drawing up this narrative for Cecil (at the very time very intimate with Sir Walter), who would laugh at the description of the scene, see its intent, and make the best use of it for the captive's delivery from prison. Ralegh, however, must have stimulated his merriment and quickened his activity in his behalf by the

---

* *Antony and Cleopatra*, Act III. Scene 1.

following letter, which commences in a very business-like manner :—

" ' Sir,—I pray be a mean to her majesty for the signing of the bills for the guard's coats, which are to be made now for the progress, and which the clerk of the check hath importuned me to write for. My heart was never broken till this day, that I hear the Queen goes away so far off, whom I have followed for so many years with so great love and desire in so many journeys, and am now left behind her in a dark prison, all alone. While she was yet near at hand, that I might hear of her once in two or three days, my sorrows were the less, but even now my heart is cast into the depth of all misery. I that was wont to behold her riding like Alexander, hunting like Diana, walking like Venus, the gentle wind blowing her fair hair about her pure cheeks, like a nymph, sometime sitting in the shade like a goddess, sometime singing like an angel, sometime playing like Orpheus !* Behold the sorrow of this world !—one 'amiss hath bereaved me of all ! Oh, glory that only shineth in misfortune, what has become of thy assurance ? All wounds leave scars but that of fantasy ; all afflictions their relenting but that of woman-kind ! Who is to judge of friendship but adversity ? or when is grace witnessed but in offences ? There were no divinity but by reason of com-passion,. for revenges are brutish and mortal. All those times past—the loves, the sighs, the sorrows, the desires— can they not weigh down one frail misfortune ? Cannot one drop of gall be hidden in some great heaps of sweetness ? I may thus conclude, *Spes et Fortuna, valete !* She is gone on whom I trusted, and of me hath not one thought of mercy, nor any respect of that that was. Do with me now, therefore, what you list ! I am more weary of life than they are desirous I should perish ; which if it had been *for*

---

* *This paragon was in the sixty-second year of her age !*

her, as it is *by* her, I had been too happily born. Yours not worthy any name or title, W. R.'"

Superlative adulation was characteristic of the period, as witness even the translators' preface prefixed to most of our Bibles ; but, notwithstanding all possible allowance for time and circumstance, it can hardly be questioned that Ralegh was somewhat of a sycophant towards Elizabeth.

Whitehead has the following to say about the material that Shakespeare may have obtained from conversation with Sir Walter Ralegh or from the perusal of his works. He also imagines that Milton may have obtained something from the same source :-

"It is certain that Shakespeare had read attentively the narrative of Ralegh's voyage. In the *Tempest* we read of 'the still-vexed Bermoothes.' Ralegh says—'The rest of the Indies for calms and diseases very troublesome, and the Bermudas a hellish sea for thunder, lightning, and storms.' In the same play, the honest councillor, Gonzala, asks, 'Who would believe

    "'that there were such men
Whose heads stood in their breasts? which now we find
Each putter-out of one for five will bring us
Good warrant of?'

"And in *Othello*, where the Moor tells of having seen men 'whose heads do grow beneath their shoulders,' we are to understand that a man of honour and veracity is speaking, not that a Mendez Pinto is telling travellers' tales to the Council of Ten.

"Seventy years after Shakespeare, Milton, in his *Paradise*

Lost, when the Archangel Michael shows the other hemisphere to Adam, says :

> " 'In spirit perhaps he also saw
> Rich Mexico, the seat of Montezume
> And Cusco in Peru, the richest seat
> Of Atabalipa, and yet unspoil'd
> Guiana, whose great city Geryon's sons
> Call El Dorado.' "

It is thus that Whitehead deals with former biographers of Ralegh :

"However afflicted at the fatal misadventure, of his brother Ralegh was nothing daunted. The discoveries of Columbus, the conquests of Cortez and Pizarro, had formed a congenial portion of his early reading, and in his conversation as a youth these had been his prominent subjects. 'Moreover, he was,' says Southey, 'one of those who are so thoroughly possessed by the spirit of adventure, that they neither learn to be wise by others' harms nor by their own.' In other words (and this meaning may be wrung out of the ungenerous, narrow-minded, and false allegation of the recluse of Keswick), he was not a man to sit in a study, and complacently pass judgment upon more active spirits, who are content to encounter formidable difficulties, undreamed of by the fireside, when they can be of practical service to their country."*

----

* Dr. Southey should not have attempted a life of Sir Walter Ralegh, at any rate not in the space to which he confined himself, or to which he was restricted ; for, regarding his illustrious subject with no friendly eye, he sometimes makes hostile and unsupported assertions, which demand proof ; and proof, even when it is not difficult, sometimes requires a lengthened presentation of itself. Ralegh was

This is severe criticism on Southey. It may be incidentally mentioned here that Whitehead would be prejudiced against a writer who supported an assertion on the authority of the elder Disraeli. That author defends King James I. of England, and Whitehead uses a porcine appellation in speaking of the monarch.

I have in the above extracts endeavoured to convey an idea of the volume under notice, and it may be well, before concluding this chapter, to give some of the views of Southey and other writers on the same subject.

Southey, in his life of Ralegh contained in his fourth volume of the *Lives of British Admirals*, condemns Ralegh severely for his cruelty in Ireland, and

---

not a man to Southey's mind. Had the knight been a soldier-captain singly, or a sea-captain, or a courtier, or a statesman, or a chemist, or a philosopher, or an historian, Southey would have presented us with a fair, as he has not failed of giving an eloquent, life of Sir Walter; but being "the universal Ralegh," his biographer could not conceal his sympathy with the evil and heart-vexing passion which possesses myriads of inferior natures. From a man of various learning and literary accomplishments like Southey, we might have looked for no niggard admiration of that marvel of labour, learning, and genius, *The History of the World ;* but he has devoted four lines to it, and, in the forty-one words of which they are composed, has qualified the praise due to the author by calling his great work a 'compilation,' and by asserting, on the rotten authority of the elder Disraeli, that some of the best wits in England assisted Ralegh with their researches.

especially for putting to death some Spaniards who, in the license of those times, had come to help the Irish rebels. Southey further says that Queen Elizabeth "detested from her heart such cruelty," and "was greatly displeased." He also accuses Ralegh of "holding out fallacious allurements to other adventurers." Southey remarks that Sir Walter Ralegh had "many great qualities and some good ones," but that his bane was want of rectitude.

One of Hume's chief contentions against Ralegh is, that having gone on an expedition to the "inland parts of South America, called Guiana," he did not find "anything to answer his expectations," but, on his return, he published an account of the country "full of the grossest and most palpable lies that were ever attempted to be imposed on the credulity of mankind." As his authority for this assertion, Hume quotes Camden (p. 584), and likewise accuses Ralegh of sycophancy, and dwells on his jealousy of Essex. He tells a story of how on one occasion, when Essex had fallen into disgrace and was sick, the Queen sent him a kindly message. But Ralegh, the "most violent" of the enemies of Essex, "was so affected" at the prospect of his regaining favour, that he (Ralegh) likewise became sick; "and the Queen was obliged to apply the same salve to his wound, and to send him a favourable message expressing her desire of his recovery." This story is amplified in Whitehead's *Earl of Essex*, but there it is Essex that is made to be the envious courtier.

Sir John Pope Hennessy, in his volume *Sir Walter Ralegh in Ireland*, censures Ralegh severely for his conduct there, and especially, like Southey, condemns him for the Smerwick massacre. Sir John says that Bacon, Camden, and a whole chorus of historians, declare that the Queen was " much displeased " at the barbarous execution ; but when, a few years ago, the State Papers in the Record Office were calendered, two letters were found speaking of it as " greatly to our lyking." Sir John also states that Ralegh had Elizabeth's approval for " assassination and poisoning of chiefs." In Sir John's opinion, it had been well had the treaty which Essex made with the chiefs been ratified and adhered to. It was this compact which ultimately led to the downfall of Essex, as clearly shown in Whitehead's romance. The *Academy*, in reviewing Sir John's book, is exceeding severe on Ralegh ; but the *Athenæum* defends him, and expresses very forcibly the view I endeavoured to state in an earlier part of this chapter, and which had previously occurred to me on purely independent grounds. It says, " The fallacy involved in the present work is that men of the sixteenth century should be subjected to the moral code of the nineteenth century . . . . . In practical life, no intelligent person falls into this mistake. The author of this work would not judge of the conduct of a Chinese by the rules of Christian morality."

In his preface, Charles Whitehead says, " Of the many biographers of Sir Walter, a few have been, perhaps, indiscreetly panegyrical, whilst some (Hume and Southey, for instance) have attacked his fame with a virulence for which an envy of his extraordinary abilities can alone account." But further on, even Whitehead admits him to have been a flatterer, and regrets that he never sought to please the people, saying that this is "perhaps to be lamented," and remarking that during his later voyages he was jealous and envious. Conceding all this, however, he can still close his preface in these terms:

"But the operation here has not been of compression, but of extract; and I trust that they and the rest of my, or rather of his, readers, will find enough to assure them that of the three great men of Elizabeth and James's time, Walter Ralegh was one, and that the companion of Shakespeare and the friend of Bacon can neither be depressed by malignity nor exalted by praise."

Sir Walter Ralegh was a highly remarkable man, and was probably entitled to the place which Whitehead claims for him. Unquestionably subservience to the great, disregard of the people, and sometimes cruelty, were among his faults. But all of these are among the failings—shall I say weaknesses?—of the period in which he lived.

Whitehead's *Life and Times of Sir Walter Ralegh* is, as far as I am aware, the last book he published before leaving England. As to its literary merit, notwithstanding its various excellences, I cannot but think that it only shows Whitehead as a clever and competent bookmaker.

It is significant, however, that a great modern poet, who probably had never even heard of *this* book of Whitehead's, and whose mode of looking at historical personages was doubtless very different, held the same exalted view of Ralegh's character, as will be strikingly shown in the following sonnet:

"Here writ was the World's History by his hand
    Whose steps knew all the earth; albeit his world
    In these few piteous paces then was furled.
  Here daily, hourly, have his proud feet spanned
  This smaller speck than the receding land
    Had ever shown his ships ; what time he hurled
    Abroad o'er new-found regions spiced and pearled
  His country's high dominion and command.

"Here dwelt two spheres.   The vast terrestrial zone
    His spirit traversed ; and that spirit was
      Itself the zone celestial, round whose birth
      The planets played within the Zodiac's girth ;
    Till hence, through unjust death unfeared did pass
  His spirit to the only land unknown."

CHAPTER VI.

WHITEHEAD AS A NOVELIST.

Richard Savage, described on the title-page as *A Romance of Real Life*, edited with occasional notes by Charles Whitehead, author of *The Solitary*, illustrated by John Leech, appeared in *Bentley's Miscellany* for the years 1841-42. Evidently it took some hold of the public, for before it had quite completed its course in that periodical, it was produced in volume form. To the illustrations I will subsequently refer. In the magazine the contents of each chapter are summarised at the beginning of it. It is probably significant of the great carefulness with which Charles Whitehead at this period polished his productions before they left his hand to appear in the first instance in print, that in the various editions of *Richard Savage* in book-form there is not even a verbal change from the text as it appears in the magazine. In volume-form, however, the pretence or pretext of editorial function is dropped, and the title simply becomes *Richard Savage, a Romance of Real Life.*

Richard Savage has the merit of vivifying in a marvellously realistic manner an historical personage. This is a matter always difficult to accomplish, and even Whitehead, who in this case so brilliantly succeeded, subsequently failed considerably when making a similar essay in the *Earl of Essex*. In this instance Charles Whitehead has achieved the difficult task of being faithful to history, whilst weaving into the weft of his story much human passion, and creating some powerfully delineated characters. Indeed, some of the purely fictitious personages are the most finely portrayed in the book. Whitehead displayed not a little boldness in choosing such a central figure—not hero —as Savage, but the manner in which he has executed his presumably self-imposed task justifies his having done so. *Richard Savage* is not only a story of incidents occurring in the eighteenth century, but it is a story of the type to which Fielding's stories belong, though happily entirely without the gross animalism which sometimes· disfigures that writer. It partakes of the character of an eighteenth century story in the following respects:

First, its large plot—a plot embracing a greater number of incidents, and probably a larger number of characters, than are to be met with in a novel of the same kind and treatment in the present age. Second, its being the story of a life, not of an incident or series of incidents in a life. Third, its being designed to chronicle events, not to analyze character or to depict situations. Fourth, its movement being continuous, something is always going on. People come and go in its pages; that which is a prominent character now may by-and-by drop out of the narrative altogether. It is a primitive type of novel, designed before novelists had got to their wits' end to devise interesting and thrilling adventures. Fifth, it being English life it depicts, but life in England in England's well-nigh least English period. For except in the hey-day of the revulsion of feeling which ensued at the Restoration from the excessive rigidity of Puritan thought, when the returning monarch brought with him and kept in fashion by personal example the manners and habits appertaining to the worst Gallic dissoluteness and depravity, eighteenth century life in England, and especially in London, was more largely tinged and tainted by injurious French influence than at any other era. It was French in its excess of manners, French in its defective morality.

In proof of what I have just been saying, let us compare *Richard Savage* with Fielding's *Tom Jones.* Like *Richard Savage, Tom Jones* has an extensive plot, comprehending a vast variety of incidents. It may fairly be termed a life-story, designed to record events, and with little ulterior moral object. In it there is constant movement—Fielding, like Whitehead, writes of things that he sees; he does not rack his brain to devise unfamiliar situations. We find that *Tom Jones* and *Richard Savage* represent the same type of English life with similar fidelity; and that this was more remarkable in Whitehead, who

lived in the nineteenth century, than in Fielding, who
lived in the eighteenth century, and who simply described what he saw ; that there is much less grasp of
humour in Whitehead than in Fielding, who was perhaps the master of all English humourists ; and that
there is more hold of tragic passion, for Fielding has
no such terrible picture of mingled bravery and
cowardice as Ludlow—the most powerfully delineated
fictitious personage Whitehead presents. Fielding has
nothing comparable in terribleness to Ludlow's madness and death. This personage is absolutely Whitehead's own creation, no such type of character having
existed before it in English fiction. Perhaps the nearest
approach to it is in Scott, and in the madness and
awe-inspiring death of one of the abandoned friends of
Lovelace in Richardson's *Clarissa.*

Richard Savage is written in the autobiographical
form. Savage is of course represented as the illegiti-
mate son of Earl Rivers and the Countess of Macclesfield, and the spirit in which the author wishes his
character to be examined is sufficiently obvious from
the following extract from his preface :—

"In conclusion, although nearly a century has elapsed
since the death of this unfortunate and erring man, let me
bespeak for him, a ' wretch,' as he affectingly calls himself
in the dedication of a poem to Queen Caroline, ' whose days
were fewer than his sorrows ;' let me bespeak for him, I
say, that indulgent and charitable construction of his
conduct which, a year after his death, was pleaded for him
with so touching an earnestness by Samuel Johnson, his
illustrious biographer and friend."

His mother, who, very shortly after his birth, was divorced from her husband, and eventually became the wife of Colonel Brett, is a personage the origin of whose motives it is very difficult to discover. Even Dr. Johnson, in his *Life of Savage,* is unable to come to a satisfactory conclusion, though he certainly presents a very ingenious theory on the subject. But, from whatever cause, let it suffice to say that she soon regarded the child with implacable hatred, and desired to put him away. Her mother, Lady Mason, a tender-hearted but irresolute woman, steps in to succour the infant. She hands it over to a confidential servant, Ludlow, who gives it out to nurse to a sister of his own, a woman without marked vices, yet destitute of all higher principle — a woman utterly mercenary in motive, and a slave to that spirit of sycophancy which, perhaps, more frequently degraded the lower classes of her time than of our own. Her husband, a dissolute fellow, was by trade a bailiff, and early initiated Richard into the bestial amusements then so prevalent. In this undesirable household the boy remained until about the age of ten, when Lady Mason sent for him, and shortly afterwards despatched him under the guidance of Ludlow to a school at St. Albans. The master of this school, whose name was Burridge, was a remarkable man. He had once been a gay fellow about town, but meeting with losses, had matured into a middle-aged preceptor of good habits and nature, with a whim to pose as a cynical philosopher, not always even sparing his own early foibles.

After Richard has been several years at school, Ludlow rather suddenly appears, and informs Burridge that it is unfortunately necessary that the lad should be removed. The schoolmaster is naturally not un-impressed by the mystery enveloping the boy, which this sudden removal from school considerably intensi-fies. Something in Ludlow's manner also attracts his attention, and he relieves his feelings by expressing himself in the following characteristic manner :

" ' A great secret, sir !' faltered Ludlow.

" ' Yes, sir, a great secret that has outgrown its clothes, and soon won't have a rag to cover it. I was one of the close gentlemen myself, once ; and I brought myself to a fine pass with my closeness. Thus it was : I married a young and pretty woman without a farthing, and I kept the marriage secret ; but I was found out, nevertheless. Then my father disinherited me—that, also, I strove to keep *particularly* secret ; but it got wind and blew all over the town. Then my creditors hunted me in and out, and out and in, to all manner of lodgings, where I designed to be *very* secret. Next, my wife, poor dear ! died of a broken heart, having kept that, all along, a *profound* secret. Then I fell into extreme poverty, and all my friends left me ; but that is *no* secret. Never to confide or to harbour secrets—*that* is a secret worth knowing."

The reason for taking Richard from school was at first very carefully concealed even from himself; but by-and-by it became known that his father had died without leaving him anything. Ludlow brings him at once from St. Albans to London, and he is forthwith apprenticed to a cobbler, very much against his will. The restiveness which Richard evinced in what he

14.—2

deemed this menial employment was rather increased
than diminished by time.   At school he had been led
to think that his lot was that of a gentleman, and now
this contemptible position excited his chagrin.   Presently his high spirit engages him in a brawl with his
cobbler-master, and taking advantage of the confusion
he escapes, and repairs to Ludlow, at Lady Mason's
house.   On hearing his story, Ludlow is at first wroth
with him, and threatens him with Lady Mason's severe
displeasure, which he tells him may, in the present
crisis, damage him for life.   He exhorts him to return
to Short the cobbler, but Richard distinctly refuses so
to do.   Ludlow also finds him unpleasantly persistent
in his interrogatories respecting the mystery of his
birth ; he even threatens to demand an explanation
from Lady Mason, or to go before a magistrate with a
like purpose.   After a while Ludlow hits upon an expedient which he imagines will meet the difficulties of
the case.   Unknown to Lady Mason, who will still
think him with the cobbler, he will place Richard
with a friend of his, Mr. Myte.   To this person's house
he forthwith takes Richard, and installs him there.
Myte's occupation is thus described, and his quaint
whimsical character hinted at :

" ' That won't be while you're here,' returned Myte.
' Look you, my ingenious young friend, I sell houses when I
have houses to sell, to certain persons—when I can find
them ; and I buy houses, when there are houses to be bought,
from certain persons who may wish to sell them ; but at
present I have neither houses to be sold nor persons to
purchase, nor do I wish to have.   All my business, there-

fore, is to do nothing, and look as though I had plenty to do ; and all yours will be to look as though you had plenty to do, and do nothing.'

" ' An easy life, sir,' I said, laughing.

" ' So so, for that,' replied Myte ; ' I've found yawning hard work before now. But you can carry a letter, and bring an answer, and draw a bill, and say I'm out when I wish I were not in, and all that ?'

" ' Oh yes.'

" ' And all these things you promise solemnly to perform ?'

" ' I do.'

" ' And you faithfully engage to talk no more than your tongue will let you, and as little good sense as you can ; not "two and two make four—two and two make four," in the moral or maxim way, for all that I hate ; besides, I know, in morals, two and two often make five.'

" ' I promise all this, sir.'

" ' Good lad, very good lad,' said Myte. ' Kiss that book,' handing me a volume of the *Tatler*. ' But come,' said he, ' let's go upstairs and see " Heaven's last, best gift," as the poet has it—the fair creation, three samples of which I have upstairs. Why, I have a wife and two daughters.'

" ' Indeed !' said I.

" ' Why indeed ? you should have said, " Joy be with you, Colbrand," for that's *my* name. Mind that stair. That's been two summersets, seven sprained ankles, and bruised hips out of number. I've been thinking of having it mended these twelve years. When it comes to a broken leg, I'll have the leg and it set to rights together.'

" ' Here,' said he, handing me forward, and presenting me to his wife and daughters, ' good people, I've brought you a young friend whom I commend to your especial good offices. This, Ricardo, is Mrs. Myte, known in this house (but only so addressed by me) by the style and title of Flusterina. My love,' with assumed surprise, ' I once told you, many years ago, that I loved the very ground you trod upon, and you're always reminding me of it by carrying some upon your face."

"Mrs. Myte appealed to her daughters.

" 'Is my face dirty, my loves ?'

"The young ladies smiled, and shook their heads. A slight tap with the fan upon the small skull of Myte was the gentle punishment meted out to the delinquent. 'And here,' continued Myte, 'are Madam Margaret and Mistress Martha, commonly called my Goth and Vandal ; they will permit you to salute their cheeks.'

"The girls blushed, while I promptly availed myself of the privilege.

" 'And now,' said Myte, 'since you will have plenty of leisure to cultivate the esteem of these ladies, let me show you your dormitory. You must know,' he resumed, as we ascended the stairs, ' that I slept in that room for ten years, before I was married, and I used to call it—that's Signor Tomaso,'—in parenthesis, pointing to a large cat which had been asleep on the landing, but which now came forward, and placing its fore-paws upon Myte's knee-pan, stretched itself leisurely. 'I used to call it Paradise,' he proceeded, 'it was such a snug room, till the fire broke out, and I had to jump out of the window into a large blanket.'

"Having taken me into every room in the house, commenting upon each, and inquiring at intervals whether I thought I could be comfortable under his roof, he brought me back again to the drawing-room.

" 'Go in there,' said he, 'and make interest for a dish of chocolate. I am going to meet a gentleman at White's.'

"The ladies vied in their attentions towards me ; and I soon began to feel, that if I were not as happy as I could wish with Myte and his family, it would be entirely my own fault. When Myte returned, and during the afternoon, he amused me with his innocent freaks and fooleries. In the evening he played upon the fiddle, and made his wife sing and his daughters dance, and tried to sing him-

self ; and, finally, would have accomplished a dance, but
that the potency of a sneaker of punch of which he had
partaken had so impaired the stability of his small legs,
that his family judged it inexpedient that he should hazard
the feat. I, myself, confess to having seen two candles in
my hand when I retired to bed ; and had Myte's disastrous
stair been upon the flight I had occasion to ascend, I think
it very likely I might have added to the list of casualties
in his possession."

Myte's peculiar personality and quaintly humorous
conversation is further aptly illustrated by this tirade,
which he addresses banteringly to his prospective son-
in-law Langley :

" 'Toiling in a perpetual round,' continued Myte, 'running fruitlessly after happiness, when, if you stand still,
you have it. I say, Wildgoose,' he added, 'did you ever
see a kitten in pursuit of its own tail ? round and round
goes the little creature, now on one haunch, then on the
other, gravely kicking and grinning, and all for what ? Why,
if it sat still, there's its tail under its nose. Now, that's the
moral of a young fellow of pleasure.' "

There can be no doubt that Myte is a distinct
creation. His presence in the book gives abundant
evidence of Whitehead's power to invent a humorous
character of almost absolute originality.

Richard's residence at the house of Myte gave him
abundant means and leisure to see life as it then was,
and he soon aspired to the pretensions of a "pretty
fellow." But none of the occupations or diversions of
his years or circumstances could prevent his mind from
dwelling on the mystery of his birth. Dr. Johnson

tells us that about this period Savage's old nurse died, and that in reading over her papers the youth discovered some letters from Lady Mason explaining his birth and the reason for its being concealed. White-head has, however, in this instance, not adhered to the facts of history, probably deeming it better for the interest of his novel to adopt a different course. He therefore makes it appear that Mrs. Freeman, the old nurse, had herself no knowledge whatever respecting Richard's parentage, that she importuned Ludlow on the subject, and that Richard solved the enigma of his origin in the following manner: One day Mrs. Brett called on Myte, and after her departure, Myte began to narrate her history to his young clerk, telling him how she had once a son who, it was supposed, had died. Richard inquires as to dates, and perceives that if that son were alive he would be about his own age. Little by little the truth dawns upon him; he remembers with what peculiar significance Ludlow had once pointed out to him the house of Earl Rivers. Thus the mystery of his birth is dispelled. Whitehead leads us to infer that, in this matter, Savage shows considerable power of deduction for a "pretty fellow" of his years.

On discovering the all-important point, his first impulse is to seek an interview with his mother. For many days he haunts the front of her dwelling at nightfall, that, unperceived himself, he may perchance perceive her. He is satisfied for a while if he sees her crossing her brilliantly lighted saloon, or going forth in gorgeous

attire to an assembly. At length, however, a crisis
.comes, and he resolves forthwith to present himself before Mrs. Brett. In the first portion of the extract
which I am about to give, Whitehead describes
Richard's vacillating state of feeling, as previously
mentioned ; in the second, his reception by Mrs. Brett :

"It was not, however, till I got to the door that I
bethought me of the probable effect so sudden and un-
looked-for a discovery must produce upon the delicate constitution of a woman. Here, again, my imagination was
at work to magnify the consequences of my visit, and,
perhaps, to palliate to myself the weakness that absolutely
overwhelmed me, causing my fingers to withdraw from the
knocker, and my feet to betake themselves to the other
end of the street. During some hours I wandered up and
down on the other side of the way, looking wistfully at the
house as I passed and repassed it, striving to extract
resolution from the steadfast bricks and mortar, which each
successive time looked more awfully prohibitory. Ought I
to be ashamed to acknowledge that I went home that night
as wise as I came, satisfying myself with excuses for my
pusillanimity which I had occasion to make use of on the
next night—and on the next?

" I saw her once in the course of these perambulations.
She came for an instant to the window. Her back was to
the light, so that I could not distinguish her face ; but her
figure was not to be mistaken. Upon this occasion I was
so agitated, that when I recovered myself I resolved, and
fortified my determination with an oath, that on the following evening I would make my way to her feet. I could
no longer bear this state of suspense.

"I was there at the accustomed time, at my old spot,
opposite the house. Again I beheld her at the window.
She was gorgeously attired—I conjectured for an assembly ;

and looked out, as though observing the night. Presently
a footman opened the street door, and ran to the corner.
He was gone to engage a chair. No time was to be lost.
He had left the door open. I crossed the way, and entered
the house. Not a soul in the hall, or on the staircase.
The door of the room was partially open. I glided in—how,
I know not—nor did I approach her and throw myself at
her feet, as I had intended; but I stood stock-still—no,
not so: still, that is to say silent; but trembling violently.

"I think I must have looked wofully white, for when
Mrs. Brett saw me she uttered a half scream.

"'Who are you, sir?' at length she said imperiously;
'what do you want? You should have knocked before you
entered the room. Were you admitted by the servants?'

"I took courage, and approached.

"'Ha! I see—Mr. Myte's young man—Ludlow's nephew.
What is your business here, young gentleman?'

"I fell upon my knees before her.

"'Bless me, madam.'

"'Bless you!' she exclaimed, with a laugh. 'Bless *me*,
boy! what is the meaning of this? Why do you apply
to *me*? What can I do for you?'

"'Bless me, madam!' I repeated. 'You see before you
your son—I am your son.'

"'You are a mad-brained boy, who deserve a whipping
for your impertinence,' she said, after a minute's pause, and
she laid her hand upon the bell-rope. 'Rise, you young
fool, and go away, or my people shall take you where you
will be well punished. This is one of your master's sorry
jests—insolent old coxcomb! Rise——' stamping her feet.

"I found my feet and my tongue too. The worst was
over, and I was not to be so repulsed. Snatching her hand,
I said :

"'Nay, but hear me, madam; you must—you shall hear
me. This is no jest—it is the truth. I am your son—the
son you have so long believed dead.'

"Her lips were parted for a scornful laugh—her eyes dilated—her brows raised; and then she saw me—gazed at me—into me. An unmoved eye confronted hers. A sudden change—a change as ghastly as sudden. There was paint upon her cheeks and on her lips, the rest was ashy.

"'Good God! good God!' she exclaimed, not smoothing, but dashing the hair from my forehead, 'it cannot be! Who are you?' quickly—'you are Ludlow's nephew?'

"'Your son, madam,' I replied, 'your son, as there is truth in Heaven. Lady Mason knows it. Ludlow can vouch for it, and shall be made to do so. Lord Rivers——'

"I had scarcely uttered the name when she frantically flung me from her.

"'Base, unheard-of imposture!' she cried, her eyes flashing as she spoke. 'He shall answer it, Ludlow shall answer it, I say. Hence, at once, or I will alarm the house.'

"Again my eye caught hers, and again she scanned me, drawing herself up proudly. 'Cunning, clever tool of an awkward journeyman,' she said contemptuously. 'If he knew how to use you! but he does not. You will cut his fingers, fellow—or I will.'

"'You do him wrong, madam,' said I hastily, 'if you mean Ludlow. He knows not of my visit here; he is ignorant of it, and that I have made this discovery.'

"By this time she had completely regained her self-possession. I watched her face. It was calm, cold, and malignant. She rang the bell violently, slowly nodding her head to me as she did so.

"'We will make another discovery between us, young gentleman,' she said; 'we will discover whether my house is my own or no.' She heard feet upon the stairs. 'Help! murder! thieves! Lucas! John! where are you?'

"I cast myself at her feet. 'For Heaven's sake, madam, if you will not own, do not endeavour to degrade me.'

"'Where are my servants?' she said (what a hideous face

it was at that moment !), addressing a little girl about twelve years of age who ran into the room.

"'I hear them coming, madam,' answered the girl; 'what is the matter?'

"'A thief has broken into the house! Oh! you are come at last!' turning to two brawny rogues, as they entered. 'Secure that young robber!'

The fellows laid hold upon me, and began to pull me zealously about the room.

"'Oh, madam!' interrupted the girl, 'he is not a thief: I know he is not. He is a young gentleman. You did not mean to rob, did you, sir?'

"'I am no thief,' I cried, breaking from the men who held me, 'and she,' pointing to Mrs. Brett, 'knows that I am not. She *shall* know that I am——'

"'Silence him! away with him!' vociferated Mrs. Brett.

"'Shall we give him to the watch, my lady?' said one, seizing me by the throat.

"'Yes—no,' she answered; 'turn him out of the house. He will not repeat his visit, I dare say,' she added, with a shocking smile.

"'Do not hurt him, Thomas,' cried the little girl; 'you will strangle him.'

"'He's kicking my shins to splinters, miss!' remonstrated Thomas, dragging me, with the assistance of his fellow-servant, to the door.

"What could I do against the well-fed villains, who now forced me from the room with blind impetuosity, precipitating my head as they did so into the stomach of an old gentleman who had been listening on the landing?

"'I beg pardon, Mr. Lucas!' cried the more strenuous of the two; 'we have got a thief.'

"'What! eh? what! what!' cried the old man, heaving and panting. 'A thief! No such thing. He's Mr. Myte's youth; I've seen him there. A thief! He's nearly stolen all the breath out of my body, if that's being a thief; and I haven't much to lose. My lady is mistaken. I must let her know who he is. Stay where you are;' and the old gentleman walked into the room.

"'A pretty business this,' said one of the men to the other, as they waited for orders, wiping his perspiring face; 'thief-catching must be hard bread.'

"'And keeping when you have caught,' said the other; 'that's all crust.'

"Lucas now came out of the room, closing the door after him.

"'Let him go quietly now,' he said. 'You have terrified Mrs. Brett very much, young man,' he added, turning to me; 'but you won't do it again—eh? what! what!—no, you won't.'

"'They will treat me with more respect when I come a second time,' said I, 'and so will she—your mistress, and yours, fellows.'"

After this repulse Richard Savage sought Ludlow, whom he found as usual at the house of Lady Mason, and to whom he at once imparted his tale. At first the old servant is terror-stricken, and cannot understand how the youth has discovered his secret. Afterwards he is still more terrified when he hears a certain ominous sound. What that sound was the following extract will explain:—

"It was Mrs. Brett's voice; we heard her ascend the stairs rapidly.

"'There'll be high words presently,' said he, looking back; 'what if we get our hats and make off—just for a walk, eh?'

"'I'd not stir an inch for an Empress,' I replied; 'I'm glad she's come.'

"'Are you?' he rejoined. 'What a spirit you have! So am I glad!—at least, I ought to be so. Do you know, Dick, when I was a boy—a country boy—I was benighted on Corley Moor. A storm came on. Well, I saw a tree—there was but one—all waste around—the lightning showed it to me. Well—well—the lightning came down, and played around it, and about it, and seemed to lick the trunk, and run along the branches; and presently down came a thunder-bolt—down it came, and clove the tree asunder. Down I fell like a stone.'

"'Well, and what of that?' I inquired. 'Here you are, none the worse.'

"'What of that?' said he. 'I don't know; only, some-how, this reminds me of it.'

"I could not forbear laughing in the pitiable face of the narrator.

"'Pish!' said I. 'Courage, Ludlow; this is a storm that'll soon blow over. What part do you propose playing in this tempest—tree or thunderbolt?'"

Very shortly afterwards Ludlow and Richard are summoned into Lady Mason's presence, and the follow-ing scene forthwith ensues between Lady Mason, Mrs. Brett, Ludlow, and Richard. The description of this scene contains some of the finest writing in the book. The main contention is, of course, respecting Savage's origin, and the character of the whole rencounter can readily be gathered from what follows:

"'Ludlow,' cried Lady Mason, looking up, 'you must not presume to insult my daughter.'

"'Oh, my lady, but he may!' returned Mrs. Brett; 'he has your warrant for it. But not with impunity,' she added suddenly, approaching Ludlow, and striking him a violent blow upon the face with her fan.

" Ludlow bore it without flinching—nay, not merely that, but he projected his face as though courting a second salute of the same nature.

" 'What is the meaning of this ?' cried Mrs. Brett, humouring his conceit by bestowing upon him a second and a third blow with additional force, which he received in the same manner.

" After a time he spoke, calmly and quietly.

" 'Madam, you remember Jane Barton ?'

" ' Jane Barton ?'

" ' Afterwards my wife.'

" 'I do remember the creature,' said Mrs. Brett. 'Go on, sir. Well ?'

" ' Well !' said Ludlow ; ' well !'

" ' What does the fool mean ?' cried Mrs. Brett, looking around. 'Nephew,' turning to me, 'expound ; this, I suppose, is another of your joint performances.'

" 'I do not know what he means, madam,' I replied ; 'and I cannot expound mysteries.'

" ' Madam,' resumed Ludlow, ' since you remember her, perhaps you have not forgotten Mr. Bennett—the gay, the handsome Mr. Bennett—your friend Mr. Bennett.'

" 'I have not forgotten Mr. Bennett.'

" 'I say "well" again, then,' cried Ludlow.

" 'Thank you, boy !' exclaimed Mrs. Brett, turning to me, and patting my head ; 'you are a very good boy ; indeed, a very good boy. You would not second this branch of the lie. Madam,' to her mother, 'I hope you now see the gross web this poor thing has woven out of his worsted brains. And so, because his wife was young, and vain, and giddy, and he had neither sense nor spirit to control her ; and because our friend Bennett (you know the whole story) was young and handsome—and fortunate,' she added, with a provoking shake of the head at Ludlow, 'has this fellow harboured a resentment against me, which he seeks to gratify by palming off his nephew upon me for my son. Begone, thou wretched animal! Out of my path, thou base and spiritless worm!'

"Ludlow met her as she advanced, and grinned in her face.

"'Worm, am I?' he said. 'How do you know that I am a worm? How do you judge I am a worm? How do you know a worm? By its shape? By its size? By its crawl? Ha! ha! you may be mistaken in your worm; perhaps I am an adder—an adder. They are alike—but one stings.'"

When the storm caused by this angry interview had to some extent abated, Richard questioned Ludlow as to his hatred of Mrs. Brett:

"'Tell me the reason,' said I, 'why you nourish this extraordinary enmity against her.'

"'Did I not hint at it,' he answered quickly, 'last night, when we were upstairs? That hint was plain speech to her. She knows, now, how little cause I have to love her—how much—how much to hate her.'

"'You said something about your wife,' I rejoined, 'and a certain Mr.—— I forget his name.'

"'I don't,' said he; 'Mr. Bennett, that was his name.'

"'I never knew that you had been married,' I observed.

"'Oh! but I have,' he replied. 'Married? Yes,' covering his face with his hands, 'and miserable too—how miserable no one can ever know. Shall I tell you all?—very shortly—if I can. You will not despise me—you will not laugh at me; for these things *are* laughed at; they are pleasant jests to some, but not to me. I could not bear it from you, Richard.'

"I entreated him to compose himself, for, when he uncovered his face, I perceived it was ghastly pale, and assured him of my sympathy. I began to suspect what it was he was about to communicate.

"'Let me see,' he said, after a long pause. 'How shall

I begin? I entered the service of Lady Mason a mere boy
—a boy from the country. After a time I was taken into
favour by her, but found no favour in the eyes of the
daughter—your mother—then a very young woman. I
was glad when she was married to Lord Macclesfield. My
only trouble, or discomfort, rather, was removed with her.
Well, I grew up into manhood. A young girl—Jane Barton
—came into the service of my lady. She was lively, good-
natured—or seemed so—and pretty. Our fellow-servants
said that she was very vain and giddy. I did not think so.
I became attached to her, and she to me. It is a lie of those
who said she never loved me. She did love me—I know
it. At length, I mustered courage to ask my lady's permission to marry Jane. It was granted; Lady Mason kindly
adding that we should continue in her service till she could
find means to set us up in a small way of business. We
were married.' Here Ludlow sighed heavily.

" 'Oh my God !' he said suddenly, striking his bosom with
his clenched hands, ' there is no other name for it that I
feel here, and that I have felt since then—no other name but
anguish—anguish. I must go on. We had not been long
married when Mrs. Brett (oh! that cursed woman, not then
Mrs. Brett!) returned to her mother, divorced—about to be
so—disgraced—infamous. It was natural—was it not?—
although she had ever treated me with ridicule and contempt (why, she used commonly to call me a sneaking
hound, a creeping parasite, a base wretch)—still, it was only
proper, she, the daughter of my excellent mistress, that I
should treat her with all outward and becoming respect. I
pitied her (she would hate me worse than she ever did, or does,
if she knew that I pitied her), and I conducted myself before
her with more than my former reverence. This might have
conciliated—melted any other woman—but her heart is flint.
As the sense of her disgrace wore off—or, perhaps I should
say, when the time had elapsed during which it was decent
to affect some sense of her disgrace—the old unfeeling inso-

15

lence returned. My wife waited upon her as her tirewoman, and in the innocence of her heart—for she was then inno-cent—(oh, Dick!)—she would relate to me from time to time what her mistress said to her about her recent marriage—what she thought of the choice she had made—what a silly girl she was that she had not looked higher—how extra-ordinary that women *would* throw themselves away—devilish seeds that pollute the soil in which they are sown, let that soil have been as fair before as the garden of Paradise.

"'And yet to others of our fellow-servants—for she would be familiar with her inferiors—they have told me that she frequently said to them that Jane would come to no good—that she was too vain and heedless—unrestrained in her speech and manner—and that " poor Ludlow " must take as much care of her as though she were worth keeping. You may say this was light talk merely, forgotten as soon as uttered, and that I was a fool to think about it. Judge.'"

Savage found in the sequel that Ludlow had ample justification for his feeling; that Mrs. Brett had treated him infamously, had abetted his wife's dishonour, and had taken advantage of his servile position to load him with contumely and scorn almost too grievous to be borne. The passage in which this is told is a very powerful one, but bearing in mind the length of the other quotations, I have deemed it desirable not to give it.

Time goes on, and Richard's cause makes no head-way; on the contrary, Mrs. Brett persecutes him by every means in her power; and having acquired com-plete mastery over her mother, Lady Mason, now grown feeble both in body and mind, she procures the ignominious dismissal of Ludlow, averring that Richard is his nephew, whom (by a contemptible plot) he is wishful to palm off as her son. Ludlow has fortunately, while in the service of her ladyship, been provident, and is therefore able at this juncture to retire to comfortable lodgings. His wife is not dead, and now comes to him, dangerously ill, apparently dying, but humbly begging his pardon for the past. He forgives her, freely and fully, and she goes once more to live with him. Richard sees them frequently, but does not at this time reside with them.

One day he is passing along the street when a man accosts him, inquiring whether his name is Savage. On his answering in the affirmative, he is firmly seized and forcibly captured; his captors thrust him into a coach, and menacing him with threats of direst import should he seek to escape, they drive off rapidly to an unknown destination. It is perfectly evident to Richard that the ruffians who have caught him are simply the paid tools of a more powerful enemy. It is almost needless to say who the enemy is; and Savage soon learns from the dastardly hirelings themselves that his suspicions are well-founded. The men, whose respective names are Rugby and Watson, inform him that he is about to be sent secretly out of the country. The vehicle is at length stopped, and he is conveyed into an old and disreputable-looking inn. He is then made to ascend to a small room, into which he is pushed and the door locked upon him, the villains telling him that he will have to remain there until nine o'clock, when it was supposed that the ship that was to bear him away would sail. So agreeable had it been to their feelings to imprison an innocent man, that one of the servants at the inn had accompanied them upstairs to assist in this delightful employment, and to aid in jeering at their hapless captive. The manner in which Savage at length succeeded in effecting his escape is described in the following extract. The passage is almost too long for quotation, but it cannot well be divided, and it is withal so fine a piece of writing, that I have judged it advisable to quote it entire :—

"With a burst of boisterous and, I dare say, heart-felt merriment, the three rogues left me to my own reflections.

* * * * * *

"And sad and bitter they were for a time—and then, revengeful. But *her* revenge, it was too apparent, would precede mine, perhaps prevent it. Was it certain—whatever Watson might have hinted to the contrary—that my life would not be attempted—that I should not be murdered in this den? *That* I had full reason to believe would be the disposal of me most satisfactory to Mrs. Brett. For of what avail—lasting avail—to send me to Jamaica, if I chanced to come back again, the possibility of my doing which my mother, guilty, I remembered, as well as malignant and revengeful, must have resolved, before she decided upon this step? Murdered—the decree had gone forth—I was to be murdered—drowned, it occurred to me, by the jolly tars of whom Watson had spoken, whose jollity would suffer little diminution from the trivial circumstance of having sent a poor devil to the bottom of the Thames. My hair stood on end at this suggestion, and the sweat gathered into drops upon my forehead.

*   *   *   *   *   *

"The moon at the instant broke through the darkness—bland goddess! she never walked out of a cloud to supply the exigence of the hide-bound brains of a poetaster more opportunely than she seemed to visit me in my prison now.

"Through one of the small windows, high above my reach, and barred, her light streamed into the room, disclosing its dimensions. It was tolerably large and square. A huge, old-fashioned bedstead against the wall opposite the windows, the sole thing in the room, except myself—and I, indeed, a thing—entrapped, outwitted—brought to my pleas, and my knees too; yes, my prayers, my tears, my cries, my wild howlings for mercy—for life—by a woman, and that woman (it was a lie—a fiend!) my mother!

"It would have done her heart—good, I was about to write, but it had, long ago, been past that—to have heard me curse and swear, as I ran madly about the room, seeking some impossible outlet. No chimney—no trap-door in floor or ceiling; no chance of scaling the windows; no chance if I could do so. Exhausted at length by these unavailing and weak efforts, I flung myself upon the mattress. I would sleep out the interval between this and nine o'clock. I wished the time were come. Suspense was agony.

"It would not do. Sleep was out of the question. So was it to lie passive, whilst dreadful thoughts of horror and of death came quickly, the last more hideous than the former, and wreaked themselves upon my brain. I could not bear it. Starting up violently, my arm came in contact with something that protruded from the wall—was it merely the wall?—at the back of the bed. There was a sort of dingy curtain—I know not what to call it—which prevented my seeing what this something was. I rent a hole in the rotten piece of linen. It was a key—a key in the lock of a door. I tried it. It turned easily. Already I could open the door some inches—remove the bedstead, and I should at once find myself in another room—a room they had probably forgotten, and the door of which they had most likely omitted to secure.

"Ha! ha! I sprang from the bed in a transport, and was at my work in a trice. These villains were not adepts —they had something of their business yet to learn. My escape would teach them foresight, caution. They would make all fast beforehand next bout. I did not think, at the time, of my successor, whoever he might be, with whom it would go hard in consequence of their acquired caution and foresight.

"Never, surely, was there such a huge, unmanageable, impracticable bedstead. Invoking imprecations upon the joiner, I laboured away at the vast effort of woodwork, and had nearly drawn it from the wall far enough to enable me to open the door and to squeeze myself through, when a loud knocking arrested my attention and suspended my labours.

"'Hilloah! young fellow!' cried the gruff voice of Rugby.

"'Well, what do you want?' I answered in a courageous tone. 'Are you going to let me out?'

"It occurred to me that, Rugby being alone, and by no means a powerful man, if he opened the door, I would have a struggle for it. Could I force him into the room, and succeed in bolting and barring him quietly within, I might slip downstairs, out at the door, and then—"Mrs. Brett, my service to you!" My heart leapt at the possibility of it. The reply of Rugby, however, dispelled this pleasing anticipation.

"'Going to let you out?' said he. 'Not I, till your time comes. Mr. Watson's a kind-hearted, considerate gentleman, and he wants to know whether you'll have anything. If you will, me and Bill Sims 'll bring it to you.'

" ' I want nothing ; go away, and leave me,' I said.

" ' You might put a handle to my name, and call me mister,' said Rugby; ' neither hog, dog, nor devil. "I want nothing ; go away!" I should like to have the teaching of you manners. I'd cut 'em into you, I would, that you'd never forget 'em ;' and the fellow retired, muttering.

"When he was well gone, I resumed my employment with renewed vigour. I had been on tenter-hooks whilst the man stayed, lest he should be reminded of the door of the inner room, which I concluded to be immediately on his right hand. In a short time I had sufficiently removed the bedstead to press myself through the opening of the door behind it, which I did with such precipitation as to fall headlong down a couple of steps that led into the inner room. I got up regardless of the accident, and proceeded, as well as I was able, to explore the apartment. It was a small garret, or rather hole, lighted in the daytime by a casement; but this I did not at the moment observe. My first impulse was to make towards that part of the wall in which I had assured myself I should find a door. Like many other assurances which a man makes to himself, mine had no foundation in reality. After carefully (in both senses carefully) feeling the whole superficies of the walls, and of the ceiling—for that I could reach with my hands—not a door was to be found, except, indeed, the door that opened into my prison. The helplessness of my condition now returned to me with tenfold poignancy. I sat me down on the two steps, and could have wept with very anguish ; but of what avail, thought I, when I somewhat recovered my composure, to wring one's hands and to disturb one's spirits, when work is to be done, that perhaps, after all, *may* be done?

" Springing up—for a new hope broke in upon me—I hastened to the casement, which, with some difficulty, I opcued.   Could I get out, and make my escape over the roofs of the houses?   Some friendly neighbour would, perhaps, receive me, and assist my deliverance out of the hands of these murderers. Or if no window were accessible, I could alarm the passengers in the street by my outcries, who might insist upon, nay, who would compel my liberation.   But would they so?   I was not so certain of that. I decided that this should be my last resort; for I was well aware that unless I had an opportunity of telling my story first, I should stand small chance of obtaining credit for it, against the combined contradiction of three hard-fronted ruffians who could, doubtless, utter a lie with more confidence than an honest man could relate the truth.

"The great fiend fly away with Rugby, and invent a new and exquisite torture expressly for him! His house had been built for the purpose, and he had taken it with the view of accommodating young gentlemen, who might happen to fall under their mothers' displeasure, with a few hours' lodgings preparatory to their embarkation for the plantations.   I could not stretch myself sufficiently far out of the casement to distinguish whether there were houses on either side of us.   I began to fear that our house (*our* house!) was detached, in which case no hope was left to me.   All was silence.   Before, and widely extended before, was a space of ground, diversified, here and there, with patches of hungry grass and ponds of accumulated rain.   Not a soul—and I watched for half an hour—dotted the surface of this lost waste; not a house was to be seen.

"Next, as to escape from the hole in which I was.   The edge of the roof—a steep one—was barely a yard and a half below the casement.   There was not even the common wooden gutter to convey the rain from the eaves; and now I turned from the casement and placed this question straight before me.   I repeated it aloud, that, as it were, my mind should distinctly see it.

"'Shall I stay here and submit myself to certain death,

or, if that be not certain, to a life-long captivity worse than death, or shall I avail myself of this chance for my life which Providence has pointed out to me?'

"No time was to be lost; nor could there be any hesitation. Having taken off my shoes, and put them in my pockets, I fell upon my knees, and commended myself to God—and I arose, strengthened.

"It was a matter of no small difficulty to get myself, in a collected form, outside the casement, and when I had done so, to project myself upwards by its side, which was raised from the roof. One glance below would have been inevitable destruction. I threw myself forward, and on hands and feet made my way towards the ridge of the roof in an oblique direction, purposing to reach the next house, if there were one. I had proceeded some distance, when one tile, and then another, and another, gave way from beneath my feet, which could effect no hold or stay—neither could my fingers, the nails of which I vainly endeavoured to infix into the mortar. I was now sliding downwards at full length. God! what a moment was that! My eyes closed —my senses reeled—and yet one thought—one vision horribly distinct within me. I saw myself below—on the ground—on the flinty-jagged stones—and what I saw— what figure, if figure it may be called—the reader shall imagine, for I cannot, or if I can, will not, describe it.

"Merciful powers! what superhuman hand, outstretched from Heaven, has stayed—has saved me? Yes—my feet were stayed—restrained by a firm bulwark. I looked round—a secure wall it seemed, against which I leaned— against which I lay my bursting temples. A flood of tears relieved me; my heart was thankful to the Almighty; but I could not as yet speak, nor could my mind yet form a prayer.

"I had fallen against a stack of chimneys, placed, as well as I could guess, between the partition that divided Rugby's house from its neighbour. As yet, I could discover no garret-window corresponding with the one I had (and yet how long the time appeared!) just left. I decided, therefore, upon again venturing to the ridge of the roof, taking care to keep the chimneys immediately in my rear, that, should my feet betray me a second time, they might once more stand me in good stead. This time I was more fortunate. Having reached the summit, I placed myself astride upon the roof, and took a survey of the prospect on my right hand, which I had not yet seen. The river lay before me and beside me, with its multifarious craft, whose half-formed shadows hung beneath the water, black and almost as motionless as themselves. The beauty—if any there were —of this scene, was lost upon me. The picturesque must give way to the pressing, and I was in haste. Placing my hands before, and impelling myself by my heels on either side of the roof, I got forward some distance till I was on a level with the second stack of chimneys, similar to the former. I slid down to these easily; and lo! not far off—but beneath me—the flat top of a garret-window! There was a long iron bar; a hold-fast, I think it is called, attached to the chimneys and to the roof. I took off my cravat and tied it with a strong knot to my handkerchief, which I fastened to the bar; and winding the other end tightly round my wrist, let myself down to the small platform. There was barely space to crouch down upon it, which I did. The horrible yard and a half of steep tiles was under this window also. I shuddered at the thought of trusting myself to the frail security of the framework. I dare not attempt to crawl down by the side of the window, lest a single false step should precipitate me to the ground. And yet, how otherwise could I hope to get into it? Perhaps, by some blessed chance, the room was occupied. I stretched my hand over the edge, and strove to discover whether there was a light in it. I had hardly done so, when, methought, I heard voices; nor was I deceived; and the momentary radiance of a candle illumined a small portion of the atmosphere beneath me. Thrusting my arm down as low as it could reach, I laid hold of one side of the casement, and burst it open with a violent crash.

"'Christ Jesus! a ghost!' cried a voice, and then a heavy tumble upon the ground.

"'What's the matter now?' exclaimed a second and more powerful voice. 'Why, Simon, have you gone crazed?'

"'There!' cried the prostrate Simon—'there!' pointing, as I supposed, to the open casement.

"'You fool,' said the other, 'the fastening has given way, that's all.'

"I heard him approach the window. It was now my turn to join in the conversation.

"'For God's sake,' I began, 'lend me some assistance.'

"'Hilloah!' cried the man, looking out. 'Who the devil are you? What do you want?'

"'Your assistance,' I exclaimed. 'I am an unfortunate young gentleman just escaped from murderers.'

"'Where from?'

"'From a fellow named Rugby—the alehouse hard by.'

"'The devil!' said the man. 'How did you contrive— but a pretty fellow am I to be asking questions instead of lending a hand. Young man, turn yourself round, and let us see your feet over here instead of your chin; only, gently; mind, gently.'

"I was not long about that. Unwinding the end of my cravat from my wrist, I did as he directed. Taking me with a firm gripe by the ankles, he guarded my feet till they rested upon the ledge of the window; then, seizing me by the waistband with one hand, he clasped me tightly round the body with his arms, and drew me into the room."

Nothing could be finer than much of the foregoing

description. At times it is so vividly realistic that one almost trembles at the hapless fate of the poor boy, should his foot slip, or should he become for a moment dizzy. The honest tradesman in whose house he now finds himself is solicitous for his welfare, as is likewise his wife, and Simon, a grown-up son. They gather round him, and interchange glances of commiseration and sympathy. At once they supply him with the comforts which his sorry plight so pitiably needs, and of which he has too long been deprived. In the whole romance there is not a more pleasant picture than that of the Martin family. From them he learns that he is at Wapping; and after a family council, it is resolved to endeavour forthwith to capture his whilom captors. By means of a very clever stratagem this is effected, greatly to the ruffians' consternation, and they are handed over to the watch.

It transpires that the elder Martin had once been soldier, and had served under Colonel Brett. Accordingly, next morning he goes with Richard to that gentleman's house, and demands an interview. Presently Colonel Brett enters the room, and is at first disposed to appear in great anger on account of their intrusion. When, however, their story is told to him with full and circumstantial detail down to the point at which Watson and Rugby are arrested on so heavy and criminal a charge, he perceives at once not only the enormity of his wife's offence, but the fact that Richard Savage has now her, and (so complicated are such matters) even himself, in his power.   Immediately he alters his tone.

A long parley and conference ensue, and at length Savage, by the advice of several of his friends, agrees that the matter shall not be pushed further.   The watch are bribed to let the prisoners go ; and so for the present things subside into their former groove.

It is probable that Richard thought by this act of leniency and forbearance to cajole his mother into recognising the justice of his claims.   He may have thought that the very fact of his now being able to bruit abroad a tale so shameless, and so much to her discredit, would induce her to be complacent towards him, lest, stung by resentment, he should take this form of revenge.   But if such were his surmises, the result falsified them.   Mrs. Brett abated not a jot of her hatred towards him ; and though she abstained from open violence, her animosity was unceasing, and she ere long contrived what proved in the end a much more damaging stratagem for his injury.   Of this I shall speak in due course.

Richard Savage gradually drops into his former mode of life once more.   He sees a good deal of Ludlow, and also of Ludlow's wife, who still appears to be dying.   Mrs. Ludlow seems to be truly penitent, deeply grateful to her husband for his forgiveness, and quite resigned.   Presently, however, she shows signs of recovery, and before long becomes almost convalescent.   One day she goes forth and does not return.   Soon Ludlow and Richard are aware that she has become accessory to a despicable fraud invented by Mrs. Brett. She has signed a document stating that Richard Savage is her son; and very naturally terrified at what will be the consequences of her treachery, she has again left her husband. Ludlow's despair at this is most terrible. It seems to him that all his projects have been thwarted; and Whitehead has a splendid opportunity for delineating varied forms of passionate emotion, and of showing what insight he possessed into the hidden springs from whence such emotion comes. This opportunity he has availed himself of to the uttermost, and in the whole work we have nothing finer than the introspective glimpses he gives us into Ludlow's mind. Ludlow's ravings are not the melodramatic hysteria of a second-rate novelist.

The account given of his closing days is only such as an author highly dowered with the great gift of dramatic insight could afford. Ludlow's mental distress ends in bringing on physical illness, and he gradually sinks; Savage meanwhile attending him with assiduity and loving devotion.

On the last evening of his life Ludlow becomes unhappy concerning his worldly arrangements, and would have had them altered in Richard's favour, but at the moment he lacks the requisite strength, and at Savage's suggestion puts off the matter until the morrow—a morrow which never comes for him on earth. This will explain a reference in the following most pathetic extract:

" My heart was heavy when Digby [the doctor] left me, and I sat down by Ludlow's bedside.

" 'How do you feel now?' I inquired, when he awoke. There was a serenity, almost angelic, upon his countenance.

" 'Better than ever I did in my life, my dear and constant friend Dick, who are ever near me,' he replied, 'so light, so airy, as it were. Why, I feel as though I should be wafted into the air if I were to attempt to walk. I have been asleep; but what a dream has my life been ! All passing away—well; so that you were not left behind, I should be quite happy—if an humble, ignorant man, like myself, might presume to advise you—to guide you, Richard——'

" 'You shall do so—oh, Ludlow !'"

" ' No, I might be wrong, after all. I guide ! I advise ! What, then, brought me to this, my deathbed ? My wisdom ? Will human presumption never have an end ? Dick,' he added more calmly, ' I wish to see Mr. Myte.'

" 'Shall I fetch him ? Will not to-morrow do ? It is too late to-night.'

" 'To-morrow will do, I dare say; but I will tell you now why I wish to see him. The money I have saved is in his hands. It was honestly got, and will be properly left—to the grandson of my dear mistress—for dear she is to me, who had been nothing without her.'

"I was about to expostulate; for, to say the truth, I felt I had no claim to the money.

" 'I have no relations in the world,' laying his hand upon my arm; 'if I had, it might be different. I shall leave my wife nothing, for if I did, it would be] mis-spent. You must know that when she first went wrong—I can talk calmly of it now—it hurt me very much, and my mind was turned to a consideration of the influence of bad example upon young minds. I had, even then, saved some money. Well, I lodged it in Mr. Myte's hands, and with it a will, devising the whole of it, whatever the sum might be that I had accumulated when I died, to the Society for the Reformation of Manners; and many a joke has the pleasant little man made at my expense, on account of my will, which I now wish to cancel. He can tell me in a moment the exact amount I have in his hands. In the meanwhile, take all that is in the house—in the box, I mean, which was picked up. I almost wish she had taken it with her. Poor thing! But all that is gone by.'

"I insisted upon remaining with him the whole of that night. I had a book which I particularly wished to read. He was at length prevailed upon to let me stay with him.

"After he sank to sleep, I drew to the fire, and read for several hours. Unused, however, to sitting up at night (then, not since), I dropped to sleep. It was what Shakespeare calls, with wonderful happiness of phrase, the 'dead waste' of the night, when I was awakened by a slight noise—a noise as of something, or somebody, near me. I opened my eyes suddenly, and looked up. A figure—it was Ludlow—stood before me. Merciful God! I could not shriek. No face of living man was ever so shocking! Yet, as I gazed upon it, it was the face of a conscious being. He pointed to his mouth with one hand, indicating—I discovered that at last—that he could not speak, and motioned with the other as if he wished to write.

"I had arisen. 'For heaven's sake return to bed. Do you want pen and ink?'

An inarticulate sound. He nodded his head. At that moment his eyes were fixed upon the wall, and his head was turned slowly round. He appeared to see some moving object. A strong shudder—his feet carried him to the bed—he fell upon it with a groan; and then, taking my hand, guided it to his lips, and thence to his heart—pressing it to his heart. I fell upon my knees and prayed, and when I raised my head all was over. He was gone for ever!

"'Thy love to me was wonderful, passing the love of women.' So said David of Jonathan, and so say I, after many years, Ludlow, of thee. And yet no, not so. And yet, again, let the grateful hyperbole stand. Gentle and dear, and ever-remembered, and never to be forgotten whilst memory holds a seat in this distracted (and now, alas ! contracted) brain, once more—Farewell !"

Richard Savage performed in a fitting manner the various duties which now devolved upon him in making the final arrangements concerning his deceased friend.

Soon after these events he has an opportunity of seeing Mrs. Brett, and the many-sided passions of his complex nature being called into action by the occasion, the following dialogue takes place. Whoever was to blame, these were bitter words, and their impression was never obliterated by softer tones ; a pitiable last interview between mother and son :

" 'Thou foolish novice,' she said leisurely, between her white set teeth, 'and what wouldst thou be, and what wouldst thou do, and what canst thou do ?'

" ' I can tell you what you have done,' I replied. ' What you will do, who can tell ? Ludlow—he is dead.'

" ' Well, sir, proceed.'

" ' Your mother lies dying. These are your doings.'

" She turned pale at that.

" ' Insolent villain ! You dare not say this to me.'

" ' I dare—I will—I have—said it. These are your doings, Mrs. Brett. I will now be plain with you. Not satisfied with disowning your son, you would have spirited him [from England. Where was I to be sent ? To the West Indies ? or was I to be murdered on the passage ? But worse than this (I thought, madam, you were a proud lady), you stooped to accept my mercy ; and afterwards

16

suborned an infamous wretch to prop your falsehood with another. You have her hand to it, I hear.'

" ' I have,' she replied ; ' and she has signed to what is false ; I know it, and I confess it.'

" ' What of that ?'

" She laughed, but it was not carried off well. Oh, God ! how exquisitely mean she looked at that moment ; and she felt she looked so. She was disconcerted ; shockingly, painfully self-abased. Ludlow ! thou hadst had thy revenge then, couldst thou but have seen her. Too ample it had been for thy gentle spirit to have borne. I could have wept for the poor soul in that beautiful body, so cursedly employed. It was some minutes before she recovered her composure. When she did, she said :

" ' I repeat, I know that what the woman has signed is false. I tell you, that you may know me. Beware of me, Richard Freeman.'

" ' I must be Richard Savage, madam. My mother's shame is yours, my father's name is mine.'

" ' As you will,' she replied, her bosom heaving. 'Richard Savage, then, that woman is your mother. You understand me ?'

" ' I do. As you will, as you have said. Upon my word, madam, I believe, after all, you have some consideration for me. Though you yourself disown me, you kindly procure one who is willing to acknowledge me. I ought to be, and am, obliged to you. So little to choose between the two——'

She flashed forth at this, coming towards me with an eye of fire.

" ' Richard Savage——' her hand held forth ; she checked herself. 'But no, we will have no theatrical show. I hate you. When I say that, it is enough.'

" I threw forth my hand and caught her descending fingers.

" ' Mrs. Brett, I do not hate—I despise you.'

"She strove to look me down, but her eyes fell under mine. She measured me from head to foot, and I her.

" 'Am I not your son, madam ?'

"And we parted, never to meet again, eye to eye, face to face, breath to breath. And was there to be no theatrical show ? Not Booth and Mrs. Barry ever stalked from the stage at opposite sides with a more taking dignity. I am told she has a keen sense of the ridiculous. She must have laughed over the remembrance of this often, as I have done. It is well that we should have supplied each to the other one occasion of mirth, and all, perhaps, that has passed between us, rightly taken, *is* ridiculous. Then, if it be so, let others laugh."

Some considerable time before the events last narrated, Richard Savage had sought Colonel Brett in order to plead his cause, and had discovered him at Button's coffee-house in Covent Garden. There he had found that gentleman in conversation with Sir Richard Steele, who, in his kindly, bantering way, said a few pleasant words to him, and eventually they became very friendly. One day Richard Savage received a message from Sir Richard begging him to come to see him at his house. On his arrival he found Sir Richard engaged in a peculiarly characteristic occupation, namely, that of interviewing an irascible creditor. In a manner altogether his own he shuffled Savage into an adjoining room, introducing him to a young lady who was there, and bidding her entertain him until he himself was disengaged. In the course of conversation it transpired that she was the little girl who ran into the room on the occasion of Savage's first interview with Mrs. Brett, when it will be remem-

16—2

bered that she had taken his part, and deprecated, in her sweet child-like way, Mrs. Brett's coarse severity towards him. This mutual reminiscence served as an interesting link between them, and on each occasion of their meeting their interest in one another grew until it expanded into a warmer feeling, and they were affianced to one another. The lady was Elizabeth Wilfred, natural daughter of Sir Richard Steele, whose affection for her was very great, and who gave his unhesitating consent to their contemplated union. He invariably spoke of securing a desirable situation for Savage, as, according to the habits of patronage at the time, he could so easily have done; but such was his habitual procrastination that even this promise remained unfulfilled.

One of Richard's former schoolmates, named Sinclair, had now succeeded to an ample patrimony and had come to town. He met Miss Wilfred frequently, and, attracted by her beauty, paid his addresses to her. These, however, she unhesitatingly rejected, and the feelings of affection which Sinclair formerly cherished towards her became changed to bitterest hatred. He conceived the infamous scheme of inveigling her into a mock marriage. To carry out this project he formed, with Mrs. Brett's connivance, a plan which was executed as follows: One day, driving with the ladies in the capacity of *cavaliere servente*, Mrs. Brett left Miss Wilfred and himself on the pretext of some call, agreeing to meet them ere long.

Seizing the opportunity thus afforded him, Sinclair

instantly conveyed Miss Wilfred to Robinson's coffee-house, a disreputable resort near Charing Cross.   They were shown into a private room, where were already waiting two low fellows who had been hired, the one to personate a clergyman, the other his clerk and witness. An hour or two before, by the merest accident, Savage had encountered an acquaintance named Marchant, a man who, though by no means a rogue, had a rather too miscellaneous circle.   This man, in the early part of Savage's career, had been useful to him as a literary censor and guide.

Marchant incidentally told Savage, in the course of conversation, that there was to be a mock marriage that day at Robinson's coffee-house.   Savage's consternation and horror may easily be imagined when Miss Wilfred's name was mentioned, and, strangely enough, Marchant did not know of his friend's interest in the lady.   Rushing wildly to the place, Savage violently entered, and dashing aside the woman of the house, who vainly sought to detain him, he forced his way to the door of the private room.   This he found locked, but energy such as his was not long in bursting it open; to the dismay of the terrified culprits, and to the intense relief of Miss Wilfred, whom he found fruitlessly sueing for release.   Inflicting a severe blow on Sinclair, and contemptuously flinging aside the scoundrel's hirelings, he bore his betrothed away from a scene so unfitted for her, and as her father was absent from London, he left her, temporarily, with the family of Myte.   It is almost needless to say that Mrs.

Brett's share in this episode justly earned for her much opprobrium.

Time goes on, and Richard Savage finds himself increasing in literary reputation, the result of certain poems he has put forth. Miss Wilfred accepts the invitation of a noble family to reside with them, and Richard is permitted to visit her as an accepted suitor.

The episode just narrated was much conversed about, and canvassed in all its bearings, and Richard's share in it was narrated much to his advantage. The wrongs which he endured at the hands of Mrs. Brett also secured him much commiseration and sympathy, and his great ability and growing fame as an author likewise contributed to bring him into, and to keep him in, popular favour. Moreover, in each of his productions he ceased not to remind the world of his sorrows, in a more or less pointed manner, and to reserve his bitterest epigram for her who had caused them.

And now we arrive at the gravest event in Savage's career. One day he came to London from Richmond, where he was at the time residing, in order that he might have the more quiet in which to compose an important poem which was finally to establish his reputation, his purpose being to discharge a lodging which he possessed at Westminster, and which, with characteristic wastefulness of money, he had retained long after it had ceased to be needful for him. After executing his errand, he was strolling through St. James's Park, when he accidentally met his two friends, Gregory and Marchant. Dr. Johnson, in *his* account

of the affair, says that they all repaired to a neighbouring coffee-house ; Whitehead, however, says that
they all went to Chelsea, and there sat drinking for the
remainder of the day. Whitehead follows Johnson in
making Savage say that he would willingly have remained in the house for the night, but this was out of
the question, as all the beds were engaged. Accordingly the three friends, naturally in no very sedate
humour, agreed to sally forth and seek adventures till
the morning. By-and-by they found themselves near
Charing Cross, and Marchant, perceiving a light in
Robinson's coffee-house, in an evil moment resolved to
enter, and did so, rudely demanding a room. He was
told that he would be shown into one immediately,
but not satisfied with this answer, he rushed uninvited
into a room, and was followed by Gregory and Savage.
There they discovered Sinclair and a discreditable
company ; instantly a quarrel ensued, swords were
drawn, and in a moment there was a general *mélée*.
Savage, at all times incensed against Sinclair, was in
his present excited state infuriated against him, and
straightway attacked him. Sinclair defended himself,
but soon Savage gave him a mortal wound. So great,
however, was the confusion at the time, that no one
seemed aware of the exact state of matters at the
instant at which it was given. Savage and Gregory
escaped, but such was their irresolution as to flight,
that they were speedily taken, and confined in the
Gate-house, and after appearing before the justices
were conveyed, with Marchant, to Newgate.

Ere long they were placed on their trial; and although the witnesses did not agree in their testimony and were persons of a character which, as Dr. Johnson rightly observes "did not entitle them to much credit," Marchant and Savage were found guilty of murder. Their judge was the infamous Page, who prejudiced the jury against the prisoners. Four days afterwards, on the prisoners returning into court to receive sentence, Savage made a most eloquent speech in extenuation of his conduct, and in the endeavour to procure the release of his companion in bonds, having little hope for himself except through the clemency of the Crown. Considerable endeavours were made to interest the Queen on his behalf, but all efforts appeared likely to be fruitless, as her Majesty had heard a perverted story respecting his first endeavour to see Mrs. Brett at her house, which was to the effect that he had there attempted to murder his mother. It was Mrs. Brett who had circulated this tale in order to prejudice the Queen against Savage, and had it not been for the kind offices of the Countess of Hertford, who went personally to tell the Queen the facts of the case, it would have had the effect desired by Mrs. Brett. As it was, however, Savage and Gregory were pardoned. On his release, Savage, feeling more and more exasperated with Mrs. Brett, began to wonder if he could not at least obtain from her the means of support, by threatening that, if she did not allow him a pension, he would more than ever make her the subject of satire, and as the events which had taken place had brought him into still greater public notice, he could now hope to do this with more galling effect. At this juncture, Lord Tyrconnel, a connection of Mrs. Brett's, came forward with an offer to receive Savage into his house as an equal, and to allow him two hundred pounds a year. It is a little uncertain what Lord Tyrconnel's motives were in this matter. Although not denying ulterior motives, his lordship himself said that his object was mainly to relieve a man of genius, but the truth of this explanation is more than questionable. Altogether, it would appear that Savage's expedient had proved successful, and that the pension really came from Mrs. Brett. For a while all went prosperously with Savage ; for the first time in his life he was in opulent circumstances, and, if he had been able to resist his inherent temptations to unworthy pleasures, all might have been well. But Savage's was a nature which, while it knew poverty, could not value prosperity, and very soon he was driven once more from his comfortable haven of refuge, and in such a manner as to make the world feel that in expelling him Lord Tyrconnel was not wholly to blame. His quarrel with Lord Tyrconnel began in a way most characteristic. In the first flush of friendship that nobleman had told Savage that he had instructed the butler that all orders given by Mr. Savage to that functionary were to be treated as if from himself ; and had likewise given the poet some valuable books bearing his coat of arms. Great therefore was his mortification when he found that Savage was still far too fond of frequenting taverns, and not unfrequently invited his boon companions to his apartments, abusing the generous privileges granted to him by demanding of the butler in an imperious manner to supply them with the best wine. Moreover, he had soon the no small annoyance of perceiving some of the handsome volumes he had given his guest exposed for sale, as it proved to be Savage's frequent custom, when he wanted a small sum of ready money, to take a book to the pawnbroker's.

Lord Tyrconnel naturally remonstrated with Savage respecting these improprieties, urging him to discontinue them, and venturing to hint that as he was now in receipt of a settled income, he should no longer be under any necessity to resort to this paltry means of procuring money. He likewise exhorted him not to spend so much time in taverns, but to let more of his hours be passed with himself. These requests Savage took in very bad part. It was, perhaps, his gravest fault never to be able to bear patiently a rebuke, however well deserved. Thus matters went on for a long while, both parties feeling aggrieved, and, though rarely referring to disagreeable subjects, being more and more incensed against one another day by day. One night, Richard Savage having been (from a cause which I shall shortly mention) very deservedly angry with himself, went to a tavern, and found even a more rollicking and disreputable company than usually congregated there.

They reminded him of a promise which he had made, when in an unfit state to make any promise, to entertain them all at his lordly home. It was a marked feature in Savage that, at the very time when he felt most that he had been always doing wrong, instead of being humbled and made penitent by the consciousness of guilt, he seemed to run all the more eagerly into depravity. Accordingly, no sooner had he been reminded of this foolish and most culpable piece of bravado, than he agreed immediately to carry it into effect. The band of revellers at once proceeded to Lord Tyrconnel's house. Arrived there, Savage, insolently usurping all the privileges of the master of the house, demanded the best wine. The servants did all they could to prevent the accomplishment of his wishes. There was an altercation; but at length they were obliged to yield, and a scene of wild debauchery ensued, in the midst of which Lord Tyrconnel himself appeared. The next morning, Savage left Lord Tyrconnel's house for ever.

It is now desirable to revert to another phase of Savage's life, namely, that concerning Miss Wilfred. I have said that Miss Wilfred had taken up her residence with a noble family, that of the Countess of Hertford; and during the greater part of Savage's connection with Lord Tyrconnel, he was permitted to go to the house in the character of an accepted suitor. By-and-by, however, Lady Hertford began to hear accounts of the unworthy life he was leading about town, and evinced a coldness towards him. Miss

Wilfred also, though loving him with an affection as sincere as ever, was deeply grieved at what came to her ears.   At last it would appear probable that Lady Hertford had gently intimated to Miss Wilfred that she could no longer permit her to receive the visits of so unworthy a person at her house.   This placed Miss Wilfred in a very painful situation, the more so as her father, Sir Richard Steele, was no longer in a position to receive her.   She confided her dilemma to Savage, and he instantly proposed that she should leave Lady Hertford and go into apartments in the house of a respectable matron until such time as they could be united in marriage, which he promised her should be soon.   This step she consented to take. For a considerable period all went well, Savage conducting himself as a man of honour.   Indeed, during the whole of this attachment, which lasted his life, his conduct respecting it was altogether blameless, except on one occasion.   In truth, his being capable of such an attachment is one of the redeeming features of his character.   The exception just referred to occurred at this time.   Finding himself growing day by day on less friendly terms with Lord Tyrconnel, and fearing that not only his means of subsistence, but also those of Miss Wilfred (which all came through him), would be cut off in the very probable event of a quarrel, Savage is represented as on one occasion going to Miss Wilfred and making a proposal to her not consistent with honour.   It is not the description of this incident which is vile; it is the sentiment which the description may occasion to an intelligent reader. The mere idea that any man of parts would make overtures against the honour of a lady placed under the peculiarly trying circumstances of Miss Elizabeth Wilfred is unpleasant to read of, but that such an one as Richard Savage, whose writings (considering their period) evinced a somewhat lofty code of morality, and who professed not only to be guided by high principles but to be deeply devoted to Miss Wilfred should do so, makes his conduct inexplicable. But when we consider that the circumstances which he pleads as his only extenuation were circumstances arising solely out of his own bad conduct—when he attempts the rash arguments, not after weeks of physical or mental suffering which it might be presumed would have impaired or deranged his moral perceptions, but simply through being heated with wine, he is made to attempt the most serious ruin to all his prospects without any overmastering reason— this is still more inexplicable. The mysteries of our fallen natures are indeed inscrutable; and as Whitehead distinctly assumes that this incident is true to nature, I presume we must believe him. But, setting aside for the present any higher questions of the promotion of religion and morality in literature, there still remains the contention whether it is good art in a work of this sort to rob the hero (for, whatever Whitehead may say of its naturalness, this incident does so rob him) of the one redeeming quality for the sake of which we pardon, or at least condone, his

many follies and excesses, and to demean him by
parading him before us divested of all claim to our
respect. To a question of this sort there are doubtless many answers, but personally I feel that this
incident constitutes the greatest blot on Whitehead's
artistic conception of this romance.

. Miss Wilfred's conduct in this terrible ordeal was
worthy of her, and consistent with her sweet and
spotless character. She left the room, refused to see
him that day, and the next day when he called, he
discovered that she had gone, leaving no address, nor
could he by his utmost efforts find her whereabouts.
It was after a day spent in fruitless endeavours, his
mind distracted with conflicting emotions, that he
sought the tavern where his quondam friends reminded him of his luckless promise. It may well be
imagined that on the following morning, when he left
Lord Tyrconnel's mansion, he did so with a heavy heart.
Even he must have felt the bitter pangs of remorse,
when he reflected that he had in two days—and that
entirely through his own fault—lost the means of subsistence and comfort, and, what was infinitely worse,
all just claim to a love which had hitherto softened
and elevated his whole being. The cold, callous
streets must indeed have appeared cold and callous
to him then. Henceforth they were to be oftentimes
the sole place to which he could resort. Henceforth
his life lies almost constantly in the shadows; his
vices and degradations are continually before us; but
even in him we sometimes meet with good deeds

which are all the more refreshing from their being
entirely unexpected. Witness the occasion when he
relieved—himself in great destitution—that infamous
woman, formerly called Mrs. Ludlow—the person who,
after Mrs. Brett, had probably done him the most
injury. Once and again he is brought into temporary
prominence by some peculiarly bitter or effective
sarcasm launched against Mrs. Brett in the numerous
literary efforts which, appearing one by one, prevented
the public from forgetting his wrongs. But even
though he had the satisfaction of driving Mrs. Brett
from Bath, and compelling her " to shelter herself among the crowds of London," as Dr. Johnson
tells us, and though the sale of the poem which had
so decided an effect was considerable, and its reception general, yet it brought no permanent benefit to
its author. It may easily be imagined that, whatever
his pecuniary resources, bearing in mind his habits
and his reckless squandering of money, he would soon
be in debt; how much more readily, then, would this
be the case when he had absolutely no other source
of income than the pittance which he might extort
from an unwilling bookseller, the bag of guineas he
might casually obtain from a patron, or the helps
which might be given him to procure a meal or to
settle a tavern bill, by some stranger charmed by the
brilliance of his conversation. At one period he would
be able to afford some miserable lodging, at another
he must perforce lie for the night on a bulk in Clare
Market.

At last some of the most sincere of his few remaining friends, seeing, as he himself says, that he would no longer do any good in London, resolved to induce him to abandon it for ever, and to go into Wales under the conditions of receiving a small pension. He has never seen Miss Wilfred since the day the painful episode which I have previously narrated occurred, but of late he has had reminders of her unwavering love in the form of letters, and, perchance, even of pecuniary assistance.

The following magnificent passage will describe the incident set forth infinitely better than words of mine:

"My kind dictatorial friends must have their way. I must be banished from London for ever. I should do no good there. They would have it so. Remonstrance or complaint or resentment was useless. I was compelled, therefore, to feign an acquiescence in their wishes: to feign, because what they intended as perpetual banishment, I designed should be merely temporary rustication. My intention was to retire to Wales and finish my tragedy: that completed, to return to London, to bring it upon the stage, and, with the profits in my fist, to wait upon my persecuting benefactors severally, and to thrust into their hands the money they had advanced to me. They had sent a tailor to me to measure me for a new suit of clothes —(that insult shall be discharged at the same time with the other debts)—and on the following week I was to be wafted to Llanelly.

"It was a Sunday afternoon, declining into evening. I had heard—for the room I occupied was a back room on the ground floor, and not, as poets use, the garret—I had heard the old woman of the house remark to a neighbour gossip, as she returned home with her baked meat, that it was a fine day. I guessed as much as I lay on my truckle bed ; for when the sun shone, a whiter light came down between my wretched casement and a high wall, about a yard in distance from it.

"I had a reason for lying a-bed, which your men of spread cloths, your daily raisers of the knife and fork, will hardly understand : I was without money or food, and had fared scantily the day before. As the light receded from the window, however, I bethought me of rising; and, since no future opportunity might be afforded me, I resolved on bending my steps to a spot—a visit to which I had long meditated as a duty. A strange and deep melancholy, which had settled upon my spirits when I awoke in the morning, and which, though I marshalled my philosophy to disperse it, increased upon me as the day wore, favoured my intention, and to St. James's Churchyard—to Ludlow's grave therein—I directed my course.

"On my way I met my old friend Mrs. Martin, with whom I had kept up an acquaintance in adverse times and in prosperity. She was going to see her son Simon, who had left the army, and was now one of the turnkeys of the Fleet Prison, within the liberties of which I had prudently taken my lodging. The worthy old creature was rejoiced to see me. She recalled old times, and dwelt upon them, crying at one moment, laughing at the next. She wrung my hands, calling me a dear, sweet, unfortunate gentleman, and wanted to force upon me some small money, which her poor hard hands, I doubt not, had earned most hardly. The simple tones, the rapturous phrase of this dear genuine woman affected me, I cannot say how strongly, and I was glad to break away from her, which I did abruptly.

"I needed no softening to approach the grave of Ludlow. I hung over it in wrapt and mournful reflection. My gentle—my honest friend ! whose tender heart my frowardness, my obstinacy, my ingratitude, had so often made to bleed, whose life was bound up in mine—who loved me! In imagination, I supposed him to have been a witness to all the sufferings I had endured since his eyes closed upon me. That thought, how much more than my misfortunes had ever done, wrung me. The expectations he had indulged—the hopes he had cherished of me—which, perhaps, thrilled along the thread of life at the very moment it snapped for ever—all destroyed, all come to nought! And this at last! a wretch returning to a dead man's grave, craving a like resolution with himself of the weary flesh into the dust whereof it was composed—it may be (oh God! there *was* that hideous wish!) an extinction, likewise, of the soul which it contained.

"The beadle warned me from the grave once, and again. I retired before him without a word. It was evening service; I entered the church modestly, for the temple of God in England is no place for misery that wears old woollen. The woman whose duty it was to open the pew-doors was grounded in this religion. She scanned me closely and contemptuously, but presently motioned me to go into an obscure pew at the entrance of the church. I did so, and was the sole occupant of it during the service. Sinners, who came to pray for the mediation of the meek and lowly Jesus, shrank from the contamination of proximity to me.

"How many years since I had entered a church!

"The bitterness that sometimes, though not often, possessed me, rose upon my mind as I gazed around me. 'Dreadful, decent rogues, the major part of these; mumbling prayers they feel not; trembling upon their knees in mock devotion; uttering and muttering responses to appeals for mercy, whilst their hearts are hatching the young of wrath and persecution, which soon with strong-plumed pinions shall go forth to devour and to destroy.'

"But these unworthy thoughts dispersed, were chased away, when the psalm was given out—when the organ heaved forth its volumes, its throes of ravishing and still-swelling sound—when the accordant voices of the children gushed out, making one full, concurrent, sublime descant of prayer, of praise, of petition. My heart wept within me from all its issues ; my soul sank prostrate before the altar. I grasped the partition with my hands, or I should have fallen upon the ground; the sweat hung heavy upon my forehead, a trembling shook my whole frame.

" Dark as was the corner into which I had slunk, the pew-opener saw my ghastly face through the obscurity. She made signs to me to leave the church ; but I stood, or rather continued upright, where I was, spell-bound, fixed. To have left the place I must have been dragged thence. Nor did I recover my calmness during the delivery of the sermon. The preacher was a simple, unaffected, and yet earnest man; he spoke of truths that I had heard when I was a boy, and in almost the self-same language. I had not been a scoffer, for I never was a trifler or a fool. Devoutly believing in a God, and knowing perfectly well the beauty and dignity of virtue, still I had contented myself, during my whole life, with avowing my belief when it was necessary, and maintaining my opinions when they were called for. I was not a man in the practice of piety, either to myself or to the world ; that is to say, I had never prayed in secret that God might hear, or gone to church that man might see.

"Shall I wrong truth so deeply as to assert that this accidental visit to St. James' Church made a convert or a penitent of me ? No ; moved as I was, it was no motion from Heaven that called me thither. It was the memory of the past that smote me, not apprehensions of the future.

" The service being ended, I would have left, but had a difficulty in finding my hat. In the meanwhile, a concourse of gaily attired people crowded the aisle. My dress forbade the presumption of thrusting myself amongst them. I was fain, therefore, to wait till they were passed by.

" But two or three remained on this side of the church, and these not so advanced towards the entrance as to

17—2

obstruct the opening of my pew.　As I stepped out, a short sharp cry caused me to turn my head.　My arm was at the same instant gently, but quickly, laid hold upon.

" ' Richard !—Mr. Savage !'

" Had I not known the voice, I had hardly recognised that face—though it was the face of Elizabeth Wilfred. Not that the face was changed, but its expression, which was one of the most profound melancholy.　The joy of seeing me (for joy it was) irradiated for a moment that aspect of sorrow, making it more sweetly piteous.　A heavy groan burst from my bosom when I beheld her ;—a groan of shame, of contrition, of despair.　But mouths were agape, and the old pew-opener was about to interfere.　They might well marvel at a recognition between two such persons !　I turned, and fled out of the church.

" She followed and overtook me.

" For Heaven's sake, dear Richard, do not leave me.　I must not lose you again.　Stay for me one moment, while I tell the coachman to drive home.　Promise me ; say that you will wait till I return.'

" I answered, ' I will wait.'　Perplexed, confounded, I knew not what to do or to say.　She came back in a minute.

" ' Where are you going ?' she said ; ' you must let me accompany you.　You are very ill, Richard.　I wish you would take my arm.'

" ' We are observed here.'

" I knew, for I had seen, that we were observed ; indeed, some dozen humane or inquisitive people, who had been standing a short distance from us, were now approaching from several quarters, halting.　A circle would soon have formed around us.　I made an effort to rouse myself, although scarce able to stand, and moved towards the gate of the churchyard, Elizabeth supporting me.　She beckoned to a coach.

" ' Whither are you going, dear Richard ?'

"'Home—home ; I must go home.'

" I whispered my direction to the driver, and was helped into the coach.   She was instantly at my side.

" Few words were exchanged between us during the time we were in the coach.   At intervals she pressed my hand, which she held between her own, and inquired whether I was better ; questions which I answered in the affirmative. And if an unnatural strength, wrought out of a determination to acquit myself with firmness through a fearful impending scene—if this which I summoned together, and held, may be called being better—I was so.   I dreaded that she should see where I lodged.   My squalid wretchedness of figure had been seen : could I have fled, that might have been borne—that had passed.   But now, by Heaven ! when the coach stopped was the most terrible moment of my life.   Had it been a Tyburn cart, and I in it, about to be paraded before the yelling mob, a craven murderer, I could not have felt a more sickening sense of abject terror.

" We got out of the coach.   I told the driver to wait, that he might carry the lady to her own house.   The wretch bowed to the gentleman with nauseous gravity—a jaw-locked grin.   My old woman came to the door, wondering whether her spectacles were bewitched.   Such light and such darkness together !   'Never had so fine a lady stepped over her threshold before ;' so said the old woman on the following day.   True, Mrs. Markham, very true ! I borrowed a candle from her, and led the way to my room. Closing the door upon us, I set down the light upon the table, and sank upon a box placed against the wall.

"'I am at home.   Dearest, best of women, leave me. Elizabeth Wilfred, I implore you leave me.'

"'Here ?' surveying the apartment with a chilly shudder —'here ?   O Richard !'

"'Here.   This is where I live—my home.   I am better now.'

" She came and sat down by my side, and placed her arm

around me, the hand resting on my shoulder.   I dared not look upon her, and yet I could not help doing so.   It was maddening to see that sweet face as she wiped my damp forehead with her handkerchief, with a smile upon her lips, although her eyes began to fill with tears.   Her gentle nature could not bear to see the wretched ruin—the ghastly wreck before her.   Her bosom heaved, a sob choked her utterance.   She threw herself into my arms, her head upon my breast, and burst into a passion of weeping.

"'Great God of heaven! this is too much—too much!' I exclaimed, almost with a shriek, striving to disengage myself; but very gently now, for she would cling to me. 'Elizabeth, if you have pity, if a miserable man may claim——'

"'Yes, yes, forgive me, dear Richard, I would not pain you; it is but joy that I have seen you once again.'

"That dear falsehood might be forgiven.   The joy of seeing me!   Joy hath its tears, 'tis true; but never such tears upon such a face.   The misery of seeing me thus—this drew forth those tears.   She wiped them from her face, and endeavoured at calmness; but sobs would rise at intervals.

"'Do let me speak,' she said at length; 'you must not stay here.   It is not fit that Richard Savage should live here.   I have money.   What is it you owe, dear sir?   You never would permit it to be mentioned.   From those we love, I have heard you say, it is a mark of love and of confidence to receive it.   I am sure you will not disdain to accept it from me.   You will not be so unkind to me as to refuse it.   Come, now,' tenderly, and looking me appealingly in the face.

"This speech, to which at one time I had listened with rapture, now was torture to me to hear.   I left my seat hastily.   She also arose, and in alarm.   Taking her hands between my own, I held her my arm's distance from me, my teeth clenched, my eyes fixed upon her with fond bitterness.

" 'Thou loveliest, gentlest, most cruel creature !' I exclaimed, 'and is it thus you requite the wrong I have done you ? Is it thus you damn me with generosity I deserve not, with tenderness that makes me mad, with pity that blasts me ? Am I not sunk enough already—abased— degraded ? Oh, Elizabeth ! that my brain be not rent in twain ; that my heart burst not asunder ; leave me—leave me !' and I stamped upon the ground. 'On my knees I pray you to leave me.'

" 'I would not offend you for the world, she cried, in agitation, wringing my hands, 'for mercy's sake compose yourself. I will leave you. Do you wish, Richard, that I should leave you ?'

" 'Oh, my God ! yes—yes —yes !' falling upon the ground at her feet, and dashing my fists upon the floor ; 'I cannot bear this ! cannot bear it !'

" '*Hysterica passio !* down, thou climbing sorrow ;'

But it would not down : such ravings as devils might have heard—perhaps, did hear rejoicingly—followed. She was at my side ; on her knees at my side.

" 'I will go,' she said, attempting to soothe me. 'I will go. I did not know my presence would have disturbed you so, or I would not have intruded. Pray forgive me, I will rid you of my sight directly ; but I cannot leave you till you are more yourself.'

" That piteous imploring face close to mine, those hands pressing my burning temples ! Nature will have way. With a deep groan I hid my face, and wept aloud like a child. Oh ! then the world had passed away from me !

" How long it was ere I recovered from this paroxysm, I know not. When I did so, I discovered Elizabeth sitting near me on the chest, trembling violently, her hands clasped before her, and paler than ever before I saw the face of woman. I arose collected, the man of yesterday, or of to-morrow, and seated myself by her side.

"'Elizabeth,' I said, 'you have witnessed a strange weakness. I am ashamed of myself; but it is the first and last.' Then, kissing her hands fervently, 'I dare not call you my love, though that I love you—how much more than my life!—Heaven is my witness, who knows how valueless life is to me.'

"She sighed. 'Oh, Richard! not now such words. We are friends, are we not?'

"Blessed, admirable woman, yes; and I am now happy beyond expression that I have seen you once more before I leave London, perhaps for ever. I thank God for it, and shall learn to thank him for all things, knowing that His providence watches over me. Our meeting proves it.'

"It was more than an hour after this ere she left. Saying she would see me on the following day, she at length arose. I handed her to the door, and passing my arm around her waist, drew her gently towards me, and kissed her.

"'God will bless you, my Elizabeth, even for your kindness to so sad a wretch as Richard Savage.'

"'You must not talk so, Richard,' she replied. 'He will bless you too, when you ask His blessing.'

"When I could no longer hear the coachwheels, I returned to my room. She had left her purse upon the seat. By mistake, I thought at the first instant—but no. All the blood in my body rushed to my face. Any other man in the world would have shrunk, probably, even to think how he looked in such a moment. Not I. I raised the bit of glass from the mantelpiece, and gazed at this proud, honourable, lofty—scoundrel! Pitiful—very pitiful was that countenance!

"Averse as I had been from leaving London, from this night I was as anxious to go as my friends could be that I should be gone. I saw Elizabeth Wilfred every day until my departure. I promised a thorough amendment of my life, and intended to set about it. She believed me and was happy.

"My friend Johnson attended me to the coach, murmuring comfort and philosophy, whilst the tears stood in his eyes. Nor was I less affected. I embraced him tenderly, and, springing into the coach, if not with a light, with a buoyant heart, I bade farewell to London, for, as I believed and designed, a short time. Sight and sound of the vast city were soon lost to me. Longer, O London! have I kept from thee than I contemplated ; but a few days longer, and I shall be with thee once again. Already the rumble of the leathern vehicle fills my ears— mine eyes are already full of thee. I come. Foes who have rejoiced that I retired, friends who will lament that I return—I come. A little older—a little sadder— a little, also, wiser."

He never returned, however. His friends had only power to change the scene ; they had no power to change his nature. He acts in Bristol exactly as he would have acted in London. At length he is cast into a debtors' prison for the non-payment of a paltry sum. He bears his imprisonment with equanimity, until one day he receives a letter containing a charge of ingratitude which disturbs him much, and presently he becomes ill, and in a few days is dead. Dr. Johnson in his life of the poet gives no foundation in fact for some particulars which are here introduced into the story ; but Whitehead had too keen an apprehension of and insight into what is necessary in good art not to perceive that it was needful here to introduce some ray of sunshine to penetrate in some measure the prevailing gloom. Accordingly, in the novel, Miss

Wilfred is summoned to his bedside, and arrives after a long and painful journey, just in time to see the end. She herself has for a long while been in most delicate health, and is so overcome with fatigue and the shock of his death, that in a few days she herself is no more. The lovers are buried in the same grave. The close of the novel is told in a fictitious letter of a touching character, purporting to have been sent by Mr. Thomas Dagge, the keeper of the prison, to Dr. Johnson.

In this novel there are two characters most powerfully depicted—Ludlow (a pure invention), and Savage. Steele as a character is more slightly treated than we could desire, though a quarrel between him and Savage is well narrated; as when Savage says to him, "You imagined you were cheapening a dog, to bark at your bidding and to fawn and cringe at your call."

The speech just quoted brings vividly before us the mingled pride and scorn of Savage's nature. We feel that the words are true to life, but are glad that there are not many who could thus insolently forget the disinterested favour of a generous heart. It is a pity that Johnson is scarcely touched on at all; for there is hardly anything more striking, amusingly pathetic, or suitable for a novelist's use, than the traditions of Johnson and Savage walking through the streets of London at night, when destitute of a lodging, and declaring that come what might in politics, they at least (poor homeless creatures!) "would stand by their country." All this, as the *Examiner* justly said in its review of the novel at the time of its first appearance, might have been " nobly told." It is also to be regretted that the habits of Savage are sometimes more revealed in the novel than is necessary, or quite consistent with good taste or good art. The language likewise, though the language of the time, is occasionally needlessly full of expletives and undesirable expressions.

The study of this book (as indeed of all eighteenth century literature) brings before us the corruption and shameless venality of these times. In our days we hear much of the badness of public morals, and, sooth to say, they may be well esteemed capable of improvement. But in the older days, with, as far as we can perceive, even greater iniquity, there was an utter absence of shame or decent concealment. In this novel, for example, with the exceptions of Elizabeth Wilfred and Ludlow, nearly all the characters are tainted with some form of positive sin. Examined from a moral point of view, it is in truth a sorry story. The portrayal of the miscarriage of justice in the trial of Savage and Gregory for murder is most vividly shown. Consequently the whole passage, although so powerfully written as to live before our eyes, is painful reading. There is one pleasing reflection to be drawn from all of this, viz., that it clearly indicates that we have at least attained in these times to a somewhat higher level of true progress.

At the close of an edition of Fielding's *Tom Jones*, illustrated by George Cruikshank (London, George Bell and Sons, 1876), this paragraph appears in an " Appendix ":

" The following notes have been found written on some of the pages of a copy of 'Tom Jones,' of the date 1773. They are in the autograph of Samuel Taylor Coleridge, and appear to have sufficient interest to justify their being appended here :

" 'Let the requisite allowance be made for the increased refinement of our manners, and then I dare believe that no young man who consulted his heart and conscience only, without adverting to *what the world* would say, could rise from the perusal of Fielding's *Tom Jones, Joseph Andrews*, and *Amelia*, without feeling himself a better man— at least, without an intense conviction that he *could* not be guilty of a *base* act.' "

A similar remark might be fittingly made concerning *Richard Savage.*

As I have before mentioned, the first edition in volume form was illustrated by Leech, and appeared in 1842. It contains seventeen illustrations, and a second edition, also containing the illustrations, appeared in 1844. It is somewhat remarkable that the edition just mentioned is not stated to be the second one. The illustrations are, in many cases, not only admirable in themselves, but Leech has shown in them that he grasped the spirit of the situation depicted. The illustration which faces the title-page represents Richard retaliating upon the cobbler. The figure of the cobbler is very characteristic of Leech. Richard is portrayed as a fine chivalrous youth; indeed, his appearance in this illustration is more pleasing than in any other in the work.   Mrs. Short, the cobbler's wife, seems a veritable Amazon, and is about to "pommel" Richard. The hypocritical Carnaby is admirably delineated. There is an illustration of Richard's first presentation to Lady Mason by Mrs. Freeman.   Lady Mason seems old and feeble, and Mrs. Freeman smirks.   If Leech is correct in the matter, it would appear that the costume of boys at that period was exactly identical with that of men.   "The First Day at School" has nothing remarkable in it.   "Savage* with Mr. and Mrs. L'Estrange" is excessively ludicrous.   The imposing Mr. L'Estrange, with the stateliness of a monarch full of pomposity on a great national occasion, is haranguing poor little crestfallen Richard, while his lady is making fruitless efforts to faint.   I do not like the conception of the illustration wherein Mrs. Brett is represented as interrogating Ludlow. The "Interview between Myte and his new Son-in-law" is well drawn, and the figure of Mr. Myte "on his return from the wedding dinner," is humorously depicted, especially the benevolent smile on his serene features.   "The Crimps surprised by Martin" is interesting, as showing the costume of the lower classes. The "Despair of Ludlow at his Wife's Misconduct" is a painful picture.   Opposite the title-page of vol. ii. is a somewhat commonplace illustration of the "Mock Marriage."   "Savage introduced to Lovell † at the

---

* A trivial incident of his cobbler days.
† A Grub Street author.

Club" is eminently Leech-esque. Lovell, and a figure to the extreme right of the picture, are wonderfully drawn. "Savage introduced by Sir Richard Steele to Miss Wilfred" is very good. Miss Wilfred is pleasing, but Leech never depicts young ladies well. "Mr. Clutterbuck receiving a Hint that he cannot Mistake" is amusing. It would appear that the name of Clutterbuck is an invention by Leech, as Lemery is the name in the novel. "The Death of Sinclair" is the frontispiece to vol. iii. There are also illustrations of the trial, in which the smirk on the features of Sir Arthur Page is peculiarly visible. There is an illustration of the "Interview between Miss Wilfred and Richard Savage in Newgate," in which the starchy expression of the warder is particularly ridiculous. "Carousal of Savage and his Friends at Lord Tyrconnel's" is a striking picture. Tyrconnel is entering the room, and Savage is rising to address him.

The "Introduction" to this edition (the first) is different to that in the copy in the British Museum. In the earlier edition, Whitehead says that he found the manuscript in "no oak chest" from the library "of a certain nobleman," nor did he purchase it from a cheesemonger. The first remark may possibly be a humorous allusion to the preface to the *Ingoldsby Legends*.

An edition of *Richard Savage* was published by Mr. Bentley in 1845, in his "Standard Novels," a series of novels with one illustration, by Leech, facing the title-page. The introduction to the 1845 edition deals with the question of the validity of Savage's claims, to which, in the introduction to the illustrated edition, Whitehead says he will not particularly allude, or words of similar import.

There are five English editions of Johnson's *Life of Savage* in the British Museum, and a French translation. The first of these editions is dated 1767, the last 1777. On looking carefully through the book, I find that, making all due allowance for the necessities of romance, Charles Whitehead, in delineating his ideal Richard Savage, has followed very closely the model of the real one. The principal point in which Whitehead differs from Johnson is in reference to the love-making between Richard Savage and Miss Wilfred. Johnson scarcely refers to this, except incidentally; in fact, as far as I can notice, Miss Wilfred is only once referred to, and then not by name; and the engagement between Richard Savage and herself is mentioned simply as one of Sir Richard Steele's projects. Whitehead, with an artistic sense of what is correct in writing a romance, deepens and intensifies the love interest by every means in his power, until it becomes one of the salient features in the work. With becoming modesty, Johnson rarely mentions himself in connection with the subject of his memoir, and no letter of Mr. Dagge, the keeper of the Bristol gaol, such as appears *in extenso* at the close of the romance, is given by him.

We can readily point out the faults of others; it is not so easy to see or correct the same faults in ourselves. Johnson, who is not celebrated for the early hours at which he retired to rest, wrote as follows, in his serious style, at the very period when his own hours were probably of the earliest in another sense of the term. He is speaking of the time just before Savage went into the Bristol debtors' prison :

"In this Exigence he once more found a Friend who sheltered him in his House, though at the usual inconveniences with which his Company was attended ; for he could neither be persuaded to go to bed in the Night, nor to rise in the Day."

Johnson's habits apart, however, Richard Savage must indeed have been a troublesome guest. On the veracity of Richard Savage's statements as to his parentage, it is not for me to pass judgment. I have, however, compared with attention the views expressed by Johnson, Boswell, and Whitehead, and it may be desirable to state some of these opinions here, dealing with these writers in the order of their date. Johnson appears to have entertained no doubt at all respecting the justice of Savage's claims, and makes Mrs. Brett's conduct even blacker than in Whitehead's romance, saying that she put off Earl Rivers with lying answers when he made natural inquiries as to his child, and finally, that when he was dying and wished to provide for his son, she told him the astounding falsehood (knowing it to be such) that that son was dead. Johnson deems her conduct most extraordinary and unaccountable, as he thinks she had neither the fear of poverty nor of shame to cause her to act as she did. Boswell, in his *Life of Johnson*, goes at length into the whole question, and the strongest arguments which he brings to bear against Savage are that he could not obtain a legacy, and that he (Boswell) had been unable to find the entry of baptism to which Savage refers. Whitehead's answer to this objection seems a very strong one; it is that Boswell looked for the wrong name. Indeed, in Whitehead's preface to the later editions of his romance, the arguments in favour of Richard Savage's claims are most powerfully stated, but at such length that it is impossible to enter fully into them here. Of course, the strongest point in Savage's favour (even Boswell admits this), is that the three different accounts of the life of Richard Savage, one in the *Plain-dealer* in 1724, another in 1727, and another, as Boswell says, " by the powerful pen of Johnson " in 1744, should all have been published during Mrs. Brett's—or, as Boswell inaccurately calls her, "Lady Macclesfield's"—lifetime, without any public or effectual contradiction.

Boswell thus sums up his statement (which is quoted by Whitehead in his preface) :

" I have thus endeavoured to sum up the evidence upon the case as far as I can ; and the result seems to be that the world must vibrate in a state of uncertainty as to what was the truth."

Of those who have written about Richard Savage, Boswell was the most hostile to his claims; and yet, after stating that the strongest argument in Savage's favour was to be found in the fact that these accounts of his life were published under the circumstances mentioned above, he concludes with the words I have just quoted. Is it conceivable that Mrs. Brett, hating Savage as she undoubtedly did, would not have contradicted these narratives effectually had she been able to do so ? Is it not upon the whole reasonable to suppose that Savage's statement, vouched for by such a contemporary witness as Johnson, is likely to be correct ?

The characteristics of Richard Savage are a deeply interesting study; and there can be no doubt that the Richard Savage of Whitehead's romance differs in some respects from the Richard Savage of real life. He is represented as handsome, easy and attractive in manners, and with an excellent address. The chief defect in him, which a casual acquaintanceship should show, would be an unreasonableness when opposed, a quick and sometimes violent temper, not even under moderate control, and occasionally a forgetfulness of former small kindnesses. The Richard Savage of the novel, for it is about him that I am alone at present speaking, is represented as having received an excellent education for a gentleman of that period. The sole advantage which he did not receive was a University course, and for this he was himself solely responsible, for Mr. Burridge, with the large-heartedness of a true friend, offered him every facility for going to Cambridge. The manner in which Savage declined this timely offer gives us one of our first real glimpses into his inner character. Had he been a youth of discretion and judgment instead of impulse, he would doubtless have accepted the offer; and it seems at least questionable whether the reason which he gives for his conduct, viz., his disinclination to leave Ludlow at that juncture in his sickness and sorrow, was the motive which in truth actuated him. Was it not rather (though he himself perchance never perceived it) a foolish disinclination to submit to Burridge's fatherly guidance, a thing which a residence at a University in the manner proposed would have involved? His intellect appears to have been bright rather than profound; his sallies of wit were brilliant, and he could conceive admirable projects— projects which, alas! he but rarely had the industry and perseverance to carry out. He was fond, like all wits of his day, of indulging much in the satisfaction apparently to be derived from garnishing the dish of his conversation with suitable Latin quotations; frequently, however, sadly hackneyed. Of other classical allusions he was also full, and in these he was sometimes extremely happy. There is one thing which strikes us in considering his intellectual character, and we have felt the same respecting other such men of his age. In Richard Savage we have a poet and man of letters who mixes with the best class of men of letters of the period. Do we therefore find him a studious man—a man devoted to books—a man who is never happier than when in solitude and peace he is communing with them, or with a small circle of intimate friends of similar tastes—a man who, whatever his occasional excesses, deeply regretted them and speedily recovered from them? This, perhaps, is what we might have expected; but what do we find?—a man who never once refers to the pleasures of reading—a man who never seems to have engaged in research—a man of whom we do not hear that he possessed any books of his own, except those given him by Lord Tyrconnel, and these he speedily pawned, though in receipt of a handsome allowance and free board and lodging—a man who is never happier than when seated with his second bottle of wine before him at a common tavern, in the company of boon companions whose conversation was certainly not of an intellectual type, and who never once complains of the lack of intellect in others—a man who could be diverted from any work, however pressing and important, by a call to some grovelling pleasure. It is certainly remarkable, however, that in these respects he was sadly similar to, and no worse than, nearly all the men of genius of his time, such men as Locke, and perhaps Pope and Johnson, alone excepted.

It is difficult to give in a few words an adequate conception of his moral nature, there was so much both of good and evil in it. Generosity was ever a prominent quality in his mind; and there is no doubt that he had a deep and sincere reverence for good, and in the inner recesses of his soul the instincts of a good man. It is an easy thing to exemplify his generosity: to his friends he was always a friend; with his money, when he had any, even lavish; and his noble conduct towards Mrs. Ludlow, when, after all she had done against him, he not only succoured her by giving her pecuniary aid, but actually entered a den of infamy, which he had resolved never to enter more, to procure her assistance, shows fine qualities of heart. The way he bore himself towards Mr. Dagge during the latter days of his life in the debtors' prison at Bristol was magnanimous. The exquisite description of his feelings when, as a poor outcast, he entered a church once more, after many years of absence, represents him as at that moment, at least, not far from the kingdom of God. The great blot on his moral nature during the greater part of his life was his fierce and uncontrolled animosity towards Mrs. Brett. If she were his mother, such feelings were from that cause alone all the more inexcusable. If she were not his mother, even he must have felt there was something to be said in extenuation of her conduct, as, with the exception of her atrocious attempt to entrap him, and compel him by force to leave the country, her treatment of him was not so scandalous as he would wish us to believe. Even he must have thought that some blame attached to Lady Mason and Ludlow, and that his pretensions and claims could hardly fail to be a grievous trial to one like Mrs. Brett.

In his mode of life he had many excesses; gluttony, however, was not among the number of these; but he was, beyond question, a persistent and continuous drunkard. Drunkenness was a habit of his age, but he was the worst of his associates in this respect.   He speaks of going through money very rapidly; and it may with too good reason be feared that he had other excesses than the one named, although this is not hinted at in the romance.   He had, however, despite all his faults, a capacity for pure love, and his affection for Miss Wilfred seems to have been of the purest.   She, like many of the heroines in the novels written at this period, 'though beautiful and pure in character, is somewhat faintly sketched, and is consequently a little wanting in individuality.   In portraying her, Whitehead has followed closely the model set him by the novelists of the eighteenth century.   Be this as it may, however, Richard Savage's affection for her seems to have been a most real thing, and had, as all true love should, a purifying effect on his character.   Once he sinned against the purity of his love, and then almost irreparably; and this, take it all in all, is the darkest stain on his life : he expiates it by years of penitence and suffering, and at length, in a few brief moments of the old loving communion, reaped the fruits of that forgiveness which long ere then had been vouchsafed to him.   There is nothing more beautiful in fiction than the pathos of the reconciliation between the world-despised outcast Richard Savage and Elizabeth Wilfred, who, amid all the allurements of rank and wealth, loved him still.*

* Miss Wilfred had immediately before the reconciliation been residing with aristocratic friends.

The career of Richard Savage, both in fact and in Whitehead's fiction, was marred by his own want of self-control and inability to deny himself the gratification of any whim which promised a moment's pleasure. It *might* have been entirely different, but that (in his own words, prefixed to the book)—

> "No mother's care
> Shielded my infant innocence with prayer,
> No father's guardian hand my youth maintained,
> Call'd forth my virtues, or from vice restrain'd."

The character of Mrs. Brett is powerfully sketched. We see a subtle delineation of the inner motives and character of a remarkable woman—a woman, however wicked, not devoid of some traits of worth—witness her avowal of the parentage of Savage, when such avowal not only ruined her position, but placed her entirely in the power of the man who had been wicked or weak enough to destroy her honour. Had there not been true love for Earl Rivers, she could hardly have taken this course. Her conduct towards Elizabeth also, until she was cajoled by Sinclair into connivance at his rash act, seems to be animated by good feelings. Her treatment of Savage, again, viewed from what was presumably her point of view, is far from being inexplicable; indeed, a great part of the blame for this must be laid at the door of Lady Mason and Ludlow, and in any case she hardly deserved the opprobrium Savage flung on her.

Of Lady Mason not much can be said in praise. Granting that the story of Savage's parentage was authentic, she may have had reasons which she thought at the time were good ones for representing to her daughter, Mrs. Brett, that her child was dead, but there is no doubt that in this instance, as in all others, it would have been better policy to have been perfectly straightforward. Had Lady Mason not made concealment, in a case where concealment was eminently undesirable, the greater part of the misery and hate in subsequent years would have been avoided. When in early youth she removed Savage from the care of Mrs. Freeman and sent him to the good school at St. Alban's, she evidently intended adequately to provide for him ; but time went on, she procrastinated, and her good intentions were never carried out. Indeed, her feelings towards Savage probably became less warm, and there is no doubt that when she removed him from school, and made him, sorely against his will, a cobbler's apprentice, she quite hoped that she had got rid of him by enabling him in this humble manner to earn his bread. When, as was natural, Richard's pride does not permit him to brook this indignity, she first becomes angry with him, and Ludlow foolishly tells her what was not the case; viz., that Richard has returned to the cobbler. Presently she finds that she has been deceived, and also that Richard is persistent in his endeavour to obtain recognition. Her better qualities revive, and she sets herself as far as possible to support his claims ; but she bitterly feels the fruit of her former equivocation, her daughter naturally believing that it was not very reasonable to suppose that her mother would lead her to accept a falsehood in past years. Was it not more conceivable that Lady Mason, agèd and infirm, even mentally evincing signs of senility, should have been so influenced by an old servant like Ludlow as to have grown to believe that his nephew was Richard Savage, her daughter's son ? Be this as it may, however, Mrs. Brett altogether declines to believe in Savage's claims, albeit she had her mother's almost dying asseverations in their favour.

Ludlow is the type of his class—a man who, though he possessed some good, even noble qualities, was nevertheless in many respects weak and apt to swerve from the right. He seems to have been a most exemplary servant, attentive to his duties, solicitous for his mistress's interests, sober and honest. When first we hear of him, it seems evident that he simply thought there was good reason for keeping Richard Savage's antecedents quiet, and that doubtless sooner or later such concealment would come to an end. Thus his conduct during the whole of Savage's school-days is perfectly reasonable and consistent; but always granting that Savage's claims were really just ones, it does appear that after Lady Mason forcibly removed Savage from school, he exceeded in his subsequent conduct what it was proper to do in the matter. There are sometimes reasons why family affairs should not be spoken of for some years; but in a case of this sort, when a young man would become a sufferer owing to the continued non-recognition of his claims, when the

only other witness, except himself, of their justice was
an agèd lady who at any time might be stricken by the
great silencer, Death, then it was clearly Ludlow's duty
to go at once to Mrs. Brett and lay the case fully before
her. Of course, his error was merely an error of judgment. We must also remember that in these days it
was deemed far more necessary for servants to obey
their orders without reflection or appeal. He suffered
fully the consequences of his error by losing, notwithstanding, his situation, and by having his words of
truth laughed to scorn when he at length uttered
them.

He seems to have had a genuine affection for Richard
Savage, and some of the description of his latter days
is not a little pathetic. His forbearance and tenderness towards his unworthy wife is a truly generous
trait, and we can well imagine the dreadful feelings of
mortification when he discovered that she had rewarded
all his kindness by making the perjured confession to
Mrs. Brett which appeared to ruin his veracity and
certainly ruined his hopes. It might, perhaps, be said
that had he been able to carry out his intention of
leaving his money to Savage, much of the latter's
career might have been different. It might also be
said that Savage had an innate tendency to extravagance and excess, and of whatever money he had been
possessed, it would only have been a question of time
as to how long it would take to dissipate it. Savage's
real wants were prudence and self-control.

The character of Myte is a somewhat complex one.

Whilst being in some senses the comic man of the book, he is in others the type of the worldly philosopher who, although necessarily possessing a blood-circulating machine, appears utterly destitute of what is conventionally known as a heart. Yet on other occasions and from different points of view he is not without feeling. He is at all times, on the surface, a good-natured man, full of epigram, witticism, and other smart talk, ever alert and anxious to do a good turn to a friend, especially if in so doing he can contrive to do himself no harm. When his friends get into real difficulties, he prefers from prudential motives to leave them alone, and not to appear in any sense identified with them. But when without his aid they have succeeded in vanquishing the aforesaid difficulties, he is most profuse in acknowledging to them the weakness and temerity of his conduct in deserting them while in straits, and his sincere trust and confidence that the nobility of their disposition is such that they will graciously overlook his shortcomings, and admit him once more into their confidence and respect. There can be no doubt that with him mercenary motives were uppermost. He had as much love for his wife and daughters as a man of his stamp could have, and occasionally, when he was in more than a usually good frame, even a little to spare for his friends.

There are no such difficulties in determining the character of Marchant as meet us when we strive to examine Myte. Such as he is, everything about him is quite clear. A man of good parts, in the main of good impulses and principles, yet sadly too liable to swerve from rectitude. He is a thorough Bohemian in the very worst sense of the term. Everything he does or says is tinged with the influence of the haphazard mode of life which men of this class invariably lived, at least in the eighteenth century. At the commencement of Savage's career he very kindly directed him wisely in his literary endeavours; but when, following up such advice, Savage had succeeded in producing a marketable play, he was careless as to the proper steps for enabling Savage to secure the full financial results from it. He attended with Savage to see its first public representation, and forthwith resolved to have a debauch on the strength of its being so well received. On this occasion Savage joins him, and Marchant does not return to his lodgings that night, much money being uselessly and reprehensibly spent at a tavern at a time just before which they had been both starving.

Marchant's character is seen in the worst light in the way he acts during the important Sinclair incident. There, after having provoked a quarrel, like a craven he deserts his friends in the midst of the difficulties which he himself alone caused. It would appear, however, that his conduct in this instance arose rather from natural temerity at a moment of fright than from baser motives. His end is deplorable. On the whole, notwithstanding all his faults, one cannot help liking the man.

Of the Martins, husband, wife, and son, it is perhaps well that a few words should be said. With the exception of Ludlow, they are the only persons moving in humble life of whom in this romance we hear much; and their exemplification of unsophisticated virtue is a great relief after the wickedness, misrepresentations, and shams in the other parts of the book. They practise good, hardly knowing it to be so, but as it were by simple impulse. The father, probably owing to having been an old soldier, and therefore seeing a good deal of life, is not only possessed of much common sense, but worldly sagacity, and the dexterous way in which, after Richard's escape from the ruffians who had entrapped him, he (Martin) conducted the capture of his whilom captors, reflects great credit on his strategy. His conduct subsequently towards Colonel Brett is also worthy of praise. The account given later of his fatherly conduct towards Richard, when resident on various occasions in his house, is pleasant reading. Of the son, Simon, little can be said. He is a fine, straightforward young Englishman in humble life. His mother is a woman who merits our respect. Probably quite uneducated, her deficiencies are amply atoned for by her goodness of heart. To Richard she is as a mother. She must have been the only woman from whom he could learn what motherly instincts were. It is also striking that this worthy couple never seemed to forget that Richard was a gentleman, or to cease to call to mind their social inferiority to him. One of the very few patches of brightness which relieve the blackness and degradation of Richard's trial for murder is the babbling and incoherent, but touching and natural, evidence of Mrs. Martin, which was all the more natural because most probably quite voluntary and spontaneous. In Richard's last years of misery he is never afraid to make himself known to Mrs. Martin, for, whatever his plight, he can always depend upon receiving a kind word from her.

Burridge is life-like ; though of course we have met him before—that is to say, he is not one of the original conceptions of the book. He is simply the type of his class in that period. He is a gentleman of great pomposity when we first meet with him. He is fond of relieving himself by taking off his wig, and talking in classical quotations on all occasions, besides being full of moral maxims after Horace. At bottom he is a thoroughly good man, despite his foibles, although he is not one who stands in need of the Kilmarnock weaver's prayer, "Lord, give us a good conceit of ourselves." He makes the fact of having overcome his youthful errors a great source of self-glorification. Later on, however, when, giving up his school, he returns to London to spend the remainder of his days, his character becomes much more mellow, and eventually one cannot help getting to love the good old man. He does not desert Savage or Gregory in their great trouble. He honestly seeks to reconcile Mrs. Brett and her *soi-disant* son, and at the end, despite all Savage's vagaries, he is among the sincerest of his well-wishers. It is noteworthy that Savage's way of speaking about him varies considerably with varying moods on different occasions.

The character of Gregory, though it may fairly be termed one of the minor ones, is at least among the pleasantest. It is a bright ray of sunshine shed over the sombre landscape of the book. From the first time when Gregory is introduced shielding the young and friendless Richard from the boy-tyranny of Sinclair, until the last occasion when, before leaving England, he extends hospitality to his somewhat unworthy friend, we see nothing but good of him. He is always the same manly fellow : ever striving without cant to act rightly, and guileless enough to suppose that all the world are actuated by the same high principles. When he becomes attached to Martha Myte, he becomes so simply from motives of sincere affection, and is totally unable to comprehend the mercenary motives of his future father-in-law, when, for the sake of lucre, Myte is anxious that Sinclair should supplant him in his daughter's esteem. Again, when unfortunately embroiled with Savage in the calamitous escapade which resulted in the killing of Sinclair, perceiving, as indeed was the case, that his father had just ground for indignation, he was noble enough to be neither surprised nor incensed at his parent's refusal either to see him or to afford him assistance. But so little did he comprehend Myte's real character, that he was more grieved than angry at *his* refusal of aid. Indeed, he appears to have felt more keenly the pain which he was unwittingly giving to his betrothed, than fear at his own impending fate. To Savage he was always a true friend. He bestirred himself much to procure Savage, at the beginning of the latter's career, a suitable introduction to managers, when the stage appeared the most likely field for financial success, and he never, like so many of Savage's so-called friends, refused to fraternize with him when in " sorry plight."

As I have indicated in my remarks on the character of Richard Savage, the character of Miss Elizabeth Wilfred is a somewhat colourless one. In person she is represented as being very beautiful. When she is first introduced to our notice, it is under circumstances which, to say the least, are somewhat embarrassing; but she comports herself with the utmost sweetness and amiability, tempered with all due maidenly reserve. We also, then, see for the first time what soon becomes sadly evident, that one of her deepest trials is the consequence of her birth acting on a sensitive mind; and even Savage, on the first interview (Savage, who loved her at first sight), unwittingly probed the wound. We do not hear anything about her education, and therefore, although we must of course assume that she had the ordinary accomplishments of ladies of that period, there is no evidence to show that she was highly educated. Neither was she clever or witty, for in the whole book not a single smart saying or clever remark is attributed to her; and, strive as we may, we cannot rid ourselves of the impression that her character is but dimly sketched, except from one point of view, on which I will shortly speak. The way she is dealt with in the romance brings vividly before us the difference between the novelists of the present day and those of the last century. A competent novelist of to-day would not have failed to bring before us in a most striking light this sweet and most interesting personality. She would, perchance, have become the most important personage in this novel. She would have been for us a living person, perhaps almost a friend. She is represented by Whitehead as possessed of all the gifts and graces which make her sex endearing—benevolent, tender, kind, and generous. The only trait of Elizabeth Wilfred's character which is placed clearly before us is her deep, pure, and unchanging love for Richard Savage. She loves him while still with Mrs. Brett; she rebuts the insinuations against him whispered in her ear by Sinclair. After his rescue of her from the mock-marriage with Sinclair she loves him, as well she may, with even deeper devotion, and her love withstands the severest temptation by which it were possible to test it—the indubitable proof that the loved one was unworthy of it. Like a true woman, she refuses to become an accomplice in Richard's execrable scheme against her honour, but whilst adopting the only course open to her, that of leaving him in such a manner that he is unable to trace her, yet she loves him none the less. As time goes on, she writes him beautiful letters, and succours him in his self-inflicted distresses, and no doubt, with the sweet delusiveness of love, looks forward with hope and confidence to the period when they will again be united in joyful prosperity. This halcyon time was never to come. I have elsewhere referred to the marvellous pathos of their meeting at the church, and to the exquisitely tender manner with which she solaced him in the degradation of the vile spot he called home. Of their last meeting on earth, when, in weakness and sorrow, she traversed the length of England—in those days when the slightest journey was a matter of importance—to be with her loved one, no words of mine can add to the beauty. So great was her previous sickness that she had been unable to leave her room, and yet so strong was the strength of desire that, though unable to take any nourishment, she was able to undertake this great exertion. We are made happy when her wish is granted, and she is beside her darling at his end; and, as no doubt it would have been her choice, she rests beside him in the grave. Coleridge somewhere says, that the highest type of womanhood is a womanhood pure, gentle, tender, but without a too marked individuality. Had he read this romance, he might have thought of Elizabeth Wilfred when giving the definition.

CHAPTER VII.

CRITICAL SURVEY.

NECESSARILY, a man like Charles Whitehead, who lived by his pen, had to devote a great deal of time to that drudgery of literature whereby he made his living. Who shall say how many noble and immortal works have been lost to the world owing to the men who had the power' to produce them being compelled to devote themselves almost exclusively to anonymous routine journalism, or to the well-nigh equally barren labour of mere compilation ? But, nevertheless, the position of the " hack " writer is that in which most of all a man exhibits any gifts he may possess. A man of no inventive faculty would simply throw off ephemeral products which could not possibly be reproduced, because they would depend for their interest on passing events of the moment. On the other hand, a man possessed of the very highest inventive powers would so treat passing events as to give them a permanent value. Whitehead has not done either of these things, but he has taken a middle course. His fugitive work has faults, the chief being morbidity, occasional coarse-

19—2

ness, and a strong tendency to Cockneyism, if I may
be permitted the use of so mongrel a word, but it
has nevertheless come down to us in books sufficiently
good to be saleable, and it has an interest, although
not of the most permanent kind.   When, however,
one comes to estimate the actual value of the work, it
is perceived that it is not very great; but we have to
remember the mass of work by fine hands, so situated,
on which an almost similar judgment would have to
be pronounced were it criticised from the same standpoint.

It would be just as unfair to judge of Whitehead's
genius by the work produced for a living as of that of
Coleridge by his leaders in the *Morning Post*, or of
that of Chatterton by the poems written for the fees
of his conceited friends.   On the whole, I am inclined
to believe that Whitehead's fugitive work is not discreditable to his genius, and more than that can rarely
be said of similar work produced under such conditions by any man.

It is remarkable that, perhaps in the whole of Whitehead's writings, there is not an example of the essay
pure and simple, using the word in its eighteenth century sense.   It may be said that such a whimsical paper
as the *Confessions of a Lazy Man* is an essay.   So it
undoubtedly is in our modern acceptation of the term,
but it is not cast in the approved form of the essay.

I have already printed in an earlier chapter a note
on Whitehead, by Rossetti, and this testimony by a
great poet would almost express an ultimate view both

of the extent and limitations of Whitehead's poetic genius. Personal inquiry, however, justifies it. The poetry *is* unequal. Its best things are perfectly wonderful; its worst are puzzling. In estimating Whitehead's place as a poet, it must be remembered that his most important poetical work was produced at probably not more than twenty-five years of age, for, as will be gathered from my opening chapter, *The Solitary* was first published in 1831. Therefore this important poem must be compared with the work of other poets in the first period of their creative activity· It may fairly be said of it that, while not so rich as Keats's *Endymion*, or so full of impetuous passion as *The Revolt of Islam*, it is infinitely more real and human than either. Reality of passion is the distinguishing note of Whitehead's poetry. On the whole, he is a subjective poet, for even in *Jasper Brooke*, in some respects the most objective of his poems, the subjective interest largely predominates; and there moans through his song in all its cadences the burden of a soul weighed down with life's sorrows. One would be disposed to place him almost on a level with Goldsmith, but lower than Cowper.

As a writer of fiction he must be classed not as a pictorial novelist, but among the Romancists of the age of George II. That period, and not our own, was the period in which his spirit lived. If Whitehead is not equal to the greatest writer of fiction in the earlier Georgian era, Fielding, and of course he is not, he is at least equal to some of Fielding's immediate followers.   It is a matter for grave disappointment that a man with his powers should have done so little permanent poetical work; just as it is a matter for regret that one possessed of his abilities should have executed so little, comparatively speaking, in the higher walks of fiction.   But I think that even what he has done in both these departments of literature entitles him to a far higher place than he at present holds.

1804.   Charles Whitehead born in London.

1831.   First publication of *The Solitary* (a Poem), 3 parts,
8vo. London : Effingham Wilson.

1834.   Publication of *Autobiography of Jack Ketch : Lives
of English Highwaymen,* 2 vols., 8vo. London :
Bull and Churton.

1836.   Production of *The Cavalier* at the Haymarket
Theatre, 15th September. Edition (the second)
of *English Highwaymen,* 12mo. Washbourne.

1836-37. November to June (first half-year of *Bentley's
Miscellany*), *Edward Saville and *The Youth's New
Vade Mecum* (a Poem). June to December (second
half-year of *Bentley's Miscellany*), *Rather Hard to
Take* (a Poem), and **The Narrative of John Ward
Gibson.* **Some Passages in the Life of Francis Loosefish, Esq.,* was probably contributed to a popular
shilling magazine between the years 1830 and
1836 ; but its name I have been unable to ascertain. It may have originally appeared as *Jonathan Loosefish, Esq.,* etc.

1838.   *Victoria Victrix* (a Poem). Third edition of *The*

* The stories marked with an asterisk were included in
Smiles and Tears. Allibone wrongly attributed to the
author of *Richard Savage* a pamphlet entitled *Cottages of
Labourers.* Whitehead wrote a play for the Surrey Theatre,
but I have been unable to ascertain particulars respecting it.

Autobiography of Jack Ketch.   London : J. Chud-
ley, Aldersgate Street.

1839-41.   **The Stock-Broker* and *Tavern Heads.*   Both con-
tributed to *Heads of the People ; or, Portraits of
the English*—a Miscellany.   London : Robert
Tyas, Cheapside.   Later edition, without date,
David Bryce, 48, Paternoster Row.   Edition of
Lives of Highwaymen, Philadelphia.   2 vols.

1841-42.   *Richard Savage* appeared in serial form in *Bentley's
Miscellany,* illustrated by John Leech ; in 1842,
published in three volume form, 12mo.   Fourth
edition of *English Highwaymen,* etc.   London :
Henry G. Bohn.

1843.   *The Earl of Essex :* an Historical Romance ; 3 vols,
12mo.   London : Bentley.   **Orlando Griffin,* and
**Five-and-Thirty or Thereabouts : Bentley's Miscel-
lany.*

1844.   Edition of *Richard Savage,* illustrated by Leech.
Bentley.

1845.   **De Loude Chisleham,* and **Mr. Yellowby's Doings;*
**A Curvet or Two in the Career of Tom Wilkins.
Bentley's Miscellany.*   Edition of *Richard Savage* in
Bentley's Standard Novels.   *Jasper Brooke,* and
Wife's Tragedy : Illuminated Magazine.   London.

1846.   *Memoirs of Grimaldi,* edited by Boz, with notes
and additions, revised by Charles Whitehead.
London : Bentley.   8vo.   *Flora Macdonald.*
London : *Bentley's Miscellany.*

1847.   *Smiles and Tears ; or, the Romance of Life* (a series
of collected stories).   3 vols., 12mo.   London :
Bentley.   *Pizarro and his Followers ; The Wooden
Walls of Old England ; The Insurrection at St.
Petersburg : Bentley's Miscellany.*

1848.   *Memoir of Captain Marryatt ; Caricature and Caricaturists ; Sir Harry Smith : Bentley's Miscellany.*

1849.   *The Solitary, and other Poems.* London : Bentley. 12mo.

1850.   September 20th, Revival of *The Cavalier*, at Sadler's Wells Theatre.

1852.   †*The Orphan.*

1853.   *Second Edition of Grimaldi Memoirs*, with notes and additions, revised by Charles Whitehead. London. 8vo.

1854.   *Life of Sir Walter Ralegh (Illustrated Library).* London : N. Cooke.

1856.   November 3rd, revival of *The Cavalier* at the Lyceum Theatre. Third edition of *Richard Savage.* Bryce.

1857.   Left for Australia in the ship *Deamia.*

1859.   *The Spanish Marriage* in *Victorian Monthly Magazine* for July. Melbourne, Australia : Gordon and Gotch.

1860.   New edition of *Joseph Grimaldi*, with additions by Charles Whitehead. London : Bentley.

1862.   July 5th, Charles Whitehead died of destitution in Melbourne Hospital.

1866.   *Third edition of *Grimaldi Memoirs*, edited by Boz, with notes and additions, revised by Charles Whitehead. London. 8vo.

---

† A story contributed to a London weekly newspaper ; I cannot discover the name of the paper.

Elliot Stock, Paternoster Row, London.